SOLDIER SNOW LEOPARD

SOLDIER SNOW LEOPARD

PROTECTION, INC.
6

ZOE CHANT

Copyright Zoe Chant 2018
All Rights Reserved

THE PROTECTION, INC. SERIES

Bodyguard Bear
Defender Dragon
Protector Panther
Warrior Wolf
Leader Lion
Soldier Snow Leopard
Top Gun Tiger (forthcoming)

All the books in the series are standalone romances. Each focuses on a new couple, with no cliffhangers. They can be read in any order. But characters from previous books reappear in later ones, so reading in order is recommended for maximum enjoyment.

TABLE OF CONTENTS

Prologue	1
Chapter One	13
Chapter Two	35
Chapter Three	53
Chapter Four	63
Chapter Five	77
Chapter Six	91
Chapter Seven	101
Chapter Eight	117
Chapter Nine	129
Chapter Ten	143
Chapter Eleven	149
Chapter Twelve	155
Chapter Thirteen	161
Chapter Fourteen	169
Chapter Fifteen	177
Chapter Sixteen	183
Chapter Seventeen	197
Epilogue	209
A note from Zoe Chant	213
Zoe Chant Complete Book List	215
Sneak Preview: *Protector Panther*	221

PROLOGUE
Justin

Justin Kovac sat in a car parked alongside a lonely country road, getting ready to track down his enemy.

The sky looked hard as steel, and was about the same color. The leafless trees seemed to claw at it with bony fingers. Hail rattled down and piled up on the dark earth.

When Justin's gaze drifted to the rear-view mirror, he saw a face fit for the colorless landscape: skin pale as the hailstones, eyes and hair black as winter ponds. Cheekbones like knives. A mouth that had forgotten how to smile.

He could barely see a trace of the man he'd once been. That man, whose buddies had called him Red, had laughed and joked his way through life. He'd loved his team and his life in the Air Force. He'd believed that he'd lay down his life to save his friends. Then he and his team had been kidnapped by the black ops agency called Apex. And he'd learned that being willing to give your life doesn't make it happen.

The brave men and women who'd been captured with him had died trying to save *him*, leaving him the sole survivor. And then there was nothing standing between him and Apex.

Apex had made him into a shifter. Given him special powers. And taken away everything that made him who he was. He'd lost his friends. His career. His honor. His integrity. His hope. His laughter. Even the color of his eyes.

He'd become Subject Seven, their lab rat. And their assassin.

The only thing Apex had been unable to take from him was his longing for freedom.

Now he had his freedom. And he had no idea what to do with it.

I have an idea, hissed his inner snow leopard. *We should hunt.*

"You're so literal." Justin spoke aloud. His breath clouded in the freezing air. "I meant that I don't know what to do with my entire life."

But his snow leopard was right. One Apex base had been destroyed when he'd broken loose, but he knew there was at least one remaining. He didn't know where it was, any more than he knew the current whereabouts of the surviving Apex agents from the base where he'd been imprisoned. But he meant to find out.

"Just one left." A streamer of mist fluttered from Justin's lips as he spoke. "Well, just one left that I can track with my power."

You must find them all, hissed his snow leopard. *Find them and kill them!*

"I'm working on it." As Justin reached up to push a lock of hair out of his eyes, his arm brushed against the cold metal of the door handle.

Instantly, he was hurled into a memory.

The metal of the lab table was icy against his bare skin. He was strapped down, with the usual array of sensors attached to his body.

Dr. Attanasio approached him with a syringe full of blue-green liquid.

"What's that?" Justin asked, doing his best to keep his voice steady.

"A little something I designed to make you stronger," the doctor said with pride.

"Why the straps?"

"You'll see," the doctor said, with a sadistic smile hovering at his lips. He lowered the syringe to Justin's arm.

The liquid burned in his veins. Justin gritted his teeth, waiting for the sensation to die down. But it didn't. Instead, the burning spread throughout his body, getting more painful by the second, until he felt like he'd been engulfed in flame.

Maybe the stuff increased his strength a little bit, but it didn't make him strong enough to break the straps, which had been designed to hold down shifters.

But even while he was screaming and struggling, unable to stop himself, he noticed when Dr. Attanasio came a little bit closer than he should have to replace a dislodged sensor. Justin's arms were strapped down, but he managed to stealthily move one finger to brush against the tiny bit of bare skin between the doctor's latex glove and the cuff of his white coat.

Dr. Attanasio never noticed. But Justin felt that sense of imprint, impossible to describe but unmistakable, and knew he'd be able to find the doctor again, no matter where he hid.

There was a strap over his chest. A strap across his waist. Cold metal against his arm. He was trapped.

His snow leopard's shriek of terror and rage rose to an unbearable pitch.

Justin grabbed the straps and yanked. They tore, freeing him.

He came to his senses kneeling in the snow beside the car, with the ruined seatbelt dangling beside him and his fists clenched so tight that his nails had bitten into his palms. Dazed, Justin looked around, trying to orient himself.

His snow leopard was snarling, frantic and furious. *Kill! Kill! Kill!*

"Calm down," Justin said. His voice cracked; his throat was raw. Had he been yelling? "It's all right. We're free."

His snow leopard's blind rage cooled into hatred. *The doctor. Kill the doctor.*

Justin opened his mouth to agree, then forced himself to say, "I'll *find* the doctor. Then we'll see what happens."

Kill him, insisted his snow leopard. *He hurt us.*

It was tempting. But he'd had enough of killing just because someone told him to. If there was one thing that could make the man he was now different from Subject Seven, it was making his own choices.

"We'll see," Justin said firmly.

He got back in the car, closed his eyes, and cautiously recalled touching Dr. Attanasio, keeping himself at a mental distance so he wouldn't drown in his own memories.

Where are you, doctor?

Justin felt a tug inside his mind. It wasn't the knowledge of a location, let alone an address, just a sense that his target was *that way.*

Our prey, corrected his snow leopard.

Justin began to drive *that way,* following that inner pull. He hoped it wouldn't be too far. For all he knew, he was trying to drive to China.

But it turned out that Dr. Attanasio hadn't gone far; he hadn't even left the state. The sense of *that way* ended at an apartment in San

Francisco.

Justin staked out the building until he saw Dr. Attanasio leave. Then he deactivated his security system, slipped inside, and searched the place.

Based on what he found on the doctor's laptop and papers, Dr. Attanasio was no longer working for Apex, but was now busy designing extra-addictive drugs. Disgusted, Justin placed several bugs in the apartment, then replaced everything exactly the way he'd found it. He checked to make sure he hadn't missed anything and all his bugs were perfectly concealed before he stepped into a shadowy corner to wait for the doctor to return.

We lie in wait, hissed his inner snow leopard, sending Justin a sense of his satisfaction. Lying in wait was the big cat's favorite thing.

Justin sank into the calm, cool mindset of the predator within. He wasn't bored or restless. He didn't think. He just waited. It felt good. Almost like being invincible...

His snow leopard stirred in alarm. He hated Justin's power of adrenaline invincibility, which had the side effect of suppressing his inner predator.

You don't need invincibility, the big cat hissed. *You just need to lie in wait.*

I can't lie in wait all the time, Justin returned. *Now hush.*

Hours later, the door opened. Dr. Attanasio stepped inside, flicking on the light as he shut the door behind him.

Justin closed the distance between them in an instant, twisting the doctor's arms behind him with one hand and putting his other hand over Dr. Attanasio's mouth.

Kill him, snarled his snow leopard. *Rip out his throat!*

Justin mentally distanced himself from the big cat's rage. He kept his voice calm and low as he addressed the doctor. "Scream, and I'll kill you. When I take my hand away, you can talk, but do it quietly. Nod if you understand."

With his keen predator's senses, Justin could smell the acrid scent of the doctor's cold sweat. Trembling, Dr. Attanasio nodded.

Justin released the doctor and stepped in front of him.

"Subject Seven!" Dr. Attanasio gasped.

"Surprise," Justin remarked, deadpan.

"How did you find me?" The doctor's voice rose in terror. Justin dipped his hand, palm down, in a 'lower your voice' gesture. Dr. Attanasio continued, hushed but frantic. "I wore gloves every time I had to lay hands on you. And I never let you touch me. So someone must have sold me out! Who?"

Justin kept his face still, making sure he didn't reveal anything with so much as a blink. "Who do you think?"

"One of the doctors? They were always jealous of me, because *my* experiments got results." Studying Justin's face, Dr. Attanasio said, "Or was it one of the project managers? It was, right? Which one?"

Justin concealed his satisfaction. So Dr. Attanasio *was* in touch with some other survivors from Apex. In case he hadn't mentioned everyone he knew about, Justin let one of his eyebrows raise slightly and made a small, involuntary-seeming head-shake.

Yesss, hissed his snow leopard, with immense satisfaction. *We play with our prey.*

"It wasn't any of them?" Dr. Attanasio looked baffled, then even more scared. "Who was it, then? Who? There's no one else who knows where I—" He broke off, obviously realizing that he'd revealed too much.

"That's what you think," Justin said. With any luck, Dr. Attanasio would get on the phone to his evil co-workers and demand that they tell him who else was out there.

Before the doctor had a chance to collect himself, Justin slowly reached out with his bare hand, letting Dr. Attanasio see it coming.

The doctor flinched. "Don't hurt me!"

Justin had been trying to keep as cool on the inside as he looked on the outside, but something snapped inside him at those words. "Why the hell shouldn't I? You hurt me until I hoped I'd die just to make it stop!"

Dr. Attanasio flinched again, but there was no remorse in his expression, only fear. Defensively, he said, "It was necessary. We made huge scientific breakthroughs. Anyway, look what you got out of it. The Ultimate Predator process gave you powers beyond anything normal humans or even shifters can dream of. Sure, the process wasn't pleasant, but we didn't do you any harm."

"No harm?" A bitter rage burned through Justin, hot and painful as the chemical the doctor had injected into his veins while he lay strapped to the lab table. *"No harm? You—"*

He forced himself to stop. He didn't want to give the doctor the satisfaction of knowing he'd gotten to him. More importantly, he didn't want to show weakness in front of the man who would undoubtedly be reporting back to his other enemies the instant he left the room. But inside his mind, the rest of his thought echoed:

You ruined my life. You broke me.

His snow leopard hissed reprovingly. *None of that is true.*

Rather than get into a pointless argument with his snow leopard, Justin forced his attention out of his head and to the enemy in front of him. He seized his prey by the throat. The doctor let out a shrill squeal of terror.

"I'm touching you now," Justin said. "And you know what that means."

Dr. Attanasio just stared at him, his eyes bulging with panic.

"Say it," Justin said. "Say it so I know you understand."

"I can't speak when you're strangling…" Dr. Attanasio's voice trailed off as he realized that Justin had only wrapped his fingers around his throat, and wasn't exerting any pressure. "Uh, it's your Ultimate Predator power. I mean, it's one of them. You can track me now. Anywhere in the world, as far as we know. You don't need to know where I am. You just follow my—"

Scent, hissed his snow leopard. With immense satisfaction, he added, *You can run, but you can't hide.*

"—imprint," the doctor concluded.

"That's right." Justin increased the pressure, just slightly. "Are you really making designer drugs, or is that a front for Apex?"

"Apex is gone!" Dr. Attanasio choked out. "You and Subject Eight destroyed it yourselves. It's just the drugs, I swear!"

Justin considered seeing if he could squeeze more information out of him, then decided to stick with his first plan. Threatening him more might just scare him into saying whatever he imagined Justin wanted to hear.

"It better be," Justin said. "If I ever find out that you're involved in kidnapping or experimenting on unwilling subjects or anything else like what you did at Apex, I'll track you down, just like I tracked down some of your other colleagues. And I'll do to you exactly what I did to them."

Dr. Attanasio's eyes bulged even more, reminding Justin of a bullfrog. "What? Who else did you track down? Did you kill them?"

Justin stared into the doctor's pop-eyes, silent and expressionless. He knew the effect his gaze had on people, even when he didn't have them by the throat. Sure enough, the doctor gulped and looked away, blood draining out of his face until it went an unpleasant pasty color.

Without a word, Justin turned his back and walked out of the apartment, letting the door slowly close behind him.

Where are you going? His snow leopard's hiss rose in frustration. *Kill him, kill him!*

An overwhelming weariness washed over Justin. He was so tired of arguing with his snow leopard. If the big cat wasn't demanding someone's death, he was all the way on the other extreme, insisting that too-good-to-be-true things like mates and packs and happiness were just around the corner.

They are not too good to be true, hissed his snow leopard. *Remember how you insisted that your packmate had abandoned you, and I kept telling you he'd come back for you? Who was right about that?*

You were, Justin admitted. But he didn't want to talk about Shane. He could hardly bear to think about his old best friend. Trustworthy Shane, whom Justin hadn't trusted. Loyal Shane, whom Justin had betrayed.

To get his snow leopard off the topic, Justin said, *Stop calling him my packmate. Leopards don't have packs.*

Shifters do, his snow leopard retorted. *Go back inside, kill our prey, and then go to your pack. They will help us hunt down the rest of our enemies. We have spent far too long hunting alone.*

For what felt like the millionth time, Justin explained, *We need to leave him alone for now, so he thinks it's safe to talk to his colleagues. We're not doing anything to any of them until we find out where the Apex base is.* Then *we—*

Rip out their throats, hissed his snow leopard.

Justin shrugged. Maybe he'd kill them, or maybe he'd phone in an anonymous tip to the FBI and put them behind bars. Based on his own experience, suffering in captivity was a fate worse than death, so he leaned toward throwing them in jail. But his leopard seemed incapable of understanding that argument.

He ran along the corridor, his soft-soled shoes making barely more sound than a cat's paws, and opened the door to the emergency staircase. It had a sign warning that an alarm would go off if it was opened, but he had deactivated the alarm before he'd entered the doctor's apartment.

When he reached the roof, he lay down so no one could see his silhouette. Justin doubted that anyone was looking for him, other than possibly Dr. Attanasio, but stealth had become a habit, and he didn't want to get killed before he'd made sure that Apex was gone for good.

Flat on his belly atop the sun-warmed concrete, he took out his earbuds, stuck them in his ears, and listened to the sounds inside the doctor's apartment. He heard rustling, footsteps, and then the doctor saying, "Hello?"

Justin couldn't hear the response; Dr. Attanasio must be talking on his cell phone, which Justin hadn't been able to bug. But he could hear every word the doctor said, loud and clear.

"Subject Seven is alive! He broke into my apartment..." The doctor detailed what had happened, then said, "No, I'm only in touch with you. Do you know anything about anyone else? They have to be warned... if it's not too late already."

There was a brief pause in which Justin wondered who he was talking to. It had to be either a doctor or a project manager, but that could be a lot of people.

Dr. Attanasio exclaimed, "Mr. Bianchi is out of his mind if he thinks he's safe in London! You want to bet that an ocean is enough to stop Subject Seven? I wouldn't! Tell Mr. Bianchi to hire every bodyguard he can lay his hands on."

Another pause. "No, I don't know if he ever touched any of us. I thought he hadn't touched me... until now. So either we have a rat or he got our imprints on the sly or his power doesn't work the way he said it did and all he ever needed to do was fucking *smell* us!"

I wish all we needed to do was scent our prey, hissed his snow leopard.

I wish I'd had the sense to pretend my power worked differently, Justin replied. *I should've told them I needed to lay my entire palm on someone's bare skin for five minutes. Then they'd have been less careful around me, and I could've gotten all their imprints.*

A wave of self-reproach swept over him, so intense that he could taste the bitterness, like he'd chewed on an aspirin. It was such a simple idea, but it hadn't occurred to him until it was too late. He hadn't been smart or sneaky or quick enough to touch them all.

He hadn't saved his buddies.

He'd betrayed Shane. He'd betrayed himself. He'd—

Pay attention, hissed his snow leopard. *Our prey is speaking again.*

Justin dragged his attention back to the doctor, who was saying, "What's he doing there, anyway?"

Another pause. The doctor gave a bitter chuckle. "Of course. Mr. Bianchi's getting fabulously wealthy dealing weapons, and I'm stuck making goddamn designer drugs. And I can't ever go back to Apex, or Subject Seven will come back and… No, I told you, he didn't say who he'd killed, let alone how he'd done it. But I saw his eyes. That's not a man. That's a predator. I'm staying right where I am. Anything else would be suicide."

Dr. Attanasio said no more. The conversation was clearly over.

Justin rolled over and looked up at the darkening sky. At long last, he had a lead on one of the higher-up men at Apex, one he'd never been able to touch. London was a big city, but Justin felt confident that given enough time, he could find Mr. Bianchi there. And Mr. Bianchi might know where the base was, or know who did. If not, Justin could return to San Francisco and stalk Dr. Attanasio until he figured out who the doctor had been talking to.

No matter what, this was a big break. He should be glad. But he felt nothing but the pain that had been tearing him apart ever since he'd escaped Apex, a searing agony of rage and guilt, shame and loss, memories of a past he couldn't stand to recall and fear for a future stretching out ahead of him like a million miles of bad road. It was in his ears like a shriek of metal on metal, in his chest like a knife in the heart, in his bones with an ache like he hadn't slept in weeks. It was with him every moment of every day.

Except when he was invincible.

Don't, hissed his snow leopard.

Justin barely heard him. Dr. Attanasio's words were echoing inside his mind, loud enough to drown out everything else:

That's not a man. That's a predator.

All those cruel days and lonely nights at Apex, he'd dreamed and dreamed about escape. Then he'd gotten out, and realized that there was no escape. He could get away from Apex, but he couldn't get away from himself. Everything he'd done—everything that had been done to him—everything he'd become—was irrevocable. He couldn't change it. The best he could do was make himself not care.

Luckily, there was a way to do that.

Don't! His snow leopard gave a low growl that probably would have made Dr. Attanasio faint with terror. *You are doing it too much. It will kill you.*

Justin tried to squelch his automatic response, but his snow leopard caught it anyway:

Who cares?

The big cat's anger, fear, and frustration surged through Justin as he snarled in desperation, *I care! I want to live!*

At that, Justin felt guilty. He fished for some reply that his snow leopard would find reassuring and that would be honest. His inner predator was a part of him, after all; he couldn't lie to himself.

He settled on, *I have no intention of dying just yet.*

It was true, as far as it went: he had no intention of dying until he'd destroyed Apex and could be sure they'd never harm anyone again. After that, he didn't care what happened to him. But since he was wildly unlikely to survive going up against an entire black ops agency all by himself, he didn't have to worry about the "after that."

He closed his eyes and pictured himself standing alone on a vast, featureless plain of blinding white. An ice field. He imagined the ice creeping up over his feet and up his legs, at first so cold that it burned, and then numbing. When the ice reached his heart, the burning flared into agony. Justin gritted his teeth, knowing that the pain would be brief. A moment later his heart went numb, and a blessed calm washed over him.

He opened his eyes. He was alone on the roof, as alone as he'd been on his imaginary ice field. Justin couldn't feel his snow leopard. He couldn't feel anything at all. No guilt, no anger, no shame, just a cool readiness to do whatever was needed.

No pain.

He could recall anything that had happened to him at Apex, and feel nothing. If someone shot him, he'd feel nothing. He wouldn't get hungry or tired. He didn't need to eat or sleep. He was unstoppable.

Invincible.

I wish I could be like this all the time, Justin thought as he headed back for the stairs. *It feels so much better.*

The only reason he didn't was that if he stayed invincible too long, he'd die.

You have to eat and sleep to live, and when he was invincible, he not only didn't need to, he *couldn't*. And while a man could go a month or so without food, Apex experiments had shown that if he went for more than a week without sleep, his body started dangerously breaking down.

Don't worry, he said silently, though he knew his snow leopard couldn't hear or speak. *I won't keep it up long enough to do any damage. Just a few hours. Eight, max.*

Justin imagined he could hear the big cat's angry hiss:

Liar.

CHAPTER ONE
Fiona

The maid of honor speech had gone perfectly, with everyone laughing or dabbing at their eyes in all the right places. Now Fiona Payne lifted her glass to conclude it. "A toast!"

The wedding guests raised their glasses and held them aloft. Grace was radiant in the unique bridal gown Raluca had designed, of white silk with black lace and pink ribbons. Her chunky black leather heels peeked out from the bottom of the gown's artistically tattered hem. Rafa stood beaming with his arm around her and the sunshine glinting off his glossy hair. Everyone seemed happy, from Rafa's lion shifter relatives to Grace's theatre friends to Rafa and Fiona's teammates from Protection, Inc.

And their teammates' mates.

Hal, the huge bear shifter and boss of Protection, Inc., sat beside his mate, the brave paramedic Ellie, with his huge hand resting protectively over her pregnant belly. Nick, the ex-gangster werewolf, leaned back in his seat with one arm around his dragon shifter mate Raluca. Lucas, the dragon shifter and former prince, sat with red-headed Journey, who was bedecked in the gold and jewels he'd given her. And Shane, the quiet panther shifter who was Fiona's best friend on the team, was partnered with the leopard shifter Catalina, who was so much his other half that she'd joined the team to work by his side.

Of the original bodyguard team, only Destiny and Fiona were still unmatched. But it was surely just a matter of time before Destiny would find her own mate. And then Fiona would be left alone.

I won't be completely alone, Fiona told herself firmly. *I'll still have Protection, Inc.*

Her snow leopard stirred within her. *A pack is good, but not enough. We need our mate.*

Hush, Fiona scolded her inner predator. *We don't* need *anyone. Neediness is weakness.* Belatedly, she added, *And Protection, Inc. is a private security agency—a* team. *Just because we're all shifters doesn't make it a pack. Only wolves have packs.*

She suddenly realized that she'd fallen silent in mid-toast, while everyone looked at her expectantly. Hoping Grace wasn't regretting choosing her as maid of honor, Fiona concluded smoothly, "Here's to a couple who truly earned their happily ever after. To Grace and Rafa!"

"To Grace and Rafa," chorused the guests, and drank.

Fiona took a final glance at her glass. Lucas had provided a bottle of dragonfire, the unique liquor finished with a breath of flame from an actual dragon. The orange-red liquor seethed and rolled like liquid flame, sending up wisps of smoke. She inhaled its sensual aroma of fruit and fire as she tilted it to her lips.

Fiona was no stranger to high society and its expensive, sophisticated drinks. She'd had Dom Perignon champagne that cost two thousand dollars per bottle, and rare whiskey aged for eighty years beneath a Scottish castle. But nothing she'd ever drunk came close to dragonfire. It tasted of cherries harvested under a summer sun, of roses dark as blood and bright as fire, of dreams and hopes and desire, and it slid down her throat like molten gold.

She stood alone with the heat of dragonfire warming her body, watching the mated pairs turn to each other and kiss. They were her closest friends—her *only* friends—but she felt like an outsider. Being in the midst of all that love and intimacy, when she knew she'd never experience it for herself, was like getting stabbed by a million tiny daggers, right in the heart.

No, she thought. *Not daggers. Shards of ice.*

She could see her reflection in her empty glass: a woman with skin as pale as frost and hair as white as snow, in a dress the color of a frozen lake.

I'm the snow queen, she thought. *I have a lump of ice where my heart should be. I'm meant to live in the frozen peaks where nothing grows. I'm only a spy down here where it's warm. Some day everyone will find out what I really am and send me back where I belong.*

Most of the time, she could focus on her work hard enough to forget about that. But not now. Fiona wished the couples all the best, but she also wished she was anywhere else.

You just have to get through today, she reminded herself. *Tomorrow, you'll be going on another undercover mission.*

One more day, and instead of drinking rare liquor while wearing an exquisite designer gown, she'd be risking her life spying on a ruthless international arms dealer who sold weapons to terrorists, gangsters, and even small dictatorships.

She couldn't wait.

Fiona stood before a man who'd order her killed with a snap of his fingers if she made one false move. Mr. Elson hadn't risen to the top of the world of international organized crime by accident; he was ruthless, suspicious, and intelligent. The FBI had been trying to get an undercover operative into his syndicate for years. Some had failed. Others had gotten in, then turned up dead. In desperation, they'd contacted Protection, Inc. for help.

And so Fiona had insinuated herself into the syndicate by posing as an unscrupulous spy for hire. She'd proved herself to Mr. Elson, she hoped, by providing him with accurate information on some of his competitors. Another month or two undercover, and she should have enough information to pass on to the FBI to allow them to take down him, his syndicate, and several other criminal groups in the bargain.

All she had to do was keep her cool. But then, that was what she did best.

Cool, her snow leopard purred. *Calm. Cold.*

"What have you got for me?" Fiona asked. Her voice was flat, colorless, almost bored. Like her lack of makeup and gray business suit, her voice matched her persona as the perfect spy: emotionless and unmemorable. An invisible woman.

Mr. Elson laced his fingers together, irresistibly reminding her of

Marlon Brando in *The Godfather*.

Which is basically what he is, she thought. *Only minus the part where he cares about his family.* As far as she could tell, the only thing Mr. Elson cared about was getting richer.

"There's a man who's recently become a person of interest," the arms dealer replied. "He broke up a deal I was trying to make in London. He destroyed merchandise worth a million dollars, and took the million in cash from the people I was trying to make the deal with."

Merchandise, she thought. *Meaning illegal weapons.*

Whoever the man was, he had to be very tough—and very reckless—to have gone up against representatives from two different organized crime factions.

She let none of those thoughts show in her face. "What would you like me to do with him?"

"Your usual. Insinuate yourself into his life. Or bed." He gave her an unpleasant leer. "But you can pose as anyone you like. If it makes sense, you can tell him up-front that you're working for me."

Fiona allowed her real surprise to widen her eyes. "I can?"

Mr. Elson seemed amused. "If it helps your mission, which is to recruit him. If he's after money or power or revenge—you know, the usual things people want—tell him I'll give it to him. Along with forgiveness for busting up my deal. If you think revealing who you're working for will put him off, don't do it right away. Find out what his goal is, and convince him it's the same as yours. When you think the time is right, let me know, and I'll send in someone else to make you both an offer."

"And I convince him we should take it." She nodded. "Got it."

He held up his hand. "I'm not done. I would *prefer* to have him working for me. But right now, he's a loose cannon. I don't want him running around, making trouble for me whenever he feels like it. So if you can't recruit him, I want you to kill him."

Fiona frowned slightly, but behind the mild dismay she displayed, her thoughts spun rapidly. If she'd only been wearing a wire, she'd have had him right then and there. Unfortunately, he always had people searched before they came into his presence, so she wasn't. She could testify that he'd said it, but it would be his word against hers. But if he went so far as to hand her a murder weapon, she'd have both testimony and a piece of physical evidence to back her up.

But she'd never claimed to be an assassin, so it would be out of character not to protest. "I'm not a hit man."

The arms dealer gave her a sharp look that made her heartbeat speed up. "Are you saying you won't do it?"

"I'm saying I'm not the best person for an assassination," she returned calmly. "And you always hire the best, don't you?"

"I'm not demanding that you do anything that requires special skills. I know you're not a sniper. Or a kung fu master." He gave her an oily smile, as if the idea of her being able to shoot accurately or fight with her bare hands and feet was absurd.

Little do you know, Fiona thought. She'd learned to shoot and fight from the best: Hal and Rafa, who were former Navy SEALs, Destiny, an Army sharpshooter, and Shane, who really was a martial arts master, though of karate rather than kung fu.

Taking her silence for agreement, he went on, "But if you can plant a bug in someone's coat pocket, you're more than capable of dropping something into someone's drink. I just want to know that you will, if I give you the order."

"I will. But if it comes to that, I want danger pay. Double my daily rate. And not just for that one day. For the whole assignment."

"Done."

Inwardly, she relaxed. The greedy demand for a murder bonus had clearly convinced him that she was the heartless criminal she was posing as.

"I should have asked for triple," she remarked.

He let out that oily chuckle again. "Too late. You've already agreed. And while I'm certain you're far too intelligent to dream of either breathing a word about this assignment to anyone, or double-crossing me and taking your target to someone else, I must remind you that the consequences of that would be… unpleasant."

"You're right," Fiona said, deadpan. "I *am* far too intelligent."

"Excellent. Now for the dossier." He opened a folder on his desk, showing her a black and white photo obviously taken from a security camera. One man was throwing another up against the wall. The attacker's back was turned; the other man looked terrified.

"Here's the target attacking one of my men," Mr. Elson said. "His real name is unknown. Based on his skill set, I suspect that he's a former government operative who went rogue. That might be an in for you. Tell him you hate the government too, and you should get along like a house on fire."

Fiona took the folder. She found more security camera shots that didn't show the man's face, and a detailed report on his encounter with Mr. Elson's men, which she skimmed and mentally summed up as "One guy kicked all of our asses, how the hell did he do that?" Then she flipped a page over, and found a shot that showed him in profile.

He was strikingly handsome, even in grainy black and white, with sharp features that looked like they'd been carved in marble. His skin was very pale, his eyes and hair very dark. His face was an expressionless mask, revealing nothing.

Fiona barely stopped herself from letting her shock show on her face. She knew him. Or, more accurately, she recognized him. The month before, she'd been kidnapped and held at gunpoint by a gang. That man had appeared out of nowhere to rescue her. He'd asked her not to tell anyone he'd been there, and she'd kept that promise.

Afterward, she'd found herself lying awake at night, going over the encounter in her mind. So many things about the man had been so mysterious. He'd been wounded in the shoot-out, but had claimed he didn't feel any pain. She'd felt an odd jolt when their eyes had met and again when their hands had touched, and she could have sworn he'd felt it too. He'd saved her life. And before she'd been able to learn anything about him, even his name, he'd vanished.

It looked like she was going to find out now.

"We found one of his hideouts." Mr. Elson dropped two slips of paper into her file. One had an address in New York City, and another had a plane ticket to New York made out to her fake name.

Her gaze once again strayed to the photo. Those dark eyes were so haunting. So haunt*ed*. They made her wonder if he ever smiled, and what he'd look like if he did.

She smiled at Mr. Elson as she closed the file. "He's all mine."

Fiona spent the entire plane ride to New York City wondering about her mystery man. Was he really a rogue agent? That could explain why he'd sworn her to secrecy, why he'd refused to let her take him to a doctor, and why he'd fled. Or was that a cover story to conceal the fact that he was still working for the government, maybe in black ops? That would also explain his behavior.

Either way, she was relieved to know that he was alive and well, or at least well enough to fight. He'd looked pale and thin and weary *before* he'd been shot, and had disappeared without even letting her bandage his wound. She'd been so worried that he might have collapsed somewhere in the vicinity that she'd returned later and prowled all over it as a snow leopard, but had found no trace of him.

If he is a government agent, I'll tell him everything, Fiona thought. *Maybe he can help me with my mission and I can help him with his. And if he still looks that bad, I'll see if I can have a word with his handler about making him take a long vacation once he's done with this job.*

If he's a rogue...

That would be a much more complicated situation. When she'd thought he was just another criminal, she'd meant to go ahead and try to recruit him, exactly like Mr. Elson wanted, in the interests of keeping up her cover. But that was before she'd known he was the man who'd saved her life. Now that she did know, she couldn't bring herself to lure him into Mr. Elson's criminal organization—and she doubted very much that he'd be interested.

Maybe she could tell him the truth. But if he was willing to go along and pretend to be recruited, she'd be putting him in danger. And if he wasn't, her entire mission could end then and there.

I guess I play it by ear, she decided.

Trust your instinct, agreed her snow leopard.

But she wasn't going to just walk up and wing it. All else aside, she was desperately curious about him. Who *was* he?

His hideout turned out to be in a neighborhood that looked like the set of a zombie movie. Minus the zombies.

So far, anyway, Fiona thought, glancing into a deserted, trash-lined alley. But it wouldn't have surprised her if one had suddenly staggered out, maybe from behind the rusting dumpster.

It was a good location for a hideout. With streets this empty, literally anyone approaching would be noticed. So instead of trying to sneak up, which was clearly impossible, she clutched her purse in one hand and her cell phone in the other as she hurried along the sidewalk, casting nervous glances over her shoulder every few seconds. There. Now she was a lost tourist looking for a safe place to call a taxi and get the hell out of there.

She passed the hideout, a seemingly abandoned building, then ducked into the shadows of a dead-end alley. If he was home and watching, he'd lose sight of her there, but believe that she couldn't leave without him noticing. The only way out was back the way she came or else over a concrete wall far too high and smooth for anyone to jump or climb over.

Anyone human, that was.

Fiona took off her black ballet slippers and popped them into her purse. Then she stripped off her pants, blouse, bra, and panties, folded them into a tight square of cloth, and sent them to join the slippers. They were all thin silk, which she'd bought on purpose because it compressed well.

She shivered briefly, standing naked and barefoot in the cold night air. Then she summoned her snow leopard.

To leap and pounce...
To hunt in the snow...
To be one with the night...

Her chill vanished. She was warm and comfortable in her coat of black-dappled white. Her senses sharpened, allowing her to scent the air. Trash, more trash, spilled beer, gasoline, the musty smell of pigeons, and the sharper odor of rats. But the only human scents were faint and faded. Her target wasn't home.

All the same, she meant to be careful. She bent down and daintily gripped her purse strap between her sharp teeth. Then she crouched, tensing her powerful haunches, and leaped high into the air. She easily cleared the wall and landed lightly on the sidewalk, her purse swinging from her jaws.

And there was the back of his hideout, with the windows boarded up and a fire escape leading to the roof. Fiona leaped on to the fire escape, then padded up to the roof. She nosed the door to the staircase. It was locked.

She set down the purse, shifted back into a woman, put her clothes back on, and took out a set of lock picks. It was open in under three minutes. Now the hideout was all hers.

If she'd still been a leopard, she would have purred. As a human, she permitted herself a small grin.

Fiona moved soundlessly down the dark stairwell, all her senses alert. If he had been careless enough to leave a laptop here, she'd suck it dry of information. If he'd left *any* belongings, she'd learn something about him from them. She'd plant some bugs before she vanished as stealthily as she'd come. Then she'd observe him at her leisure.

At the bottom of the stairwell, she blinked until her eyes adjusted enough to see by the moonlight filtering through the few unboarded windows. She was in an abandoned warehouse cluttered with empty crates and the hulks of rusted machinery. Then she spotted a mattress in one corner, and a duffel bag beside it. Fiona hurried toward it.

A hand clamped over her mouth, and a strong arm clasped her against a man's chest.

A voice began to speak in her ear. "Who—"

Fiona didn't give him the chance to finish the sentence. Her heart was pounding with shock, but she reacted instantly, kicking backward to knock her attacker's feet out from under him.

Her foot met empty air as the man holding her shifted his weight, avoiding her attack.

He's fast.

But his grip loosened. Fiona dropped down, slithering out of his grasp and diving away.

She rolled, then immediately leaped to her feet. The man before her stood in a slight crouch, like a cat ready to pounce.

Even in the dim light, she knew him immediately. The moonlight transformed him into a black-and-white image like the one in the photo: black pants and shirt, white skin, black hair falling across his forehead and casting a shadow that made his eyes vanish into darkness. But he moved with a grace that no photograph could capture, as beautiful and deadly as a leopard in the jungle.

When she'd met him a month ago, she'd thought he looked too thin. He'd lost more weight since then, and the lines in his face were deeper. He moved his head slightly to get a better look at her, and the moonlight illuminated his eyes. She'd seen them before, but they were still startling. They were wells of darkness, and not just because of their color. Something about them made her think that he'd seen things no one should ever see.

He looks like he's been through hell, she thought.

He has, hissed her snow leopard. *You need to help him.*

Fiona had no idea how her snow leopard knew what he'd been through, since Fiona sure didn't. She pitched her voice low and calming as she said, "I won't hurt you. Don't worry."

"I'm not worried." He also spoke calmly—no, flatly. The total lack of emotion in his voice was unnerving. She couldn't even tell if he recognized her. "What are you doing here?"

Fiona was rarely caught off guard, but she hadn't prepared anything to say for what to do if he'd caught her breaking into his home when she still didn't know anything about him. Finally, floundering, she asked, "Do you remember me?"

His expression didn't shift. "Of course."

She had no idea what to say, but she had to say something. Hoping it would come to her before she had to finish the sentence, she began, "Well…"

A flash of light moved across the floor.

It was the kind of reflection that would shine off the barrel of a rifle.

Fiona instinctively lunged to shield him. At the same instant, he dove toward her. They collided hard and painfully, knocking each other down.

As they fell, the crack of a gun sounded, and the window they'd been standing by shattered. Glass tinkled to the floor. A split second later, another gunshot blew a tiny crater in the concrete floor, two inches from Fiona's face.

They grabbed each other and rolled together. Their combined strength sent them into the opposite wall. More shots were fired, thudding into the walls and ricocheting off the floor, as they scrambled into the safety of the stairwell.

They bolted up the stairs together. With the strange attention to detail that sometimes comes with an adrenaline rush, Fiona was very conscious that they had somehow ended up holding hands. He had a strong grip, and with his longer legs, he was practically hauling her up the stairs, even though she could run faster than most men.

"The shots were coming from the west," she gasped. "We could get down the fire escape—it's on the other side."

"Maybe we're meant to think that," he replied, his voice harsh and ragged. "Maybe there's a second sniper."

They stopped at the door that led to the roof. It was pitch black. Fiona couldn't see him at all. She couldn't even see her own hands.

"Is there another way out?" she asked.

"Yeah." He was standing so close that she could feel his warm breath on her cheek. "I have a rope hidden up there. We could cross our fingers we're not surrounded on all sides and climb down."

"If you have a cell phone hidden too, I could call for backup," Fiona suggested. She'd lost her purse in the warehouse. "Or the police...?"

"Tell you what. You stay here. I'll climb down. If I don't get shot on the way down, I'll make the call, then run. If I do..." He shrugged. "Well, they weren't shooting at *you*. You were just in the way. And you never saw their faces, so you're not a witness. I think if you waited a bit, they'd go away and you could leave safely."

Do not let him go into danger alone, hissed her snow leopard. *You must protect him!*

I'm on it, Fiona replied silently. She'd felt an instinctive horror at his lack of concern for himself.

"I don't know about that," she retorted. "Don't be so sure they're after you. They could just as easily be after me."

There was a brief silence. Then he said, "Really?"

"Really. I have enemies too. And if we stand here talking much longer, someone will come inside to finish the job. If rope is what we have, we'd better start climbing."

Another silence. Then, with what sounded like reluctance, he said, "All right. But stay here till I get it set up."

He opened the door, letting in a flood of moonlight, then flattened himself down and swiftly belly-crawled across the roof. She saw him pry something up, then reach down and remove a backpack. He wriggled to the edge of the roof, took a coil of rope from the backpack and tied it around a sturdy pipe, then turned back and beckoned to her.

Fiona crawled to him. "Ready?"

"I was about to ask you that." He tossed the rope over. "I'll go first.

Don't start climbing till I'm all the way down."

"In case you get shot?"

He shrugged. "My rope, my rules."

She bit her lip, hating the thought of it. "Got another gun in there? I could cover you."

"Oh, sure." He opened the backpack again and handed her a pistol in a shoulder holster, then slung the backpack over his shoulders and took hold of the rope.

Don't let him get away, her snow leopard urged her.

"Wait!" Fiona grabbed his wrist. "One more thing. Don't run off on me."

His eyes flickered, but she couldn't read his expression.

She searched for something he'd find persuasive. It was so hard when she knew so little about him, not even his name. But he'd risked his life to save hers when they'd first met, and jumped to shield her when the shooting had started. Whether he wanted to help her specifically or whether he was just the protective type, she didn't know. But either way, she could use those instincts to keep him by her side.

"I need your help," she said. Making sure he could hear the truth of her words, she said, "If you disappear on me now, I'll be on my own. I could get killed."

"If you need me, I'm not going anywhere," he replied instantly.

I knew it, Fiona thought. *He'll stay with me if he thinks he needs to protect me. And that gives me the perfect excuse to stay with him so I can protect* him.

As soon as she had that thought, she wondered about it. Why was she so set on protecting him?

Well, he had saved her life. Twice. She owed him. That was all.

"If I get down, I'll cover you," he said.

"*If?*" Fiona echoed. "I'll have you know, I'm an excellent shot. You *will* get down."

"That's true, you are. I remember from the last time we met. You fired three times fast with an unfamiliar gun and made all three shots." His comment seemed sincere, but he didn't seem reassured by his own belief that she could cover him. Nor did he sound worried. He spoke flatly, as if he didn't care one way or another. Then, without warning, he swung over the edge.

She watched intently, searching for any telltale movement or glint of light that might be a sniper, but saw nothing. He climbed the rope with catlike agility, and had his feet on the sidewalk within seconds. He drew his gun with a lightning-fast move, then melted into the shadows.

Fiona replaced the pistol in its holster, slung it over her shoulder, and followed him down, hoping he'd just taken cover and hadn't vanished for real. But when she reached the alley, he stepped out of the shadows and beckoned to her. He quickly led her through a maze of dark and narrow alleys, sometimes scrambling over fences, until she saw the moving lights of a busy street at the end of an intersecting alley.

"Hold on," she said. "I'm sure we've lost them by now. Let's get a cab to my hotel. I'm staying at the Ritz Carlton."

He gave her a dubious glance. "The Ritz, as in the most famous hotel in New York City? Not very stealthy."

"I didn't check in under my own name," she said. "And we won't take the cab right there, just close enough to walk. Like you said, it's famous. That means it's got good security. Anything happens there, it'll be swarming with police within minutes. And if someone got murdered there, it'd be a huge news story. Even if we get tracked there, which we probably won't, no one will try anything till we leave. It'll give us some breathing room."

She could see that he had qualms about the idea, but no real arguments against it.

"Unless you have a better place to go?" she asked.

"No. You're right, anywhere I'd go would be like the place we just came from. There'd be nothing stopping us from getting ambushed again. Hold on a second. Let's see if I can get less conspicuous."

He opened his backpack, took out a tightly folded suit jacket, and buttoned it over his shirt. Fiona turned her back when he pulled out a pair of suit pants and polished shoes.

"I'm done," he said after a moment of rustling.

She was startled by how different he looked when she turned around. It wasn't just the clothes. He'd also put on a pair of black-rimmed glasses. As she watched, he slumped a little bit, ruining his perfect posture. He couldn't completely disguise his striking features or catlike grace, but he now looked much less dangerous: a handsome professional athlete, maybe, rather than a lethal weapon in human form.

And where did he learn to do all that, I wonder? Fiona thought.

She watched, fascinated, as he unzipped some closures on his backpack and re-zipped them in a different configuration, transforming it into a small duffel bag of the sort a businessman might carry for an overnight trip. She passed over her pistol and holster, which he tucked away in it.

"Did you lose your wallet?" he asked.

"Yeah, but I have my credit card and room card in my pocket," Fiona replied. "I can cover the cab."

"I'll do that," he said. "I assume you already paid for the room."

The room. She'd forgotten about that part. If they were staying together, they'd be in the same room; if they wanted to attract the absolute minimum amount of attention, they couldn't ask to add another bed. That could make people wonder why she hadn't asked for one when she'd booked the room, and what relationship they had. Whereas if he simply showed up with her, everyone would assume they were a couple on vacation.

Which meant they'd be staying in a room with just one bed.

If Fiona was the blushing type, she'd have blushed. In fact, she did feel a little warm. The thought of sharing a room with him—sharing a *bed* with him—made a shiver of… something… go up and down her spine. It wasn't fear; she'd never feared him and certainly didn't now. Excitement? Anticipation? Not desire, surely. He was a handsome man and he intrigued her, but he was too strange and distant for her to want him that way…

Well, maybe it *was* desire. Just a little bit. A side effect of the combination of his stunning looks, the fact that he'd repeatedly saved her life, and the lingering traces of her adrenaline rush. A purely instinctive reaction, not something real. She didn't know him well enough for that. She didn't even know his name.

She wanted to at least find that out, but if she asked now, he'd probably just give her an alias. Still, she had to call him something if they were going to impersonate a couple.

"What name is on your ID?" she asked.

"Andrew Wright. What's on yours?"

"Anne Burns."

"Anne and Andy. What a coincidence. I assume you're my girlfriend?"

He sounded completely unruffled by the idea: not excited, not flustered, not anything but maybe mildly amused.

For some reason, that annoyed her. But she didn't let it show. "Yeah. I'll let you know when we're close enough to the Ritz that you should hold my hand or something."

"Shall we?" He indicated the street.

They hailed a cab to a different hotel near Fiona's, then walked to the Ritz. The street was alive with locals and tourists, so they didn't talk. Anything they could possibly say, they didn't want to have overheard.

But as they came closer to her hotel, she said, "It's around the corner."

"Ah." He put his arm around her waist.

Fiona swallowed. She'd been trying not to think about that one bed, but having his arm around her was really not helping.

Fine, she thought. *I'll think about it. It'll help me get in character as his girlfriend.*

His arm was warm and strong. His hand was settled on her hip in a way that suggested tenderness and sensuality, as if it might slide over—and lower—at any moment. What would it be like to be touched—*really* touched—by those long, clever fingers? What would his stubble feel like on her face if he kissed her? What would it feel like on her body if he went on kissing her, all over?

Heat pooled in her belly. And lower down. Her heart was beating faster and faster.

That's enough!

She wrenched her mind away from those fantasies. In-character was one thing. Turning herself on so much that sharing a bed would be horrifically embarrassing was another. This was all strictly business.

With his arm still around her waist and drawing her attention as much as if it was on fire, she strolled up through the lobby and into the elevator. Another couple stepped in with them, so they rode up in silence. It felt like an eternity before they got to her floor. She opened the door to her room. He stepped in. She hung up the Do Not Disturb sign.

The door swung closed behind them, leaving them alone together.

His arm was still around her waist. Probably he'd forgotten it was there, but she hadn't. She didn't want to step away from him, but she forced herself to. Once he was no longer touching her, she couldn't help regretting that she'd moved away.

I had to, she told herself. *That was just for show.*

He took off his glasses and replaced them in their case. Now that she was facing him in a brightly lit room, her attention was caught by how exhausted he looked. His skin wasn't just pale, it was *white*. The shadows under his eyes were smears of black.

"Are you all right?" Then, remembering how he'd been shot and not felt it when they first met, she asked, "Could you have been hit?"

"No."

"Are you sure? You might not feel it."

"I checked when I changed my clothes," he said. "I'm not."

That answer didn't satisfy her. "When was the last time you slept?"

He made a sound like a chuckle, but without any real humor. "You caught me. A week ago."

"A week!?" Fiona stared at him. She'd sometimes gone without sleep for several days, but a week was far longer than even a shifter could manage. "That's impossible. Three days without sleep, and you start hallucinating!"

"No." He sighed. "No, not for me. But I do need to let it go."

"Let what go?"

He gave her a long look, as if deciding whether or not to reply, then sighed again. "I have a… a thing… that lets me go without sleep for long periods. Without food, too. But I'm at my limit for how long I can keep it going. Tell you what. I'll set an alarm on the door. Then I'll let… it… go, and we can both get some sleep. We can do our explanations in the morning. I promise you, I won't disappear in the night."

"A *thing?*" she echoed, baffled. "You mean a drug?"

With a long-suffering expression, he said, "Why do people keep accusing me of being on drugs? No, it's nothing like that. It's just something I can do."

Before she could quiz him more, he opened his backpack and took out a small portable alarm, which he attached to the door and activated. It was the sort of thing Fiona would have used herself, if she hadn't lost her purse.

They knew so many similar things. How to put on a character. How to disguise yourself. How to shoot. How to avoid attracting attention. How to protect yourself if you needed to sleep.

Who *was* he?

"My name's Fiona," she said. "It's my real name. You don't have to tell me your last name, but what's your first? Just so I can stop thinking of you as 'he' and 'you.'"

He didn't reply for so long that she was about to tell him to forget it, she'd call him Andy. Then he said, "Justin."

Fiona barely stopped herself from making the idiotic reply, "That's a nice name." She couldn't help thinking it, though.

Before she could come up with anything sensible to say, Justin said, more to himself than to her and in a voice so low that it was almost a whisper, "All right."

He closed his eyes and seemed to brace himself.

An unsettling feeling of anticipation came over Fiona, as if she was watching a horror movie and didn't know whether the next scene would be the heroine slaying the monster or being torn to shreds by it.

Her snow leopard let out a long, hair-raising growl.

What is it? Fiona asked silently.

Her snow leopard made no reply in words, but the growl slowly shifted into a purr that made Fiona feel as if *her* body was vibrating.

What? Fiona demanded. *What the hell is going on?*

Justin opened his eyes. They were black, so black, but no longer mirrors. At last, she could read them. Could read *him*. The lines in his face spoke of the grinding weariness of pain, and the darkness of his gaze told her that he hadn't just been through hell, but was still living there.

But that wasn't all she saw. The faint lines around his eyes and mouth had been carved by laughter. And beyond what she could literally see, she sensed courage and compassion, endurance and loyalty, a passion for justice and an immense capacity for love.

There was something else, too. Before, her attraction to him had been more of a possibility than a reality: an appreciation of his looks and competence, plus a bit of "I could be into that if he showed a little more emotion." But the instant that they'd locked eyes, desire caught fire within her. Suddenly, she *wanted* him on the most primal level possible. She wanted to rip his clothes off, she wanted him to rip *her* clothes off, she wanted to press their naked flesh together until it felt like they were merging into a single being, a single soul...

Ahhh, said her snow leopard in a rumbling purr. *So that's it.*

So what's what? Fiona replied.

He's our mate, her snow leopard purred.

"No way!" Fiona exclaimed aloud.

But she spoke in shock, not in denial. Her snow leopard's words felt deeply *right*; not simply correct, but expressing a profound truth. How else could she have sensed so much about him just by looking in his eyes? Why else would she have felt so driven to protect him when he was so clearly capable of looking after himself? It had to be because her big cat was right: she and Justin were perfectly compatible. All they had to do now was get to know each other.

My mate, she thought, awestruck.

She'd seen the bonds between mates, and had never imagined that much trust and love could ever be directed at her. She'd done nothing to earn it. But apparently she'd been given that treasure whether she deserved it or not. After a lifetime of loneliness and cold, she'd finally be allowed to come inside and warm her hands at the fire.

Justin recoiled, staring at her in shock and horror.

"No," he breathed. Like her, he too seemed to be replying to an inward voice. His own voice rose in a startlingly loud shout, "No! I can't have a mate! I won't do it! I—"

He broke off, swaying as if he was dizzy. Instinctively, she reached out to steady him. He sprang backward, hands held up to ward her off.

Then his eyes closed. Before she could react, he crumpled to the floor in a dead faint.

Fiona dropped to her knees beside him, cursing herself for having been too surprised to catch him and break his fall. She felt at his throat for a pulse, and was immensely relieved to find one. When she rolled him on to his back, she saw his chest moving evenly as he breathed.

He's probably just exhausted, she thought. Given what he'd said, the only surprising part was that it had taken him that long to collapse.

All the same, she took off his jacket and shirt to check for injuries. She found none, but did notice a star-shaped scar just below his heart. Fiona knew what made scars like that; both Hal and Shane had them. Justin had been lucky to survive getting shot so close to his heart. That must have been a close call.

He lay sprawled on the floor, head tilted back and throat exposed. The position made him look terribly vulnerable. She eased her arms under him, supported his head and neck in the crook of her elbow, took a deep breath, and stood up. Her knees cracked, but her shifter strength enabled her to carry him to the bed and lay him gently down. He didn't stir as she took off his belt and shoes, then pulled the covers over him.

Once she knew he wasn't hurt and was as comfortable as she could make him, her urgency faded, giving her space to think about what had happened right before he had collapsed.

My mate, she thought. *This man is my mate.*

At last, purred her snow leopard. The big cat was so filled with contentment and satisfaction, she was practically licking her paws and sunning herself.

Fiona's own feelings were considerably more complicated. She couldn't deny that she felt deeply and instinctively drawn to Justin, nor that she also had more rational reasons for feeling that way. He'd saved her life—twice! He was quick to think and quick to act, skilled at fighting and subterfuge, competent and intelligent and brave. From the first moment they'd met, they'd worked together as smoothly as she did with teammates she'd had for years.

There was also the little matter of him being devastatingly handsome and incredibly sexy. Especially when he was in motion. She'd never seen anything to match his predatory grace, not even from her shifter teammates.

He could be—he *was*—the partner she'd always longed for, and never believed she'd find.

And yet.

She had so many questions about him. Why was he on the run? What the hell was the *thing* that enabled him to go without food or sleep for a week, and why had it prevented them from recognizing each other as mates? He was clearly a shifter, since he too had known they were mates, but what sort? Had he been born one, or had he been made into one?

She didn't even know his last name.

We will learn everything about our mate, purred her snow leopard. *When he awakens.*

Yeah, Fiona thought grimly. *When he wakes up, we're going to learn a whole lot of things we'd rather not know.*

Her snow leopard snorted a dismissive denial.

But Fiona's mind had already sped back to the moment her snow leopard had told her Justin was her mate. She'd been overwhelmed with happiness—and desire. But though he'd obviously gotten the same news from his own inner beast, whatever it was, *he* hadn't been glad. Hearing that she was his mate was such bad news to him that the shock, coupled with exhaustion, had actually made him pass out!

What made it even worse was that she already knew why he'd reacted like that. He must have gotten a glimpse into her soul at the same time that she'd gotten a glimpse into his. And what he'd seen had horrified him.

Did he literally *see my past?* A wave of panicked shame swept over her at the thought. *Does he know what I was—what I am?*

Of course not, hissed her snow leopard. As if Fiona was a toddler, the big cat went on, *Did you see his past? No? Then he didn't see yours.*

But that didn't make Fiona feel any better. If Justin had reacted like that just from a general sense of her personality, what would he do if he learned what she'd actually done?

The same thing anyone would, she thought. *Run screaming.*

Her snow leopard hissed, *Does he look like a man who runs? Or screams?*

I didn't mean it literally, Fiona thought. *But he wouldn't want to have anything to do with me.*

It was hard enough keeping that secret from her teammates. It would be impossible to keep it from a mate.

She sat in a chair by the bed, where she could keep an eye on Justin, and forced herself to do what she did best: coldly analyze the situation.

Justin obviously needed help. He reminded her a bit of Shane, when Hal had first brought him on the team: wary, haunted, dangerous yet also fragile, as if he had a crack running straight down the center of his soul. But he'd gotten better with time, and much better since he'd moved in with Catalina. He might still bear a scar, but the wound had closed. Maybe if she could recruit Justin for the team, he too could be healed.

But if she wanted him to stick around long enough for her to befriend him and convince him to join her at Protection, Inc., she could never let him get any closer to her than her teammates. A friend could accept being kept at a slight distance. A friend could accept knowing nothing about her past. But her mated teammates kept no secrets from each other. It wasn't even that they didn't; as far as she could tell, they *couldn't*.

Fiona couldn't deny the devastating truth. She'd found the man who was supposed to be her true love. And they could never be together.

CHAPTER TWO
Justin

Justin surfaced from a deep sleep, becoming slowly aware that he was warm and comfortable. He wasn't used to feeling anything pleasant when he woke up after being invincible for that long. But when he reached within himself, as cautiously as if he was prodding a broken bone, he found neither the blank numbness of invincibility nor the physical misery and mental anguish that normally crashed over him when he emerged from that state. He felt dizzy and weak, but nothing worse than that.

Also, he was in a real bed, with a firm mattress beneath him, a pillow under his head, and soft blankets over him. That too was strange. He lay very still, keeping his eyes closed and his breathing exactly the same as before, feigning sleep. He might have been captured—

No, purred his snow leopard.

That was also unfamiliar. His snow leopard hissed and growled, snarled and screamed. He didn't purr. Justin hadn't even known he *could* purr. Until…

With that, his memory returned in a flood. He recalled how Fiona had broken into his hideout, how they'd been attacked and escaped together, and then holed up at, of all places, the Ritz Carlton. He remembered his decision to let go of his invincibility, and how he'd braced himself for the return of gnawing hunger and crushing exhaustion, bitter guilt and bleak despair, a desperate need for sleep and nightmares that would make him wish he'd never sleep again.

And he remembered looking into Fiona's eyes.

He'd seen them before, of course, but he'd been invincible then and so he'd perceived them without emotion. Just as he'd perceived *her* without emotion. Both times they'd met, he'd felt driven to protect her. He'd supposed that was due to the remnants of his sense of duty and desire to do the right thing. But it had been a bloodless compulsion, shorn of the blazing determination he'd felt in combat to save his buddies or die trying.

As for Fiona herself, he'd noted that she was tall for a woman and slim, moved like she'd been trained to fight, had blonde hair and green eyes, and was about his age.

When he was invincible, nothing was beautiful. Nor was anything ugly. Everything simply *was*, with no value attached to it. He could look at a rainbow arching over a green hill and a heap of rotting trash in a dark alley, and have no desire to see one rather than the other.

When he'd taken off his shield of ice and let his snow leopard back into his heart, he'd been deluged with *feeling*. Fiona wasn't just a tall blonde woman, she was the most beautiful woman he'd ever seen. She wasn't just capable of moving quickly, she'd leaped like lightning to shield him with her own body.

And her eyes—he could have looked into her eyes forever. They were a bright clear green like rain-washed grass, like tiny leaves unfurling in spring, like beach glass held up to the sun. When he'd seen them, really seen them, he'd felt his heart start to open like a flower.

And in that instant of gazing into that incredible green, he'd somehow seen straight into Fiona's soul. He'd sensed courage and intelligence, discipline and pride, kindness and loyalty and a smoldering passion hot enough to burn him to ash if it ever caught flame. He couldn't imagine that he'd mind.

For a split second, he'd been overwhelmed with feelings he'd thought he'd never experience again. Hope. Joy. Desire.

Then his snow leopard had purred, *She's the one. She's our mate.*

The big cat's words sent Justin crashing back to Earth. He couldn't have a mate. *Him,* paired with this amazing woman? She should be free to fly to the highest of heights, not be chained down to a broken soldier. His life was a shambles. He'd done terrible things he could never atone for. His body was a ruin, his mind a battlefield.

And he was going to die.

No, his snow leopard had snarled. *We will live for our mate!*

I will not! Justin had shouted silently, stumbling backward as if his snow leopard had been a real beast crouched in front of him rather than a voice inside his mind. *I can't. I won't.*

You will! His snow leopard's voice had risen in a terrified—and terrifying—scream. *You must!*

Do you still think I'm getting a happy ending? Justin had demanded with bitter sarcasm. *Seashells and wedding bells and babies on the rug? What a joke! I'm going down in flames, and I won't take her with me!*

Justin frowned, trying to recall what had happened after that. He had a vague recollection of darkness closing in on him, as if he was peering into a shrinking tunnel. He must have passed out. And then Fiona must have laid him on the bed. She'd have to be strong to have wrestled him off the floor—but she must be a shifter too. He wondered what kind. Maybe a big cat, like him. She moved like a cat.

Yes, purred his snow leopard. *We are two of a kind.*

Justin knew what his inner predator was implying, but he ignored it rather than arguing. Fiona had said she needed protection, so he'd protect her. If that required laying down his life for her, he'd do it gladly. But he could never be her mate.

"Justin?" It was Fiona's voice, clear as crystal and pitched soft. "Are you awake?"

"Yeah." His voice was hoarse, his mouth and throat dry. He coughed, then opened his eyes.

Fiona sat in a chair by the bed. She was so beautiful. His glimpse of her in the short time between when he'd been able to see beauty and when he'd passed out hadn't been enough. He drank her in unashamedly, savoring every detail.

She had fine hair so blonde it was nearly white, braided and wrapped around her head like a crown. She'd put on a more casual outfit than the ninja-like clothes she'd worn before, black pants that showed off her long legs and a blue blouse that clung to her breasts and gave her eyes, her incredible eyes, the aquamarine shimmer of a tropical lagoon.

She examined him with concern. "How do you feel?"

"Fine," he said automatically.

Embarrassed to be lying there in bed while she sat over him, he tried to sit up. Before he was even fully upright, his vision grayed out and the room spun around him

Fiona put her hand on his chest, pushing him back down. "Are you trying to make me pick you off the floor again? Stay where you are. I'll get you something to drink."

He lay still, breathing deeply, willing his dizziness to subside. The room came back into focus, and he watched her open a well-stocked minibar.

"Jack Daniels," he called. "On the rocks."

"First thing in the morning?" she called back. "No wonder you can't sit up."

"I was kidding." In fact, he hadn't had any alcohol in… years, he realized. Apex didn't put minibars in their prisoners' cells.

"I know." Fiona pulled a small plastic bottle of orange juice from the back of the minibar and brought it to him. "I can hold it for—"

"No!" He wanted to protect her and be strong for her. It was bad enough that he'd passed out and made her pick him up; he was hardly going to make her hold the bottle to his lips like he was an invalid.

Then, realizing that she'd made him a kind offer and he'd responded by shouting at her, he added, "Sorry. I didn't mean to yell. But I only got dizzy because I sat up too fast. I should be fine if I take it slow."

"Okay." She sounded doubtful.

She probably had reason. Justin still felt light-headed. "You can give me a hand, if you like."

"Since you ask so nicely…" She leaned over and wedged her arm under his back.

The action brought her so close that her breasts almost touched his chest. He could feel her body heat, and smell a faint scent of flowery soap and an even fainter one beneath that, a warm and living aroma that had to be her own natural scent. Justin inhaled deeply, taking it in. It gave him a strange feeling, partly like he was dreaming and partly like he was more awake than he'd been in his entire life.

A rush of heat went through his body, making him very aware that he had one. When he was invincible, his physical self was nothing more than a tool, something he was aware of but couldn't feel himself, like a gun in his hand. Now he was suddenly alive within his body, experiencing scent and touch… and desire.

He wanted Fiona. Wanted her with an intensity he hadn't felt in… years, it must be. He wanted to strip off her clothes, cup her breasts in his hands and feel her nipples hardening against his palms, press her nakedness against his own—

Sit up first, purred his snow leopard, sounding distinctly amused.

Jolted back to reality, Justin hurriedly helped Fiona raise him, bracing the heels of his hands on the mattress and pushing himself up. Once he was leaning against the headboard, she removed her arm and slid a pillow behind his back.

"Thanks," he said, wishing he could ask her to put her arm back.

"No problem. Here you go." She uncapped the orange juice and held it out.

He reached out, but his hands were shaking. He'd spill it all over the bed if she gave it to him.

"Sorry," he muttered again. "I really did a number on myself this time. If I was my patient, I'd tell me off. And then put in an IV drip. Don't worry, though, orange juice is lower tech but just as good. I'll be fine once I get my blood sugar back up."

Fiona gave him a curious glance, then slid the bottle into his left hand. She cupped her own hands around his, holding it still.

"You remembered," he said.

"Remembered…?"

"That I'm left-handed." It touched him. She knew him, even in such a small way. There were so few people left who did.

"I never forget a person's gun-hand," she replied. "Now drink."

The warmth of her hands steadied him deep down, as much as her grip steadied his tremor. With her support, he brought the bottle to his lips without spilling a drop.

The juice was sweet and tangy and cold, fresh with no chemical aftertaste. Justin couldn't remember the last time he'd had real orange juice. Probably it had been before he'd been captured by Apex. Unexpectedly, a memory stole into his mind, of sitting at a kitchen table at dawn, drinking a glass of fresh-squeezed orange juice and watching the sun rise. He didn't remember why he'd been up so early or how long ago it had been. But he could recall the peaceful quiet and the gold-streaked sky as if it had been yesterday.

When he'd finished drinking, Fiona asked, "How do you feel now?"

"Better." He'd felt strength flowing back into him with every sip. "I should eat something before I try to get out of bed, though."

She gave him a sharp glance. "A week on that too, huh?"

He nodded, trying to think of a way to change the subject. He didn't want to lie to her, but he didn't want to talk about it either. Every aspect of his power was painful: what it was, how he'd acquired it…

"Why?" Her tone wasn't demanding, but neither was it one that he could ignore. "What were you doing that was so important that you couldn't stop to eat or sleep for an entire week?"

And then there was the part he least wanted to discuss: why he used his power.

Tell her, hissed his snow leopard. *She is your mate. She needs to know.*

"I…" Justin abruptly felt shaky again. His skin prickled as he broke out in a cold sweat. "Can we hold off on that for a bit? At least until after breakfast?"

Fiona touched his forehead. Her fingers were cool and comforting, and he couldn't help wishing she'd leave them there. "You look like you need a doctor, not breakfast—"

"No!" The yell burst from his throat without his intention, loud enough to make his own ears ring. She jerked her hand away. Lowering his voice, he said, "No doctors. Seriously, I don't need one. I've done this before and I recovered fine, with no help at all."

"How'd you manage that?" she asked dubiously.

"Lay where I'd fallen until I managed to fish a few granola bars out of my emergency supplies," he admitted. "I'm all out, though. I was going to buy more today, but…"

She shook her head, clearly unimpressed with his emergency planning. "I'll call room service. I'm hungry too, actually."

He didn't like the idea of some stranger walking into the room when he couldn't even get out of bed. But the alternative was Fiona going out alone to fetch something, and he liked that even less.

"I'll give you the code to turn off the door alarm," he said. "But can you pass me my bag first?"

She handed him his duffel bag, and he took out his gun. He gripped it, making sure his hand was steady enough to shoot.

"You're fine," Fiona said. "You could balance a dime on the barrel."

He glanced at her, startled and a little alarmed. He'd trained doing exactly that. "You're not active-duty, are you? On some kind of mission…?"

To his immense relief, she shook her head. He wanted nothing to do with the military. There was no telling who might be passing info on to Apex. "I've never served. The people who taught me were vets, though. You?"

"Air Force." He hesitated, wondering how to describe his current status. He was listed as killed in action, but saying so himself was a contradiction in terms. Finally, he said, "Not any more."

"Were you a doctor?"

"No. I have paramedic training. But I was a PJ—that's Special Operations pararescue. Parajumpers."

Fiona was nodding. "I know. One of the guys who taught me was a PJ."

For all that he thought he'd left that life behind, he felt the stirrings of pride. "No wonder you shoot so well."

To forestall any further questions, he bent over to stash his gun under the covers, where he could feel its cold metal against his hip. It made him feel better to know it was there. He might not be able to leap up and punch anyone, but he could shoot from where he was. If he needed to, he could protect her. "Do you want my other gun?"

She tugged at the collar of her blouse, exposing an exquisitely sculpted collarbone and the strap of the shoulder holster.

"I should've guessed," Justin said. "Keep it, it suits you."

"Thank you, don't mind if I do." She passed him the room service menu. Deadpan, she said, "Order anything. My treat."

"That's very gentlemanly—I mean ladylike—of you, but I'm an old-fashioned kind of guy. I insist on picking up the check."

"See if you still want to when you read the prices," Fiona remarked.

He thought of the million dollars he'd confiscated from Elson. Then he opened the menu and read the prices. "Whoa."

Now she was openly laughing. "You should see your face! This *is* the Ritz."

"Twenty-eight dollars for sausage and eggs!?" Justin exclaimed, indignant. "Twenty dollars for sliced fruit and a Danish?!"

"The Ritz," she reminded him. "Seriously, I can cover it. I'm on the job. It's a business expense."

Justin couldn't help asking, "What is your job, exactly? *Are* you FBI?"

She shook her head. "Private security. Very well-paid private security."

"Well, I'm a very well-paid vigilante. So eat up. On me. But since you're obviously an independent woman who likes to pay her share, you can buy me a cup of coffee."

"I'll buy you an entire *pot* of coffee. Which in this place is a substantial financial sacrifice, let me tell you. What do you want? I'll call it in."

He tossed the menu back to her. "Steak and eggs. And a side of bacon and hash browns. And the pastry basket, whatever that is."

"That's a lot," she said doubtfully. "Especially when you haven't eaten at all in a week. Won't it make you sick?"

"No. I've done this before, remember?"

With a shrug, she picked up the phone and ordered. When she was done, she reminded him of the alarm code. He gave it to her and watched her deactivate the alarm, then stash it in his duffel bag. Then she went back to the minibar and rummaged until she found a bottle of apple juice.

"To tide you over till breakfast comes," she said.

"Thanks." Justin took it from her, half-regretting that he no longer needed any help holding it. Being able to drink a bottle of juice without assistance was a pretty low bar. But he missed having her fingers covering his.

"You look better," Fiona said as he drank it. "I think you need another six nights' sleep, though. At least."

"Did *you* get any sleep last night?" He hoped she hadn't stayed up all night to make sure he didn't stop breathing.

"I did. I watched you for a while, but you just seemed to be very deeply asleep. So I went to sleep too." A faint pink blush stained her cheeks. "On top of the covers."

"You could've gotten under them," he remarked. "It's not like I was in any condition to try anything."

"You wouldn't have anyway," she shot back. "You're an old-fashioned gentleman."

"Absolutely. So you'd have been doubly safe." But the banter about the beds reminded him of something. "Hey, we need to get ready before the waiter comes in. We're posing as a couple. And you asked for a tray table, so presumably we're both having breakfast in bed. I'm fine,

I've got my shirt off and the blankets over my pants. But you should be in pajamas or a nightgown or something."

Her flush deepened, though her expression didn't change. "I know. I'll go change into something more breakfast-in-bed-like."

She snatched a small suitcase from the closet and vanished into the bathroom with it, leaving him alone in a bed that suddenly seemed big and cold and empty.

My mate, he thought.

He'd been trying not to think about it. The whole thing was a cruel cosmic joke. But Fiona knew it too, so they'd have to discuss it sooner or later. Justin winced, thinking of everything he didn't want to talk about and would soon have to. Maybe if he just gave her the absolute minimum she needed to know, it wouldn't hurt too much. And once he told her, she'd know, and then it would be over. He'd never have to talk about it again.

Like pulling off a band-aid, he thought. *One quick rip is the way to go.*

She took her time in the bathroom. He wondered if she was avoiding getting into bed with him. He'd thought joking about it would make it less awkward and embarrassing, but maybe he'd only made it more so.

She emerged from the bathroom. Justin felt his jaw falling open, and closed it with a snap.

Don't stare, he told himself.

It was hard not to. She stepped delicately across the floor, catlike in bare feet. He tried to just watch her feet, since that wasn't one of the sexier parts of the body. Only on Fiona, they were. Hers were narrow and graceful, with high arches and slim ankles. The more Justin fixed his gaze on them, the more he felt like he was developing a foot fetish.

He raised his eyes. Fiona's legs seemed to go on forever, slim but strong-looking, like a ballerina's. Her light blue nightgown was short and silky, swirling around her knees and floating upward with every step she took. She'd taken off her bra to preserve her cover, as no one wears a bra under a nightgown. Her nipples were hard enough to make points against the thin fabric. Because the air was cool? Or...?

Justin forced his gaze upward from her breasts, reminding himself that he was trying *not* to embarrass her. The lace around the low-cut neckline clung to her chest, its creamy color only a little paler than her skin. She'd taken her hair out of its braids and brushed it out, so it fell down her back like a cascade of white water. It stirred and floated with static electricity, adding to the impression of flowing water.

It was going to be rough sitting in bed with her in that barely-there outfit, feeling her body heat just inches away, and not being able to touch her.

Then touch her, hissed his snow leopard impatiently.

Be quiet, Justin replied.

A faint pink flush colored Fiona's chest and began creeping upward toward her face. He had obviously been staring at her much too long. To break the tension, he said lightly, "You're much better prepared than me. I completely forgot to pack my pajamas."

Her blush faded as she replied with apparent relief, "No pajamas. No granola bars. Did you at least remember your toothbrush?"

"'Fraid not."

"Well, I'm not sharing mine. You'll have to hit the gift store."

"At the Ritz? Bet it costs a hundred bucks."

"That's because it's gold-plated," she said promptly.

Justin chuckled.

A knock at the door made him start. His fingers closed over the gun over the covers.

Fiona went to the door, looked through the peephole, and gave him a nod. But he noticed that she stood behind the door as she opened it, so as not to be in the line of fire if there was any. She opened the door and let in a maid with a push-cart.

"Good morning!" The maid pushed the cart to the bed. To Fiona, she said, "You can get back in bed. Snuggle up!"

Fiona smiled at the maid, and got in bed beside him. She snuggled in next to him as the maid began setting up a large tray table. He sucked in a deep breath at the feeling of her warm body pressed into his. He could feel her chest rise and fall as she breathed.

"Isn't this nice, honey?" she said sweetly.

He leaned his head against hers. Her loose hair was just as silken as it looked. Strands lifted with static electricity, and clung to his cheek and throat. He had to swallow to make sure his voice would come out smooth before he could say, "It sure is. What a break from the office."

"You two just relax and enjoy your breakfast," said the maid as she set an array of dishes on the tray. Then she indicated a remote control on a small table within reach of the bed. "I don't know if you noticed, but the door has an electronic lock with a remote control. So you don't have to get up when I leave—you can lock the door from the bed."

"Oh, thank you," said Fiona. "No, I hadn't noticed."

Justin hadn't, but he suspected that Fiona had. But she smiled and nodded as the maid demonstrated, then set it back on the table and went out with a wave. When the door closed behind the woman, Fiona raised the remote control and pushed the button. The door clicked as the lock engaged.

For a moment, neither of them spoke or moved. Justin could feel his pulse thundering in his ears. He was excruciatingly aware of every square inch of his skin that was touching hers. It was impossible to focus on anything but that, and on knowing that he should move away from her that instant, and being completely unable to bring himself to do so.

You have to, he told himself. *You know her beast spoke to her too. Leading her on is cruel.*

"About the mate thing..." he began.

Beside him, he felt her stiffen.

When you had something hard to say, you had to just say it. "I can't. I'm sorry, but... I just can't."

What are you saying? growled his snow leopard. *Quick, apologize and beg her to forgive you for your moment of madness!*

Be quiet, Justin said silently.

Stop telling me to be quiet, hissed his snow leopard.

Be quiet, or I'll make *you be quiet,* Justin retorted.

With a final angry hiss, the big cat subsided.

Fiona had pulled away from him but was watching him intently, her face unreadable. He couldn't tell if she was hurt or just felt incredibly awkward.

"Look," he said. "I'm a mess. I think that's pretty obvious. This has nothing to do with you. You're great. I just..."

"You just can't," she finished. Her voice was chilly. "I get it, all right? That's all you have to say. I don't need a detailed explanation."

Justin was immensely relieved. The last thing he wanted to do was give her a point-by-point breakdown of the extent of his damage and the bleakness of his future.

The next moment, he was ashamed of his own relief, which he had gained at her expense. He'd started a conversation that had obviously made her uncomfortable, when he knew she needed his protection and couldn't just leave. In fact, he realized, she was literally trapped: with a full tray table over her legs, she couldn't even easily get out of bed.

Justin picked up the remote control. "Do you know what this is?"

Her eyebrows rose. "Weren't you listening to the maid?"

"It's a time-reversal device." He indicated the light dimmer. "I'm going to hit this button and jump time back… Let's see… Two minutes."

She was staring at him as if he was a lunatic, but he was used to that sort of look.

"And then this whole conversation will have never happened," he went on. "We'll be back where we were before it began, a well-paid private security agent and a fucked-up vigilante pretending to be a couple, about to enjoy their three thousand dollar breakfast in bed."

Her mouth quivered with reluctant amusement. "A *well-paid* fucked-up vigilante. Don't forget that part."

"Well, of course. Otherwise I couldn't afford the time-reversal surcharge."

As if against her will, a laugh burst from her lips. Then, shaking her head, she settled back against the pillows. "Okay. Hit it."

Justin pressed the button, dimming the lights, then brightened them again. He looked down at the tray-table in simulated surprise. "Ah! We have breakfast!"

"It seems to have magically appeared." Her voice was distinctly sarcastic. "How nice."

"This *is* the Ritz," Justin said, imitating her inflections.

Once again, he startled a laugh out of her. Though their bodies no longer touched, they still sat close enough that he could feel the shift as she relaxed. "Stop talking and eat. I keep worrying that you're going to pass out again."

A pang that had nothing to do with the lousy shape he was in pierced his chest. Despite her light tone, he could hear that she meant it. He wasn't used to anyone caring about him for his own sake, rather than because he was a useful tool they didn't want to break.

Shane cares about you, hissed his snow leopard.

Justin didn't want to think about Shane. Hoping to distract his snow leopard and satisfy Fiona in one fell swoop, he grabbed the first thing within reach on the tray, a bite-sized pastry from the basket, and stuffed it into his mouth.

His snow leopard wasn't the only one it distracted. The flavor and textures burst in Justin's mouth like a firework. Rich cream, tangy lemon icing, fluffy cake. Like the orange juice, the taste wasn't just good, but shocking to his senses. It was as if he was tasting food for the first time.

Justin raised his mug of coffee, breathing in its scent, then took a sip. It was objectively excellent coffee. Especially compared to all the terrible coffee he'd had in his life. He'd sometimes gotten desperate enough in the field, when he'd needed to stay awake but hadn't been able to take the time to heat water, that he'd torn open the instant coffee packets in an MRE and poured them into his mouth. Even burned *and* cold coffee was better than that, let alone the mellow smoothness of the cup he had now.

"Good, huh?" remarked Fiona.

"Best coffee I've had in my life. Best pastry, too." He examined the basket. It was a treasure trove of pastries, from the vaguely healthy (blueberry muffins with a crumb topping) to the decadent (miniature chocolate cheesecakes) to the even more decadent (little pies that appeared to be entirely composed of salted caramel). "Want one?"

"Thanks, I will. When I'm done with my eggs." She was working her way through a plate of eggs scrambled with lobster and topped with caviar, with fresh fruit on the side.

With that reminder, Justin turned his attention to his steak and eggs. He'd ordered them on the theory that he'd needed the protein. But now he wondered just how delicious they'd be, given the coffee and pastry. He cut into the steak and the fried eggs on top so the orange yolk oozed out over the char marks, topped his forkful with hash browns, and took a bite.

It was, unsurprisingly, the best steak and eggs he'd ever had. The meat was perfectly cooked and juicy, the egg flavorful, the hash browns just the right mix of crisp and soft. He finished it all, along with the (also best ever) bacon in record time. When he was done, he knew that he'd have no trouble getting up. He probably needed a bit more rest to be at his physical best, but his weakness was gone.

But he had no desire to get up. He felt perfectly content to stay where he was, in this comfortable bed with the best-ever pastries and coffee in front of him and Fiona beside him. Stealing a glance at Fiona, who had finished her eggs and was scooping up the last black pearls of caviar with a piece of toast, he thought, *I'd be happy to pour a packet of instant coffee into my mouth, as long as she was there with me.*

But that thought made him realize something. The Ritz's food and coffee *were* great. But it had been a long time since he'd registered the taste of anything at all, good or bad. When he thought back to his last meal, he had a vague recollection of a burger and coffee in a diner. But he had no idea if the coffee had been burned or fresh-made, or if the burger had been juicy or overcooked. The meal had only been fuel to him, and eating nothing but a task he had to perform. He hadn't even cared enough to find it unpleasant.

"Fiona? Thank you. This was wonderful." He waved his hand over the breakfast tray.

"Thank *you*," she replied promptly. "You're the one who's paying."

He debated if he wanted to say more, so she'd understand how he was feeling—he didn't want to open the can of worms that was *"What's wrong with you, really? What* happened *to you?"*—but she'd given him something too precious to let it pass without even telling her.

Justin touched her shoulder. She didn't jump, but he felt her draw in a startled breath. He dropped his hand, but didn't turn away. "I haven't enjoyed eating for… years, maybe. It's been such a long time that I didn't even realize till I did enjoy it, just now."

He braced himself for her pity. But it didn't come. Instead, she gave him a long, thoughtful look, then picked up something from her own plate. It was a tiny, plump, perfect strawberry, brilliant red and speckled with seeds no bigger than grains of sand.

"Here." She raised it to his lips.

He didn't have time to think of what a bad idea it was. He just saw her long, elegant fingers, smelled the tart scent, and opened his mouth.

She placed the berry between his lips. He chewed and swallowed in a bright burst of sweetness. Then, unable to resist, he closed his lips over her fingertips before she could pull them away. Her emerald eyes opened wide as he explored her fingers with the tip of his tongue, feeling the soft skin and gemlike smoothness of her nails, tasting the tanginess of berry juice and the faint salt of her skin.

All he was doing was kissing the tips of her fingers. Once, years ago, he'd have thought of that as the smallest of gestures, a bit of foreplay to be enjoyed briefly before getting down to the main event. But now, with Fiona, it had a dizzying intensity. His heart was pounding as hard as if he was halfway through a marathon.

Her gaze was locked on his as he dropped his hand down to the pastry basket. But he didn't need to look down. He knew where everything was. Justin picked up a bite-sized lemon cake.

He'd never in his life seen anything as sexy as watching her pink lips open for him. She tipped back her head and closed her eyes as he placed the cake in her mouth. Like he had done, she ate it in a single bite, then captured his fingertips with her lips. The inside of her mouth was soft and wet and hot, so hot. She licked at his fingers as if she was hungry to taste him, then sucked, first gently and then harder, making him imagine what other parts of him she could suck on. A wave of desire broke over him at the thought, so intense that it made him feel half-crazy with desire. He *had* to have more.

They moved at the same time, two bodies with a single thought, dropping their hands down and leaning in for a kiss. Fiona's lips were soft as rose petals, soft as velvet, and her mouth was hot as fire. Her scent surrounded him, delicate and sensual as the woman it belonged to. Everywhere she touched him, his skin tingled as if it had fallen asleep and was prickling back to life. But it wasn't painful. It was ecstatic.

Justin was overwhelmed with sensation—and emotion. Not only his body, but his heart felt suddenly alive again, filled to the brim with feelings so strong that they were halfway to pain. He wasn't just sexually attracted to Fiona, he was drawn to her as a person—her banter and her brittleness, her strength and vulnerability, her competence and intelligence and kindness. She was so much more than he deserved, and yet here she was.

Maybe, just maybe, his long nightmare was finally over. Maybe there was hope.

He reached out blindly to push the tray table out of their way. Hot liquid spilled over his hand.

Dr. Elihu squeezed a few more drops of liquid on to Justin's hand. Burning agony penetrated down to his bones, but the gag in his mouth stopped him from screaming.

"It isn't acid." The doctor smiled like he'd made a joke. "Of course not! Even with your healing abilities, that would risk permanent scarring. And we don't want to damage our weapon. This is a harmless nerve agent Dr. Attanasio concocted to send pain signals to your brain. All you have to do to get rid of it is wash it off."

Dr. Elihu smiled again. "Or invoke your adrenaline invincibility. Then you won't feel a thing."

The pain made him feel cold and sick. Every inch of his skin was sweating. Justin tried to concentrate on ice creeping up his body, *but his hand felt like it was on fire. It was impossible to focus on anything but how much he hurt.*

Kill the doctor, *hissed his snow leopard.* Rip out his throat!

Justin knew fighting was useless, but the pain cracked his self-control. His snow leopard took over his body, flinging himself against the straps…

Justin slammed into a hard surface. Something soft was on top of him, smothering him. He flung it off, frantic to escape.

Only then did he realize where he was. He'd apparently thrown himself out of bed in a tangle of blankets.

Fiona had scrambled to the edge of the bed and was leaning over, reaching out to him. "Justin! Are you all right?"

"No," he managed.

"What's wrong?"

He couldn't even begin to answer that. His snow leopard was screaming inside his head in an ear-splitting keen of terror and rage. He could barely hear his own thoughts.

Justin staggered to his feet. "I—I have to be alone."

He bolted for the bathroom and closed the door behind him. It slammed with a bang that made him jump. Justin stumbled to the sink, twisted the tap, and began splashing cold water over his face.

Stop, he ordered his snow leopard. *Stop it!*

The big cat fell silent. Justin stood trembling, icy water dripping from his face to his chest, hands gripping the cool porcelain sink.

You're at the Ritz, he told himself. *Not in Apex. The lab they held you in is gone. Dr. Elihu is dead. Shane killed him.*

Gradually, he managed to catch his breath. His heartbeat slowed and the shaking subsided. The shock and fear ebbed away, leaving only weariness. And guilt. What had he been doing? What had he been *thinking?* How could he have given in to temptation and led Fiona on, when he knew—and had just proved beyond the shadow of a doubt—how unfit he was as a mate for her? It had been selfishness verging on cruelty.

Now that it was over, the whole thing felt surreal. He'd kissed her. Felt a desire intense enough to take his breath away. And before that, they'd been enjoying breakfast in bed together. He'd been joking. Teasing. Even laughing.

For that brief moment in time, he'd felt like himself again. His old self, the one he'd lost. The one who had died at Apex.

You did not die, his snow leopard hissed impatiently. *You are here now, living and breathing.*

I'm not that guy any more, Justin replied. *I'm just what's left of him.*

CHAPTER THREE
Fiona

Fiona stood outside the bathroom door, her hand frozen in the about-to-knock position. She'd been there for at least a minute, debating with herself whether she should bang on the door, like her frantic snow leopard kept insisting she do, or hold off, like she herself was certain Justin would prefer.

But he's not in any physical danger, right? Fiona asked for the third time. *You'd know if he was, right?*

Reluctantly, her snow leopard hissed her agreement. But she immediately added, *He needs us. If he doesn't answer, break down the door. You must go to him and lick his wounds!*

"Ew," Fiona muttered. Silently, she went on, *I'm not doing any more licking. I licked his fingers a minute ago, and look what happened.*

As usual, the big cat failed to understand irony. *If you won't lick him, at least stroke his fur and make him feel better.*

Fiona sighed. Whatever was wrong with Justin, it was obvious that the last thing he wanted was her touching him in any way whatsoever.

Still, she had to check. "Justin?"

But just as she spoke, the shower turned on. Her voice had undoubtedly been drowned out. Well, at least now she knew he wasn't on the floor again. She pried herself away from the bathroom door and quickly changed back into her street clothes, then summoned the maid to collect the tray table, which she was sure he wouldn't want to be confronted with.

When the maid appeared, she indicated the mostly-untouched pastry basket. "Shall I leave that for later? And the coffee?"

Fiona would have been happy to see the last of the pastries, but they belonged to Justin and he might not feel the same way. Plus, he probably could use the calories. "Sure. Thanks."

The maid removed the rest of the breakfast stuff, then made the bed. Fiona locked the door behind her and sat down on the bed, listening to the shower run.

With no more tasks to perform, she was left alone with her thoughts. Normally they ran on orderly tracks, but now she felt completely at sea. She was used to being presented with a problem and coming up with a plan to solve it. But now she was overwhelmed with some problems that didn't have solutions and some she couldn't solve because she didn't even understand what the problem was. Not to mention her own guilt over giving in to temptation and kissing Justin when she knew perfectly well that they could never be mates. She'd not only led him on when she couldn't follow through, she'd apparently pushed him into some kind of breakdown.

And, overlying everything and making it impossible to focus on anything else, she kept thinking about the raw pain in Justin's eyes and her own inability to help him. It made her heart hurt.

Of course you can help him, her snow leopard hissed. *Lick his wounds and—*

"Be quiet!" Fiona burst out. "Or at least stop saying that!"

"You got an animal that never shuts up, huh? Me too."

Startled, Fiona looked up. Justin had emerged from the bathroom. His chest and feet were bare, and his wet hair hung in glossy strands around his face. She bit her tongue on asking him if he was all right. She didn't know much about him, but one thing she'd figured out was that he didn't like that question.

"Mine's a snow leopard," she said.

Justin actually smiled at that. It looked fragile, but real. "No kidding! So is mine."

"Really?" Fiona was both surprised and not; he moved with the grace of a stalking cat. A bit like Shane, come to think of it, who could become a panther.

He nodded, then sat down on the bed an arm's length away from her.

"Can we talk?"

"Sure," she said, surprised. She'd expected him to pretend nothing had happened. "Fire away."

"Ball's in my court, huh?"

He tried to smile, but she could see that he was already beginning to regret opening up the conversation. If she was going to get any answers out of him, she'd have to move fast before the moment slipped away. She knew lots of ways to get people to open up and think it was their idea…

He is your mate, her snow leopard hissed. *Do not manipulate him.*

Guilt stabbed at Fiona. She knew the big cat was right, and that made it worse. It was so easy and natural to fall back into lying and manipulating. It was what she *was*, deep down. If she wanted to be different, to be better, she had to defy her entire nature. And that meant being on guard every second of every day.

She tried again, as honestly and straightforwardly as she could manage. "There's obviously something wrong, but I have no idea what it is. I want to help you, but I'm not a mind-reader. If there's something I should know, you're going to have to tell me."

He took a deep breath, then another. "All right. I'll do my best. Thing is, you might get some nasty surprises anyway. Half the time I don't know what's going to set me off till it happens. When we were, uh, when we were kissing, I spilled some hot coffee on my hand. It gave me a flashback to when they poured this stuff on me, this burning chemical—"

He stopped to take another breath. Fiona wished she could put her arm around him and hold him tight, but he was so wound up that she was sure he'd jump out of his skin if she tried.

Finally, he went on, "The thing that lets me not sleep or eat. It's called adrenaline invincibility. I was kidnapped by a black ops agency and held in a lab. They gave me that power. Made me a shifter, too. They said they were doing experiments and maybe they were, but it was torture, too. They made me—"

Justin swallowed. His fists clenched so hard that his knuckles went white. "I used to be a soldier, an airman. I rescued people. Saved their lives. Then Apex took me, and they made me into an assassin."

He stopped as suddenly as if someone had put a hand over his mouth.

His dark eyes seemed to be looking past her or through her, not at her. It was as if she wasn't even there: as if he was once again in the lab, forced to endure terrible things, alone.

Fiona's mind was racing. She could tell from the difficulty he was having that he'd never told anyone this story before, but it was all too familiar to her. Apex, the black ops agency that kidnapped people, made them into shifters, and gave them powers at a terrible price. The sadistic "experiments." Being forced to become an assassin.

The same thing had happened to Shane. And as far as she knew, only one other person had survived it.

"I know who you are," she blurted out. "You're Red!"

Justin's eyes came back into startled focus. "Yeah, that's what they called me in the PJs. How did you know?"

"I'm friends with Shane Garrity. He told me you and he were PJs together until Apex captured you both. He said up until last year, he thought you were dead."

"You and Shane are buddies?" Justin shook his head in amazement. "Small world. How do you know him?"

"We both work at Protection, Inc. It's an all-shifter private security agency."

"Even smaller world. I've met a couple of your teammates. Sort of."

"I know. Shane said you turned up out of nowhere and helped Nick when he was hurt."

"Nick," he said thoughtfully. "Young guy with green eyes and a lot of tattoos? Broken leg, broken ribs, dislocated shoulder, bite wounds, gunshot wounds, and shock? How's he doing?"

"He's fine," she assured him. "Completely recovered."

"Let me ask a weird question. Do you remember what you were doing three days before Nick got…" Justin spoke as if he couldn't quite believe what he was saying. "…bitten, shot, and fell from a height?"

"I do. I was undercover with some nasty characters who started suspecting that someone was spying on them. They interrogated me at gunpoint. There were a couple moments that were touch-and-go. But by the end of it I convinced them that someone else was the spy. They let me go, and I slipped away with the information I'd come for. The FBI broke down the doors just in time to stop them from murdering the man I'd pointed the finger at."

"Huh. Well, that explains a lot. I'd been thinking my power had gone haywire. But I bet I was actually tracking *you*. Even though I'd never touched you—never even met you."

Fiona had no idea what he was talking about. "What?"

"It's something else Apex did to me. When I touch people, I can track them down, no matter where they go. Three days before Nick had his terrible, horrible, no good, very bad day, I got the feeling that someone was in trouble and needed my help. That's not how my power normally works, so I thought I'd better go see what was up. The problem is, I don't get an address delivered into my head. I just get a sense of 'that way.'" Justin pointed in demonstration.

"So I got in my car and started driving that way," he went on. "By the time I arrived, the feeling was gone. But I was in Santa Martina and I knew Shane lived there, so I thought maybe he was in danger and I started tracking him. I found a guy who wasn't Shane, but he sure as hell needed help. Shane turned up a couple minutes later—he was close. But I think the person I was originally zeroing in on was you."

"Was that how you found me when those gangsters were about to kill me?"

"Yeah, same deal. I had a feeling someone was in trouble, I followed it, and I found you."

"Because of the..." She'd been about to say, *"the mate bond."* But there was no bond. Justin didn't want to be her mate, and she could never be his even if he did. She stopped without finishing the sentence.

"Yeah. I assume because of..." Justin obviously found it as awkward as she did, because he finished with, "...*that*."

But there was something that was both more important and easier to talk about than the odd interaction between their not-a-real-mate-bond and Justin's power.

"Shane's been worried sick about you," she said. "I'll call him right now and tell him you're with me—"

"No!" Justin grabbed her wrist as if he thought she was about to reach for a phone. Then he released it like it was a hot potato. More quietly, he repeated, "No. Don't tell him. Don't tell anyone."

"Why not?" Fiona was puzzled. From the way Shane had talked about him, she'd thought they were best friends. "He can keep a secret. You should call him, just to let him know you're all right."

Justin sighed. "Well, that's the thing. I'm not."

"That's exactly why you need to get in touch with him. Apex took him too. And let me tell you, when I first met him, he was very much not all right. But he's a lot better now. He'd understand what you've been through. He could help you."

He turned his dark gaze on her. "I said no. I promised to protect you, and I meant it. But I'm asking one thing in exchange. Don't tell anyone about me. If you can't promise me that, I'll take you somewhere safe, and then I'll disappear. For good."

Fiona drew back. After fighting for their lives together, after the personal connection it had felt like they'd had, even after kissing her in a way that had sure as hell felt like he'd meant it, he was talking like she was nothing but a client who'd hired him.

"I was giving you my opinion," she said icily. "That's all. I had no intention of going behind your back. You don't need to give me an ultimatum. If you're dead-set on suffering all by yourself, far be it from me to stop you."

"Good." But he didn't sound happy.

Then she remembered something. Awkwardly, she said, "There's just one thing. I won't tell anyone about you. But someone already knows. That is, he doesn't know your name or who you are. But the reason I was in your apartment was that I'm on an undercover mission, posing as a freelance spy to infiltrate the organization of an arms dealer named Elson."

Justin looked up, interested. "I know who that is. I broke up an arms deal he was trying to make with a terrorist group—Oh. Did he sic you on me?"

She nodded, then outlined her two missions: the real one, and the one Elson had sent her on. "And then he ordered me to murder you if I couldn't recruit you."

His eyebrows rose. "What did you say?"

"I made him double my salary."

"In that case, you can buy me another pot of coffee."

"I'll buy you a *cup*," she replied. "I didn't make him triple it."

Justin smiled, and the tension between them eased. His smile was so rare and bright, it was like a glimpse of sun on a cloudy day, turning everything to gold.

She noticed once again that his eyelashes were a bright coppery red, startling against his midnight eyes. "Did they call you Red because of your lashes?"

"Huh?" Then realization spread across his face. "No. I dye my hair. If I don't, I draw too much attention. People actually turn to look at me when I go by."

I bet they do anyway, she thought.

He picked up his mug and took a drink. "Thanks. This really is great. Or maybe I should thank Elson."

She slid the pastry basket toward him. "To go with your murder-bonus coffee."

Justin took a lemon square, then passed her the basket. She helped herself to a cream puff. "Are all your assignments this glamorous?"

"I wish." She ate the cream puff, thinking about what it would be like to not taste food for years. It went some way toward explaining why he was so thin, and why he didn't seem to care if he didn't eat for a week at a time. Even so, she didn't understand why he didn't try harder to keep himself in good shape, even if he didn't enjoy it. It wasn't as if he didn't have the willpower or discipline to do so.

But she was sure that was one of the many things he didn't want to talk about. So instead she asked, "Why *did* you break up Elson's deal?"

"I was chasing a guy named Bianchi. He was middle management at Apex, but he's an arms dealer now. While I was trying to close in on him, I ended up eavesdropping on a terrorist group that had been considering buying weapons from Bianchi, but Elson offered them a better deal. I couldn't let those weapons get into the hands of terrorists. So I had to drop my original plan and break up the deal. I blew the weapons sky-high, and left an anonymous tip with MI-5 to collect a bunch of tied-up terrorists and illegal arms dealers."

"And the million dollars?"

"I still have it. I put it in a safe deposit box under a fake name. I figured I could survive on some of it while I do my thing—I'm supposed to be dead, so I can't access any of my own money—and whatever's left over, I'll give to charity. I don't think it has a legitimate owner I could return it to."

Now there's a man with integrity, Fiona thought. *Give him a million dollars of untraceable dirty money, and he takes what he absolutely needs to survive and gives away the rest.*

As if I needed even more reasons why we can never be mates.

Justin frowned. "Fiona? Is something wrong?"

"No." Before he could pursue it, she asked, "What happened to Bianchi?"

"I lost him. Apparently he heard about what happened with Elson's deal, and it spooked him. I eventually figured out that he'd gone to New York, so I came here. But it looks like he's in Venice now. He owns a house there, apparently."

"Venice, California?"

"Venice, Italy. I was going to buy a ticket today."

"Along with granola bars." She remembered him calling himself a vigilante. "So what's your big plan? Track down everyone who ever worked at Apex?"

"Yeah. But not just for revenge. The base Shane and I destroyed wasn't their only one. They've got at least one more, but I don't know where it is. I'm hoping Bianchi can lead me to it, or lead me to someone who can lead me to it. I want to destroy their entire operation, so they can never hurt anyone again."

Justin's voice rose commandingly, and his eyes blazed with passion. For all the damage that had been done to him, he was still the man who had parachuted into combat zones and single-handedly defeated a gang of terrorists *and* Mr. Elson's thugs, simultaneously. If anyone could do it, he could.

"Want a partner?" Fiona asked.

"You'd team up with me?" Justin looked astonished, as if he couldn't imagine anyone wanting to stay with him.

"If you want me to." She tried to sound casual, as if she didn't care if he did or not. But she thought, *I'd follow you to the ends of the Earth.*

That brilliant smile of his lit up his face. "Of course I do! I just—I didn't realize you had it out for Apex too."

I have it out for anyone who'd hurt you, she thought.

She said, "I blew up their base in the Sierra Nevadas."

"Really? You, personally? I figured your team did."

"I set the charges. Me, personally. With my own two hands." She held them up for his inspection.

Justin looked at her solemnly, then took off an imaginary hat and made a very creditable bow from a sitting position. "I doff my hat to you. And also, I owe you a drink. Would you take a glass of Italian wine in Italy?"

"I will." She thought quickly. "Elson expects me to be cozying up to you. So if we keep pretending to be a couple, that's our cover for the trip, and it's also our cover with Elson. We can kill two birds with one stone."

"Sounds good." He sprang up, suddenly filled with energy, and offered her his hand. "Shall we run away to Venice together?"

There was nothing she wanted more. But before she could take his hand, every reason the entire plan was a terrible idea popped into her mind.

She was going to be a triple agent in a deadly game of deceit, matching herself against two different international arms dealers, a powerful black ops agency, and whoever it was who'd shot at them the night before, all without the help or even knowledge of her team.

Her entire team would want to help Justin with his plan if they knew about it, but she'd promised not to say a word. In effect, she'd agreed to lie to all her friends. Shane was desperate to help Justin, but Fiona couldn't even say she knew him. Would Shane forgive her if—when—he found out? Or would she destroy the best friendship she'd ever known with yet another lie?

Worst of all, she'd be alone with Justin in the most romantic city in the world, pretending to be a couple, and knowing all the while that they could never touch except to trick observers with a show of fake love. Fiona couldn't imagine anything more excruciating.

Justin was still standing there, brimming with excitement and hope. He'd gone through so much. She couldn't take that away from him.

Not only that, but she had to stay with him to protect him. He was dead-set on taking on Apex, and if they parted ways, he'd do it all by himself. No one person, no matter how tough, would have a chance. He'd saved her life twice over. She couldn't let him throw his away.

He is your mate, hissed her snow leopard. *You cannot walk away from your mate.*

Her leopard was right, in a way. When it came down to it, Fiona couldn't bring herself to leave him. No matter how much it hurt.

She took his hand. Like the very first time they'd touched, when he'd slipped her a gun under the watchful gaze of six hit men, a jolt went through her body.

What is that? Fiona asked.

The mate bond, her snow leopard purred. *Trying to make you stop denying it and connect.*

Justin's snow leopard apparently told him something similar. With a gentleness that stung more than a slap in the face, he said, "Believe me, if I could be your mate, I would. I just can't."

Fiona felt like she'd lose her mind if she heard him say that one more time. "Let's get this straight. You're not the only one making that call. I am too. So you can stop saying that."

"You don't want to be my mate?" Now *he* sounded hurt.

"It's not that I don't want to. I just can't." She replayed her words in her mind, realized they were identical to what he'd said earlier, and hurriedly said, "Sorry. I wasn't making fun of you. It looks we're in the same boat here. If we were different people with different lives, we'd get together and it would be great. But we're the people we are, with the lives we have. And it's not happening."

He nodded sharply. "Hey, we're both adults. So we're attracted to each other. So our leopards keep telling us to go for it. So what? We've agreed that we're not going to, so we won't."

"Right," Fiona replied, keeping her voice calm and cool. "We won't."

It wasn't until she turned away to start packing that she realized that neither of them had released the other's hand.

All the choices that gave me the life with no room for a mate, I made years ago, she thought. *And now it's too late. The time-reversal device was just a joke.*

She let go.

CHAPTER FOUR
Justin

Justin looked around warily as they left the Ritz. Neither he nor Fiona had any idea who had shot at them the night before, nor if the attempted killers had tracked them. He walked beside her with all his senses extended, ready to shield her if he caught the slightest hint of danger. But all was peaceful as they hailed a cab to the airport, nor did they have any trouble buying tickets for the next departing flight to Venice.

He had to admit, posing a couple made that request much more plausible. Especially the way Fiona giggled girlishly and hung on his arm. The clerk even winked at them. Justin forced a smile. Half of him wished he hadn't agreed to that particular cover story—he knew perfectly well that it was frustrating Fiona, not to mention that it was torturing him—and half of him was guiltily glad of the opportunity to touch her at all.

You can touch her all you like, hissed his snow leopard. *You idiot.*

Justin ignored the big cat. But he kept his arm around her slim waist as they strolled around the airport. He bought a toothbrush and other travelling supplies, and she bought a cheap disposable phone to replace the one she'd lost at the warehouse.

"And a new purse?" he asked.

She glanced at a display of designer purses, then shook her head. "I'll get one in Venice. A wallet too. It's Italy, they'll be nicer there than anything I could buy in an airport."

"Have you been there before?"

"I've been to Rome. Not Venice. I've always meant to go, but I never got around to it. What about you?"

"I've never travelled anywhere outside of the US." As soon as he said it, he realized how completely wrong that was. He'd not only spent quite a lot of time in Afghanistan, he'd just come back from England. But it wasn't as if he'd been able to see the sights in either country. "I mean, not for fun."

She seemed to understand what he meant, which was good because he couldn't explain in public. His cover identity, Andrew Wright, was the head of HR for a car wash chain, and had never served in the military. With a mischievous glint in her eyes, she remarked, "Those business trips keep you shut up in offices the whole time. You might as well have never left America."

"Eight hours a day in air-conditioned offices that all look the same," he replied, keeping a straight face. "Endless power point presentations about integrated software platforms. Sometimes I really wonder if I'm on the right career path."

"Well," Fiona said after a pause in which he was sure she was trying not to laugh. "That's what happens when you choose job security over a more varied workplace environment."

Their boarding announcement cut the conversation short, but he was still smiling to himself as they joined the line. He'd never get tired of talking to her, even when they had to maintain their characters and couldn't speak freely. Her sense of humor was so sly and unexpected. But he couldn't wait till they were alone together, so he could learn more about her.

He wanted to know everything: not just crucial life events like where she'd grown up, why she'd become a bodyguard, and whether she'd been born a shifter or made into one, but little everyday things like what she liked to read, what her secret junk food cravings were, and whether she followed sports. If she didn't, maybe he could convert her. He'd love to take her to a ball game, share a beer and a bag of peanuts, and see what she looked like in a baseball cap. (Mind-meltingly sexy, he bet.) She'd literally let down her hair when they'd had breakfast together, but he was dying to see her do it metaphorically.

Stop it, he ordered his own treacherous imagination. *You're not taking her to any ball games.*

We'll see about that, purred his snow leopard.

Justin shook his head in disbelief as they boarded the airplane. Ever since he'd met Fiona, his inner cat had done a complete turnaround from its usual mode of snarling and hissing in fury or panic, to purring with what Justin could swear was satisfied smugness. It was so bizarre that he didn't even know how to argue with it.

"Window or aisle?" Fiona asked.

"Aisle," he said instantly. He didn't expect anything to happen on the flight, but on the off chance that it did, he wanted his body between her and any attackers.

They took their seats. He would have bought economy tickets, out of sheer habit if nothing else. But Fiona had done the booking and she'd gone business-class. The seats were unexpectedly comfortable.

"This sure beats..." *Military transports,* he thought, but substituted, "Economy."

Once again, Fiona gave him that bewitching smile that told him that she knew the truth behind the words. "It does. Look, they tilt all the way back."

She tipped his seat back until he was lying nearly flat. "Get some sleep, honey. You've had a rough week."

"I took the aisle seat to make sure no one bothered you," he protested.

Smoothly, she replied, "And no one will, if you're in it. Any flight attendants try to reach over you to hand me snacks I don't want, you'll wake up in a flash and stop them. Right?"

He considered it. No matter how exhausted he was—and he *was* still tired—he couldn't imagine sleeping through an attempted attack on Fiona. And she was right that any attackers would have to reach over him. "Yeah. No unwelcome packets of peanuts will get by me."

"Then go to sleep. You don't want to still be worn out in Venice and miss your vacation."

She was right that he'd be less efficient—and less able to protect her—if he was still sleep-deprived when he arrived. But the thought of sleeping in a public place filled with strangers unsettled him, even knowing that he'd wake if there was any danger.

Justin chewed on his lower lip, trying to figure out how to convey that. "I'd hate to miss the in-flight movie. Might be something exciting."

He reached for the seat controls.

Fiona caught his hand. "I'll keep a lookout. If something comes on that I know you'd want to see, I'll wake you up."

He, too, understood her perfectly: *Go to sleep. I'll stand guard so you can feel safe.*

It was the sort of thing PJs did for each other. It required absolute trust. But he did trust her.

"Thanks." He let go of the seat controls and curled his fingers around hers, trying to convey with his clasp and eyes alone how much that meant to him. "I'll do the same for you, any time. You'll never miss a movie you've been looking forward to. Not while I'm around."

Fiona's green eyes glistened. With tears? Then she blinked, and they were gone. "I'll hold you to it."

He closed his eyes, and drifted off to the comforting warmth of her hand holding his, the familiar vibration of jet engines, and the unfamiliar sound of his snow leopard purring.

Justin was awakened by the increased air pressure as the plane came in for a landing. It was hours later, but her hand was still wrapped around his. He blinked up at her. "Are we there yet?"

She gave a distinctly unladylike snort. "Almost. And if you don't stop asking, I'm going to turn this plane around."

He raised the seat. To his regret, that made her disengage her hand. "No movies I wanted to see, huh?"

"Nothing with gun fights or martial arts battles or explosions." With a slight edge to her voice, she said, "Just people talking about their feelings. And kissing. Getting naked. Nothing you'd be interested in."

"Getting naked on an in-flight movie?" Justin inquired. "That's different."

Fiona stealthily kicked his ankle. "Naked with sheets covering the R-rated parts."

"If they ever get naked for real, wake me up."

She kicked him again. He kept a straight face and looked past her, out the window. It was night. Venice was an island of sparkling lights in the middle of a dark sea. As the plane touched down, he felt as if he wasn't only entering an unfamiliar country, but stepping into an unfamiliar life. His snow leopard, purring. Fiona, guarding his sleep.

Himself, with someone to protect.

They collected their checked bags from the luggage carousel. Justin immediately grabbed his duffel bag and headed for the bathroom, where he could take out his gun and strap it on without alarming anyone. As he did so, he saw Fiona take her small suitcase to the ladies' room, presumably for the same reason. That too felt surreal. The last time he'd been in company with someone who also always carried a weapon, he'd been a PJ. It was as if he'd traveled back to a better time.

The sense of strangeness increased when they left the airport and, instead of catching a cab, caught a vaporetto—a motorboat the size of a bus. It sailed along, engine humming, and deposited them in a city of old buildings with water lapping at the thresholds of the front doors. Moonlight sparkled on the water of the canals, the flowers growing in the houses' window boxes perfumed the air, and night birds sang.

Justin felt like he was still in a dream—a very pleasant one, for once—as he and Fiona walked along the canals. But he woke up in a hurry when she pulled out her phone and programmed the address he'd given her into its GPS. Venice was such a small island that everything was walking distance—including Bianchi's house.

They headed toward it. Once they were alone in a dark alley, he caught her arm. "Hold on."

He closed his eyes. But before he could summon the ice, she grabbed him by the shoulder.

"What are you doing?" she whispered fiercely.

He opened his eyes. "It takes me a minute or two to become invincible."

"What? Why would you do that?"

"I know we said we were just going to check it out when we arrived. But we might see an opportunity to go in now. Or someone could spot us and attack. So I thought I'd better do it now. It takes time and focus, and I don't want to miss my chance."

"That's not what I meant. Why are you doing it at all?"

Justin thought back to when he'd explained it to her, and decided that he must have been so shaken up by having to tell her about Apex that his explanation of his power had made no sense to her. "When I'm invincible, I can't feel pain."

"So?" she demanded. "You're a PJ. What do you care about pain?"

"It's not just pain. It's the effects of damage. Wounds don't always hurt right away, but if you get shot, it'll drop you whether it hurts or not. If I'm invincible, it won't."

"If you get shot, we've got bigger problems than whether or not you collapse on the spot," she said drily. "Don't do it."

She is right, his snow leopard hissed.

Justin ignored him. His leopard always voted against his power. "Why not?"

"Why not?" Her eyebrows rose. "Have you looked in the mirror lately? For your information, you look like you just got out of a war zone."

"It'll be for a couple hours at most," he pointed out. "And it's not as if I'd be eating or sleeping then anyway. I'll take it off as soon as we're done."

"Hmm." She didn't look happy, but clearly didn't have a good argument against it.

She doesn't know you can't shift when you're invincible, hissed his snow leopard. *If she thinks you can, she may take actions based on that. You cannot let her walk into danger believing a lie that could harm her!*

Justin had forgotten about that. Reluctantly, he said, "I can't shift when I'm invincible. Just so you know."

"WHA—" Fiona lowered her voice. "Then forget about it! It's not worth it."

"It is!" Justin insisted, then remembered to lower his voice too. "It's not like we want to turn into snow leopards in Venice. Talk about conspicuous!"

She folded her arms. "I want to have that option. For both of us. Look, this is supposed to be reconnaissance. Let's just go and check the place out. If it looks like we can get in, we can revisit this discussion then."

Justin glanced around uneasily. They'd been standing in the alley arguing, and not always in whispers, for minutes now. "Fine. Let's get out of here."

They slipped out of the alley and continued toward Bianchi's house in silence. Justin no longer noticed Venice as a beautiful place, but merely observed all the areas where assassins could be hiding and the places where they could take cover if attacked. Fiona moved beside him like a cat, her feet soundless.

When they neared Bianchi's mansion, he felt his vulnerability like a gun to his head. How was he supposed to protect her when all it would take to put him down was a dart or a bullet or even a knife? He edged closer to her, his senses on high alert, ready to throw himself in front of her.

"Stop crowding me," she whispered. "I feel like I'm going to trip over your feet."

Reluctantly, he moved aside.

We can protect our mate better this way, his snow leopard hissed. *If anyone attacks, we can pounce and rip out their throats!*

His leopard's ferocity reassured him as they slipped into a shadowy gap between buildings to observe Bianchi's home. It was patrolled by a whole lot of armed security guards, all of them alert and professional. Justin watched unseen from the shadows, looking for gaps in the security, but saw none. He glanced at Fiona in case she'd spotted something he'd missed, but she shook her head. They left as stealthily as they'd come.

Once they were in another empty alley, she said, "I might be able to go undercover and get into his house as a maid or assistant or something like that."

"Alone?" Justin hated that idea.

"He knows what you look like," she pointed out. "He even knows you're after him. There's no way you're getting inside. Or we could wait for him to leave and catch him outside. Unless you have a better idea."

"No..." He considered a third possibility, then shook his head. "No."

"What were you thinking just now?"

"Well, I could kill the guards. But I'm not sure I could get all of them before one could sound an alarm. And even if I could, they're probably just hired security, not Apex workers. They're innocent."

The look she gave him made him feel like she could see every person he'd ever killed for Apex. Her gaze was unblinking, her eyes colorless in the moonlight.

"I'm not Subject Seven any more," he said. "At least—I'm trying not to be."

"Oh, Justin." Her expression changed so completely that he wondered if he'd misinterpreted it the first time. She caught his hand in hers. "I know you're not. I don't think you ever have been, really."

"You don't—" The words stuck in his throat. He swallowed and went on, "You don't know what happened there. The people who died because of me."

"I know it wasn't your choice."

He wanted to tell her that didn't matter, but all he could focus on was the warmth of her hands, the touch of her skin like an electric current, and the sympathy written all over her face. And not just sympathy, but empathy. As if she not only felt bad for him for being torn up inside with guilt, but felt the same thing herself.

Which made no sense. She hadn't done anything wrong. He'd seen into her soul, and it shone bright as the sun. He was the one with only darkness inside of him.

"I…" His hands closed tight over hers. Even as he held her hand, it was breaking his heart that he knew he'd have to let it go. "Thank you."

She didn't reply, but simply stood there, looking into his eyes. She was so beautiful. And kind. In the cool night air, he could feel the heat coming off her body. Her head was tilted upward, her eyes half-closed, her lips parted. It would be so easy to bend down and taste the velvet sweetness of her lips, pull her close and feel her body mold itself into his…

…and take her down with me, like a drowning man pulling his rescuer under.

Justin straightened up with a jerk. At the same time, Fiona yanked her hands out of his grip like she'd been burned. She ducked, avoiding his eyes, and tapped at the GPS coordinates on her phone.

"We're not far from our apartment," she said. "Let's get some sleep and figure out a plan in the morning."

"Right."

They walked along the canals to the place they'd be staying. They'd booked an apartment at the airport, but because it was peak tourist season and last minute, they hadn't had a lot of choices. The apartment they'd gotten had been selected more for security than comfort, up a narrow flight of stairs that would be impossible to climb up without being heard, and with a nice view of the canals that also meant they could jump out the window if they had to.

They used the code the owner had given them to open the mailbox to get the key, unlocked the door, and carried their luggage upstairs. The apartment consisted of a small bathroom, an even smaller kitchenette with a mini-fridge and a hot plate, and a medium-sized bedroom with a bedside table and chair, but no sofa.

It also had only one bed. Again.

Fiona sat down on it, avoiding his eyes, and took her laptop out of her small suitcase. "Let me do some research on Bianchi. See if I can figure out where we can ambush him."

"Sounds good."

To avoid staring at that damn bed, Justin went to the balcony and stood looking out at the canals. Moonlight transformed the still waters to liquid silver and the arched bridges to glowing ivory. The full moon was reflected in the water like an immense pearl. He'd never seen anything so beautiful in his entire life, except for Fiona's eyes.

If he'd been invincible, he wouldn't have thought it worth a second glance.

"Justin?"

He went back inside and sat on the bed, a prudent distance away from her. "Find something?"

"I did. Bianchi seems to be a homebody. He throws lavish parties and entertains guests, but he doesn't leave home much. He gets most of what he needs delivered. If we stake out his house and wait for him to leave, we could literally be waiting for weeks."

"It's not like I have somewhere I need to be," Justin pointed out. "But if you do..."

"Oh, wait." Fiona bent over her laptop. "There's one time he does leave. He's a big fan of Carnival."

"He goes to *carnivals?*" Justin had a hard time picturing the cold Apex manager cheering on a demolition derby or throwing golf balls into goldfish bowls.

"Not carnivals. The Carnival of Venice. It's an ancient festival they still celebrate here. Back then, kings and queens would mingle with commoners, but everyone wore masks so no one knew who was who. And the masks gave people permission to do things that they never could if they were their real selves."

She turned the laptop around. He examined the photos of people posing on the streets and plazas of Venice in elaborate costumes and masks. Some wore lace-covered ball gowns, some sweeping black cloaks, Some masks were white and sad, some looked hammered out of gold, and some had long bird beaks.

"It's next week," Fiona said. "It's why we had such a hard time finding a place to stay—it's a peak time for tourists. And apparently Bianchi likes dressing up in incredibly fancy, show-offy outfits to show everyone how rich he is. Like, masks made with real gold. And Carnival happens on the streets, not inside."

"Ah-ha. We could nab him while he's wandering around and weighed down with gold."

"Exactly. And we'd be in masks too, so he wouldn't see you coming. We'll have to get costumes too, of course."

Justin looked dubiously at the outfits, which tended toward the enormous, elaborate, and puffy. "Are there any we can move in?"

"I'm sure we'll be able to find something. It'll be expensive, though, since it's so last-minute."

"My million dollars is going fast. I feel bad for the charity I was planning to give it to."

"Think of it as supporting local craftspeople," she advised. "That's a good cause."

"True. Well, maybe this is for the best. We're here anyway, so we can take a week and see the sights. If Bianchi's a shut-in, we don't have to worry about him spotting me. Could be fun."

Fiona's eyes sparkled with delight. "Oh, it'll be more than fun. I've wanted to come here for years. We can see the Doge's Palace, and St. Mark's Basilica, and the Bridge of Sighs, and—"

"The Bridge of *Sighs?*" Justin repeated.

"It's because convicts would be marched over it on their way to prison. They'd sigh at their last view of the beauty of Venice before they were locked up in their windowless cells."

"Must be a good view. Though if you're going to be locked up, a parking lot is probably enough to make you sigh, if it doesn't have walls." He yawned. "Excuse me."

"Let's get some rest." She shot him a half-amused, half-concerned glance. "You've still got five nights to catch up on."

"It doesn't work exactly like that."

"Oh?" The edge in her voice was back. "How does it work, exactly?"

"I don't need one night of sleep for every night I missed. That's all."

To avoid further conversation on that topic, he grabbed his pajamas out of his bag, went into the bathroom with them, and closed the door. He normally slept in boxers, but he'd bought pajamas at the airport given that he was rooming with Fiona. He'd deliberately selected the worst ones, not that any pajamas were especially sexy. But when faced with a choice between a plain black set that clung to his body and a baggy set the color of a glass of milk forgotten under the sofa for a week, he'd gone for the latter. No point tempting fate. Not only would he ensure that he didn't look appealing to Fiona, they'd hopefully also make *him* not feel in a sexy mood.

When he came out in his mildew-colored pajamas, he caught her look of disbelief. Then, shaking her head, she grabbed an armful of fabric and went into the bathroom. While she was changing, he set alarms on the doors to the stairs and the balcony. He took his time doing it. He had extremely vivid memories of her short, floaty nightgown, and he didn't want to be caught staring.

But when Fiona emerged, he had to suppress a laugh. She'd bought new sleepwear too, and apparently with the exact same idea he'd had when he'd acquired his. She wore an excessively modest nightgown of red-checked flannel, with long sleeves, a high collar, and a hem that nearly reached the floor.

If she'd been auditioning for a movie with a title like *Showdown at Sagebrush Ridge*, it would have been perfect. But as a lust-discouraging device, it was a miserable failure. She *still* looked sexy. Also, adorable. She'd taken down her hair but left the braids in. They hung nearly down to her waist, giving her a schoolgirl air. Justin had the near-irresistible urge to grab one and give it a tug. He had to fold his arms across his chest to stop himself.

He let her take her choice of the side of the bed, then slipped into the other one, keeping as much of a distance as possible. It was a full-sized bed, not a king or even a queen, so that wasn't much. If there had been more than two pillows, he'd have been tempted to pile them into a barrier. But maybe it was just as well that there weren't. Constructing a wall would be childish and do nothing but make an awkward situation more awkward by drawing attention to its awkwardness.

Like he'd said, they were both adults. They were perfectly capable of sleeping in the same bed and doing nothing but sleeping.

"Good night, Fiona."

"Good night, Justin." She turned out the light.

The bed was comfortable, but sleep didn't come. She lay so close to him that he was warmed by her body heat. Every tiny movement she made was transmitted to him by the covers and mattress. He could hear her soft, even breathing, quiet but as attention-catching as a live concert at full blast. Even the air around them was perfumed, faintly but unmistakably, by the lingering fragrance of her shampoo and, beneath that, her own natural scent.

But more distracting than the simple fact of her presence was the knowledge that all he had to do was reach out his hand, and he'd be touching her. All he had to do was ask, and he could have her in his arms and feel the raw passion of her kisses. The willpower it took to not touch her left him gritting his teeth and lying there rigid as a toppled statue, his muscles quivering with tension.

Touch her, hissed his snow leopard. *TOUCH HER.*

If he lay there for one more second, he was going to do it. Justin sprang out of bed.

Fiona's voice rose sharply. "Are you all right?"

"Yeah, I'm fine. Sorry. I couldn't sleep."

"Oh." She sounded relieved, but not surprised.

He looked down at her. The moonlight coming in from the windows made her hair shine like silver. And she hadn't moved at all since they'd gotten in bed together, even though that had been—he checked his watch—over an hour ago. She'd obviously been lying awake too.

He took his pillow and dropped on the rug by the foot of the bed, then began rummaging in the closet. He found a lamp with no bulb, several shoeboxes, a set of elephant-shaped bedroom slippers, and—jackpot!—a blanket, which he spread out below the pillow.

"What are you doing?" Fiona sat up and turned on the bedside light.

"I'm going to sleep on the floor," he said.

"No, you're the one who hasn't slept in days. You take the bed. I'll take the floor."

"Don't be ridiculous," Justin protested. "You stay in bed. I'm the one who doesn't want to be there."

"Only because I'm in it. Well, not anymore. I was getting out anyway. You were distracting me too." She climbed out of bed. "Get back in bed. I'll take the floor."

"No!" He saw her eyeing his blanket and sat down on it before she could lie on it and claim it. "Look, I'm used to sleeping rough. You're not. So you take the bed."

"You're right, you haven't slept in a nice bed for—what? Years? So you should have it."

"That's by choice," Justin countered. "At least, the last couple months, it's been by choice. If I wanted a nice bed, I could've gotten one."

"That's true," Fiona said thoughtfully. But instead of getting back in bed, she went on, "You have plenty of money. You have *a million dollars*. Why were you squatting in an abandoned warehouse?"

"I didn't want anyone to know where I was."

"You have a fake ID. The one you used to stay at the Ritz."

"It didn't occur to me to stay anywhere nice," he admitted.

"Then enjoy being somewhere nice now." She pointed firmly to the bed.

"No."

"Why not?" Fiona demanded.

"I can't sleep in a bed while you're on the floor," Justin said, frustrated. "Forget it. I won't do it."

"Well, I won't either." She began bundling the pillow and blankets from the bed into her arms.

"What are you doing?"

She marched into the bathroom with them, disappearing from view. Her voice slightly muffled, she called back, "I'm sleeping in the bathtub!"

"What? Why?"

She didn't respond, but he heard her noisily flapping blankets. He was sure she was doing it on purpose. The blanket-flapping and pillow-thumping went on for much longer than it needed to, and then silence fell.

Unable to believe that she was really going through with it, he got up, went to the bathroom door, and knocked.

"Come in," she called. "Door's open."

"I can see that." He went in. Sure enough, she had constructed a sort of nest for herself in the bathtub. "You have got to be kidding me."

She folded her arms across her chest. "Nope. I'm done with the bed. If you don't sleep in it, it'll just sit there. Empty. So you might as well take it."

"Same to you!"

They glared at each other. Then Justin looked down at the bathtub nest and began to laugh. "You do know this is ridiculous, right?"

She kept her scowl locked and loaded for a few moment longer, then a snicker escaped. "Yes."

"So you'll take the bed now?"

"Not a chance."

He idly contemplated scooping her up, blankets and all, and dumping her back on the bed. But he quickly discarded that notion. For one thing, she'd get right back in the tub as soon as he let go of her. For another, she'd undoubtedly fight him. And for a third, he had a feeling that any physical struggle between them would lead to the exact thing he'd left the bed to prevent.

"Fine," he said. "Good night."

"Good night," she said. "Sweet dreams."

"Don't hit your head on the faucet when you wake up."

Fiona rolled her eyes at him, then grudgingly moved the pillow to the other end of the tub.

"Sweet dreams," Justin said, and returned to his blankets on the floor.

CHAPTER FIVE
Fiona

Fiona squirmed around in the bathtub, but tried to do it quietly, so she wouldn't wake Justin up if he'd managed to fall asleep. It was incredibly uncomfortable. But she was hardly going to return to the bed if he was on the floor. Maybe if she stayed in the tub, he'd eventually decide that since the bed was right there and empty, he might as well sleep in it.

She'd fluffed the pillow for what felt like the thirtieth time when she heard a sound from the other room. Fiona froze, abruptly on high alert. Adrenaline surging through her veins, she quietly rose from the tub and edged to the bathroom door, which she'd left ajar. But when she peered through, she saw no one in the bedroom but Justin, lying on the floor with his head turned away from her. As she watched, she heard the sound again. This time she could identify it as a soft moan.

"Justin?"

He sat bolt upright with a gasp. His left hand clutched at his hip, found no weapon, and fell away.

"Fiona." His voice shook slightly, then steadied. "Is something wrong?"

"No. Are you all right?"

He pushed his hair out of his face. "I'm fine. Go back to sleep. Take the bed if you like. I'm sure it's comfier than the tub."

"I'm sure it's comfier than the floor," she retorted. "You take it."

He lay back down on the rug and closed his eyes. She returned to the tub.

When she woke up the next morning, stiff and cramped and with a crick in her neck, she found him doing stretches on the floor. She sat down and joined him. He didn't look any more rested than she felt, but she didn't mention it. What was the point? He'd just say he was fine and be annoyed at her for asking.

She took a shower, and felt better after an infusion of hot water. When Justin went to take his, she contemplated her phone. She had to call Mr. Elson, but she could wait till Justin got out to make the call, so he could listen in on it. That would save her having to recap it to him afterward. But the thought of him watching and listening while she put on the persona of that heartless spy made her cringe. He'd know it was just an act, of course. But all the same, she didn't want him to see her do it.

More than that, she didn't want him to see just how good she was at being fake.

She closed her eyes, took a moment to get into character, then called Mr. Elson. She had his direct line, and he picked up on the first ring.

"Speak softly," she whispered. "He's in the shower in the other room."

"So you're in," Mr. Elson replied in low voice, sounding pleased. "*Very* in, if he's showering around you."

"Well, he's not showering *with* me. But I'll get there. Just give me time." As she spoke, she patted herself on the back for making the call out of Justin's earshot. The thought of saying those lines while he was listening was so horrifying that she wasn't even sure she could bring herself to do it.

Mr. Elson gave his oily chuckle. "Good work. Where are you?"

She made a lightning-fast calculation of how likely he was to have her phone call traced, and decided not to risk a lie. He certainly had the technical capability, and in the world of organized crime, it paid to be paranoid. "Venice. Italy."

"How romantic," he said drily. "He must be smitten. Has he told you why he's really there?"

"He gave me the impression it *was* because he was smitten."

"I think it's actually a business trip," Elson replied. "A business rival of mine lives there. The same man who was the subject of your boyfriend's hostile takeover. The one that brought him to my attention."

As usual, he was careful to say nothing too incriminating over the phone in case someone was recording or listening in.

"If he is here on business, what would you like me to do about it?"

"I don't care if my rival's company goes under," said Elson. Fiona easily translated that as "Let Justin kill Bianchi if he wants." "Just keep on with your assignment. It sounds like it's coming along nicely. Learned anything about him yet?"

"Not much. He's closed-mouthed. I'm still—Gotta go," she whispered, then hung up.

The shower was still running, but she'd gotten what she wanted. Suddenly ending the call would reinforce the idea that she was going behind Justin's back. And she didn't want to spend any more time talking to that sleazy arms dealer, or being that sleazy fake person, than she absolutely had to.

The shower turned off. A few minutes later Justin stepped out, fully dressed and toweling his wet hair. His face was flushed from the heat and his eyes were bright.

I wish I'd been in the shower with him, she thought. *Wonder if he gets that pink all over...?*

"Hey, I just got off the phone with Elson." She recapped the conversation to Justin, who listened with interest.

"Should've let me listen in. I'd have loved to see you do your thing."

When Hell freezes over, she thought.

"Some other time," she said.

"Shall we get our masks and costumes now?" he asked. "I bet you already found a place to get them."

"I did, actually."

"You're good with computers."

"I just googled that. Anyone could've done it."

"I'm not so sure about that. I'm going to go out on a limb and guess that you found the best place in Venice to make the sort of costumes we need that can do a rush job if you pay enough—and you figured that out even without knowing much Italian. Am I right?"

"You're right."

"And the information you found on Bianchi took a bit more than googling, didn't it?"

Fiona nodded. "I had to do a little hacking for that."

"And you pick locks, right? I assume that's how you got into that warehouse I was hiding out in."

"Yes."

"What else do you do?"

"What is this, a job interview?" Fiona demanded.

"Uh-huh. I'm looking to hire a bodyguard who can turn into a snow leopard, but she's got to be multi-talented. Otherwise I could just hire myself. Obviously."

She laughed, then said, "I'm good with mechanical and electronic stuff in general. We have a tech room at Protection, Inc., and I like to go there and tinker around. Make alarms and trackers and little robots and so forth."

"You've got to be careful with robots," he said. "They're always trying to take over the world."

"It's okay, I'm careful not to make them too smart."

"So, you build not-too-bright robots, pick locks, hack computers, and turn into a snow leopard. In addition to being an undercover agent, a marksman, and a hand-to-hand fighter."

Justin sounded both amused and genuinely admiring as he listed off her skills. Lots of men were intimidated by a competent woman, and some expressed it by getting hostile. But he seemed sincerely delighted by everything she could do, like he'd waited his entire life to partner up with a woman who could build wobbly robot dogs.

"Is there anything you *can't* do?" he asked.

I can't be honest, not even with the people I care about most, she thought. *I can't love or be loved.*

Putting on a wry smile that did nothing but make her feel even more fake, she said, "I can't cook."

"Good, I was starting to feel inferior. *I* can't build robots. But I'm an excellent chef. If we buy groceries, I'll prove it tonight." Then, after a perfectly timed beat, he frowned and said, "Wait. Let me re-phrase that. I'm a reasonably good amateur chef who's mastered the art of cooking with ingredients you can afford on an Air Force salary."

"I don't have lobster and caviar every day," she replied. "And anything homemade would be a treat. I only get that when a teammate invites me over for dinner."

"What? Shane learned to cook?"

"Shane absolutely did not. And Catalina is even worse, if that's possible. When I go to their house, we order in. I peeked in their cupboards once and there was nothing in them but MREs and cat food." Seeing Justin's expression, she added, "For their cats."

"That's a relief. You had me worried for a second."

She laughed, then said, "Hal and Destiny cook. And Nick barbecues."

"Of course he does. Barbecuing is a manly art beloved of young men with lots of tattoos."

"Also of middle-aged dads. Which I think Nick aspires to be some day. He was awfully excited over Ellie getting pregnant."

"Which one is Ellie?" Justin asked.

"She's our boss Hal's mate. She's a paramedic. Hal met her when he bodyguarded her after she witnessed a murder and agreed to testify."

"I think I met her," he said. "Or saw her, anyway. Built like Catalina, but with curly blonde hair?"

"Don't tell me you rescued her too!"

"No, no. I saw her with some of your other teammates after you blew up the Apex base, but before you showed up at the meeting point." He swallowed, the brightness fading from his eyes. "She and Catalina were treating Shane for a gunshot wound to the chest. He looked bad. Shock, respiratory distress—I think he was bleeding internally."

He brushed his fingers over his scar, then rubbed it like it still hurt. "He asked me to stay with him. But I had a couple Apex guys on my trail and I was afraid of leading them to him. All the same. He needed me, and I walked out on him."

"He would've done the same if he thought it was the only way to protect you. I must've gotten there right after you left. I held his hand…" Fiona could recall the scene like it had happened yesterday. Shane lying there on the ground, eyes closed, face ashen. She hesitated, then confessed, "I was sure he was dying. I felt so helpless. And—and scared."

Justin laid a comforting hand on her shoulder. "Someone should have told you he wasn't going to die. The paramedics would have known."

"Oh, they did. But it's one thing to hear it and another to believe it."

"Ain't that the truth."

Justin's hand still rested on her shoulder, warm and reassuring. She wished he hadn't had to leave back then. If he'd been there, she was sure he could have convinced her that Shane would recover.

She wished she'd known Justin earlier, period. She didn't flatter herself that if she'd met him immediately after he'd escaped from Apex, she'd have been able to convince him to join Protection, Inc. Shane had told her he'd asked Justin, and he'd refused. But if they'd met before that, before he'd been captured and she'd... gone wrong... maybe everything would have been different for both of them.

And now it's too late.

As if in answer to her thought, Justin stepped away from her. "Let's get some coffee before we get our costumes. This is where they invented espresso, right? Bet it's good here."

Putting on another one of the perfectly convincing fake smiles she'd grown to hate, Fiona said, "All those fancy drinks you order in Starbucks were invented in Italy. Espresso. Cappuccino. Macchiato."

"Pumpkin spice latte?"

"No, that one's all-American."

"Unicorn frappucino?"

Her fake smile melted into a real one as she realized he was teasing her. "Order one of those here and see what happens."

"Maybe we can find the guy who invented it. I'll look for a princess-pink awning."

"And a sign with a horn." She slung her purse over her shoulder. "Come on, let's go."

"Hang on." Justin put on a pair of sunglasses and a baseball cap, then tilted the visor down to cast a shadow over his face. It was a simple disguise, but it was a good one; no one would recognize him unless they got close, and he'd hardly allow Bianchi to do that. It also made him look much more like the tourist he was supposed to be.

"Nice," said Fiona.

Justin tipped his cap to her. "Thank you."

They found a café right outside their apartment. Unlike American coffee shops, it had no tables. You stood up at a polished wood bar as you drank your coffee.

"What do you want?" she asked.

"A unicorn frappucino, of course." When she stepped on his foot, he said, "But if you've taken me to the wrong place and they don't have one, I'll take a cappuccino. And that, and that, and that." He pointed to several pastries behind glass.

Fiona, who spoke a little Italian, ordered for him and herself, then fished out the correct amount of money from his wallet to pay for it.

"You *can* do anything," he remarked. "Except make these yourself. Tragic. I could, of course."

She cast a skeptical glance at his almond cake, crisp pastry ribbons sprinkled with powdered sugar, and little fluffy buns topped with candied fruit. "You could not."

"I could. Really. I mean, I'd need a recipe. Baking is very precise. You can't just improvise how much flour and how much butter. But sure, I could do it. Ask Shane."

Fiona bit her tongue on "I could if you'd let me tell him you're alive." Instead, she said, "Did you bake cupcakes for your—" She couldn't say "Air Force buddies," so she smoothly substituted "Car wash buddies?"

Justin, who obviously wasn't used to being undercover with a partner, looked completely blank for a second. Then he said, "Absolutely. Always had a tray ready for when we went on... uh... business retreats." He looked irritated, and she stifled a giggle when she realized why: he'd wanted to say something like "combat missions," and had been forced to ruin his own joke with a substitution that made it not funny.

"Seriously, did you?" she asked.

"I did."

"Literally cupcakes?"

"Literally cupcakes. Some of my buddies were dads. Or moms. Their kid had a birthday, I'd make custom cupcakes. I'd do little drawings of Darth Vader or Rainbow Dash or Harry Potter in icing."

"You really need to meet my friend Grace," Fiona said. "She just married another friend of mine. They had cupcakes instead of a wedding cake. Their friend Paris baked them, in something like twenty different flavors. Red velvet. Pink lemonade. Key lime pie. Rose."

"Forget Grace, I want to meet Paris. We could trade recipes."

Fiona nudged him. "Stop talking and eat. You haven't touched your pastries. Or your coffee."

She picked up her own coffee and took a sip, stealthily watching him over the rim of her cup. His black hair fell forward as he bent his head to drink. She wondered what he'd look like if he stopped dying it. Black eyes and brilliant copper hair: no wonder people stared at him.

The unselfconscious happiness that lit up his face as he tasted his coffee gave her a pang of joy and sadness, swirled together like the pinks and purples in a unicorn frappucino. She was happy for him that he was enjoying himself at last, and heartbroken that he'd suffered so much and for so long that something as ordinary as enjoying a cup of coffee was so significant to him.

Those feelings only grew stronger as she watched him try each of his pastries with startled delight, as if he couldn't quite believe that he was actually experiencing pleasure. As for her, she couldn't quite believe that this was the same person as the expressionless, emotionless man who didn't seem to care about anything, not even his own life. Why would being unable to feel pain or hunger or weariness also seem to take away everything else you could feel?

Oh.

Fiona felt stupid for not having figured it out earlier. Of course. Justin's "invincibility" power was actually the inability to feel, period. Pain. Pleasure. Everything. No wonder he couldn't shift while he was using it—he couldn't feel his snow leopard, either.

She'd thought that power was bad for him even before she'd realized what it was, just on the basis that it was obviously damaging his health. But now that she'd watched him eat pastries and laughed at his jokes, kissed him and held his hand while he slept, a cold horror came over her at the thought of him deliberately erasing everything that made him who he was.

Justin glanced up, smiling, and she made sure to erase any trace of her thoughts from her expression. He offered her a twist of sugar-dusted pastry. "You have to try this. It's delicious."

She took and crunched it. "Thanks. It is."

Encouraged, he broke off bite-size portions of his cake and buns for her to try, then quizzed her on her favorite. She offered him a bite of her biscotti in return.

But all the while, she was thinking about his invincibility. It allowed him to power through hunger and injury and weariness, but because of that, he let himself get hungry and hurt and exhausted when he didn't have to. Why not just eat and sleep and exercise more caution? He called it a power, but it seemed more like a Devil's bargain. And using it at the cost of his health—worse, at the cost of his very self—was sheer madness.

Fiona dabbed the last crumbs from her lips. "Let's get those groceries.

I warn you, I'll be expecting genius after all that baking bragging."

"I only have a hot plate," Justin protested. "Genius requires an oven."

She made herself smile, but his playfulness and ease made her heart ache. It seemed so fragile and temporary, and he was so willing to throw it away.

Well, she wasn't going to stand by and let him do it. As they walked out, she silently vowed to make sure that he never used his invincibility again.

The nearest market was a set of docked boats. They stood on floating wooden platforms to examine baskets of plump tomatoes and pink shrimp, violet artichokes and tangerines with leaves still clinging to their stems. She had to stop him from buying more than would fit in their small refrigerator and narrow shelves.

They returned to the apartment and unloaded their groceries, then set out to get their Carnival disguises. Despite her GPS and maps, they got lost. Venice was a maze of twisting alleys, and it was impossible to walk in a straight line. Again and again, they'd head in one direction, then have to walk out of their way to cross a bridge arching over a canal, make a few more detours, and find themselves back where they started.

But there was no rush. She kept an eye out for trouble and Justin obviously did too, but she had an eye for the beauty of the city as well. Everywhere they went, there was something lovely to see: an ancient cathedral, a window box of blooming poppies, a gondolier plying his boat down a green canal, a statue of a winged lion, a glimpse of a woman dancing through a foggy window. The streetlights were made of pink glass. The air was fresh, with a hint of salt. A chilly wind blew, but the sun shone bright. Some of the gondoliers were singing.

And through it all, Justin was beside her, walking so if any danger struck, he'd be perfectly positioned to place his body between her and it. But while he did, he also cracked jokes, pointed out gargoyles on rooftops, and tossed saved biscotti crumbs to the pigeons. She knew he'd been through terrible things, and she'd seen some of the scars he bore. The one on his chest was probably the least of them. But despite all that, he was so vibrant and funny and engaged with life. So *alive*. It made her feel like she'd lived her whole life behind a sheet of glass, never getting her hands dirty or her feet wet.

If he took my hand and led me to the water, I'd go in with him, she thought. *Into the ocean. Into the mud. Into the fire. Anywhere.*

Her GPS beeped, startling her. They'd gotten so lost that they'd come across their destination by accident.

"Honey," she said, reminding him of their masquerade, "We're here."

Quick on the uptake, he put his arm around her waist. She shivered involuntarily. That was why they hadn't touched coming here. Every time they did, it made it difficult to focus on anything but how much she wanted to be able to touch him all she wanted. How much she wanted him to take his other hand and cup her breast. How much she wanted him to run his fingers through her hair, and kiss her as passionately as he had at the Ritz, but not stop this time. How much—

Goddammit.

She pushed open an old wooden door, beautifully carved with men and women in elaborate costumes and masks. Inside, exquisite masks hung on the walls, some decorated in feathers and others with jewels, each one a work of art. Mannequins wearing beautiful costumes stood like frozen party-goers.

An old man sitting at a work table greeted her in Italian.

Haltingly, Fiona replied in the same language. "I and my—" She didn't know the word for 'boyfriend,' so substituted "—the man I love want Carnival costumes and masks."

The man I love. No way was she ever telling Justin that was what she'd said. But now that she'd said it, the mask maker was smiling at them the way old people smiled at young lovers.

He answered her in a flood of rapid Italian. She only understood about a third of it, but she got that his name was Mr. Toscani and that this was a rush job so it would cost them much more than it normally would and his wares were expensive to begin with because they were the best, and by the way this shop was three hundred years old and passed down from father to son. Had he mentioned that it was very expensive because it was the best?

Fiona assured him that she had plenty of money, and she was there because it was the best.

That seemed to please Mr. Toscani, who spoke faster than ever. All she could understand was that he wanted to know if she had something specific in mind, or if she would be wise and let him design something perfect for the two of them.

The thought of attempting to describe specific costumes and masks in Italian was so appalling that she gratefully said, "You design. But we are... um..." She searched for the words for "street performers," then finally said, "people who play for money on the road."

"What!?" Mr. Toscani exclaimed. A flood of Italian, plus hand gestures, made her realize that she'd apparently said that they caught roadside mice for dinner. Or maybe lizards. There was definitely eating and small scurrying things involved.

"What?" echoed Justin. "What's he saying? Wait. Never mind that. What did *you* say?"

She made a face at him, then tried again. "We are like... Cirque du Soleil."

"Ah!" In English, Mr. Toscani said, "Acrobats!"

"Yes, acrobats," she said gratefully. In Italian, she added, "You design. But we must..." She made a hand gesture that she hoped conveyed a backflip.

"Yes, yes," said Mr. Toscani in English. "I can do." Then he yelled, "Chiara! Giovanni!"

A man and a woman appeared from the back of the shop with tape measures. The woman seized Fiona and the man seized Justin. Next thing she knew, they were being measured more thoroughly than she'd ever been measured before, and she'd been fitted for custom ball gowns.

When Chiara was done with the measurements, she held up a thick sheet of moistened paper. Carefully, she said in English, "For mask. Hold breath. One minute."

Fiona held her breath, and Chiara pressed the paper against her face. It was cold and wet, and it clung unpleasantly to her mouth and nose. Sixty long seconds ticked by before it was removed. An impression of Fiona's face remained on the paper, which Chiara carefully set aside.

Fiona looked over just in time to see Giovanni approach Justin with the same paper. The briefest flash of alarm widened Justin's eyes before he held up his hand to ward off the paper.

Giovanni said something in Italian, in a reassuring tone. In English, Chiara said, "Is safe. Do not worry."

"I know it's safe. I just..." Justin looked at Fiona, clearly hoping for some kind of rescue.

A burst of white-hot fury burned through her as she realized what the problem must be. One of those sadistic monsters at Apex must have put something over his face to cut off his breathing—suffocated him or waterboarded him or something like that—and he was afraid of having a flashback.

She stepped between him and the mask makers. In Italian, she said, "The man I love is, is—"

"Claustrophobic," said Mr. Toscani, in English.

"Yes," Justin said with relief. "I'm claustrophobic."

In Italian, Mr. Toscani said, "It's common. We can wait. Would he like some water? Fresh air? An herbal remedy? Brandy?"

"Wait," said Fiona, and pulled Justin into a corner.

"Sorry," he said in a low voice. "I keep tripping over these—these fucking random land mines in my head."

Fiona didn't stop to think. She just put her arms around him. His muscles were hard and tense, but they relaxed under her touch. "What can I do?"

She felt him take a shaky breath, then a steadier one. "Well. Seems like that's good."

"Mr. Toscani also offered you water, some sort of herbal medicine, and brandy."

Justin managed a smile. "You don't get customer service like that in the US. Actually… If he was serious, I'll take the brandy. It might help if I had something in my mouth that's really different from—" He broke off.

Water? A gag? She wished, not for the first time, that she had those Apex sadists in front of her now. She'd smother *them* and see how they liked it.

But her anger wasn't what he needed right now.

"Brandy, and I keep my arm around you?" she suggested.

"Yeah. I think that'd do it." Justin sighed. "You'd never believe I used to—uh, do extremely manly things."

Fiona turned, making sure he was looking her in the eyes as she said, "Yes. I would. And there's no 'used to.' You still do."

She wasn't sure he quite believed her. *It's one thing to hear it and another to believe it,* she thought.

But he straightened up anyway. "Hope it's good brandy."

"In Venice? Of course it is. It's probably been aging in a cask for a hundred years."

Mr. Toscani sent Chiara for it, all the while telling Fiona to let Justin know that customers freaked out over the mask imprint all the time. He included a vivid pantomime of a big, tall, strong man passing out, which got a half-smile out of Justin. When Giovanni returned with a small glass of brandy, Justin drank most of it, then held the last sip in his mouth and gave the mask maker a nod. Fiona kept her arm tight around his waist as Giovanni pressed the damp white sheet over his face.

Justin stood stock-still, his body rigid. Sixty seconds ticked by like an eternity. But he didn't move until Giovanni took off the paper, and she felt him sag in a sudden release of tension.

The mask makers congratulated him on his courage, which she could see embarrassed him. She paid and got a promise that it would all be ready in time for Carnival, and then they hurried out.

Justin went straight for a sunny spot, glanced around, then took off his hat and sunglasses. He looked up into the blue sky, breathing deeply. Fiona supposed he was reminding himself that he wasn't in that underground torture chamber at Apex, and was livid with rage all over again. If she ever got her hands on those monsters, they'd regret the day they'd laid hands on him. They'd regret the day they'd ever been born.

Tear out their throats, hissed her snow leopard.

Don't worry, Fiona replied. *We'll get our chance.*

CHAPTER SIX
Justin

Justin stood in the sun, focusing on its warmth on his skin. The lab had always been so cold, and the metal table and instruments colder. The lights were a bleak fluorescent white. But he wasn't underground anymore. The sunlight proved it. If he just stayed in it long enough, maybe all of him would believe it.

Fiona put her arm around him. He leaned into her, thinking all the while that he shouldn't even do so much. She deserved a man who was undamaged, whole.

He didn't want to talk about what had happened. But no one was around to overhear, and she needed an explanation. "They called it an experiment. They strapped me to a table and put a cloth over my face, and Dr. Mortenson poured water over it until I—"

"I know what that's called," Fiona snarled, sounding remarkably like his snow leopard. "And it's not an 'experiment.' It's torture."

"She did it once when I wasn't invincible. Then when I was, to see if it I could hold out longer before I passed out. No idea what the results were, if there even were any beyond her getting her sadistic kicks and me getting permanently fucked up."

Her fist clenched against his belly. "You are *not* permanently fucked up, all right? Fucked up would be if you'd run out of there and then refused to tell me what was going on."

"You're my partner. I can't do stuff that affects you and not even tell you why."

Oh? hissed his snow leopard. *Did I miss you telling her why you really use your power? Or how you got captured in the first place? Or—*

Justin spoke loudly, to drown out anything his leopard might say. "Let's walk around, okay? Do some touristy stuff. Take my mind off things."

She curled her hand around his, which took his mind off things all by itself. "I vote for the Bridge of Sighs."

The week that followed was the most frustrating yet exhilarating, excruciating yet wonderful time of his life.

They were pretending to be tourists, so they did all the things that tourists did: fed the wheeling flocks of pigeons in St. Mark's Square, went on moonlit gondola rides, explored twisting alleys, photographed beautiful old churches, and had pasta and pizza, gelato and pastries, and a tongue-twisting array of fancy coffee drinks. Fiona was the best possible traveling companion, even when they had to talk in code because he was pretending to be a car wash manager and she was pretending to be a high school history teacher.

And, of course, they were also pretending to be a couple. That was where the excruciating part came in. They'd hold hands, link arms, and stand so close that he could smell the light perfume of her hair. But they never kissed, even when it would have made their performance more convincing. He assumed Fiona never tried for the same reason he didn't, which was that if they did, they'd either end up having sex up against the wall in some dark alley, or they'd have to throw themselves into the nearest canal to prevent themselves.

And, of course, every night she stubbornly went to sleep in the bathtub, and he on the bedroom floor, no matter how much he coaxed her to just take the damn bed. She wouldn't even agree to let *him* take the bathtub. Every morning, he woke up stiff and tired, and he could see that Fiona did too. By the second morning they'd gotten into a routine of stretching out together before they went for their morning coffee and pastries.

The pastries were purchased, of course. But as he'd promised, Justin did cook for her. He couldn't do anything fancy with just a hot plate, but on the other hand he had access to fresh-caught seafood, beautiful fruits and vegetables, and an amazing array of cheese, not to mention pasta with names Fiona translated as "little moustaches" or "clown hats" or "priest stranglers." When in Italy, cook Italian, he figured. So he sautéed little pink shrimp with oil and garlic, draped prosciutto over slices of ripe melon, and layered mozzarella with dripping slices of ripe tomatoes.

He hadn't cooked from scratch in years. But it came back to him as if he'd never stopped. And while he'd always liked cooking, he'd never enjoyed it more than when Fiona leaned on the counter, intently watching him chop and stir, then ate his food with expressions that started at blissful and ranged into the positively orgasmic. Sometimes he had to dig his nails into his thigh under the table to stop himself from impulsively leaning across the table and kissing her.

She said no, he'd remind himself, only belatedly remembering that he'd said no too. But his reasons for that, which had seemed so compelling at the time, felt increasingly hazy as the days went on. They came back to him at night, though, when he lay sleepless on the bedroom floor. Even when he didn't have nightmares, he didn't sleep well, waking suddenly every few hours with a sense of foreboding or else lying awake with a hard-on he couldn't do anything about due to Fiona being in the next room.

But the worst was when he woke from a dream of Apex, sweating and disoriented, his heart pounding and his leopard screaming in his head. Every time, he'd strain to hear Fiona's soft, even breathing from the bathroom. It was both reassuring and maddening to have her so close yet so far away. He'd lie there biting his tongue to stop himself from calling to her to come and hold him, to prove to him with the warm touch of her body that he'd really escaped and was never going back. She was *right there…*

Still. Even when he felt like he was going to lose his mind from sexual frustration or just sheer longing, it was wonderful to be with her. Even discomfort and pain were feelings. After years of drifting through the world like a ghost, Justin finally felt alive.

Two days before Carnival, they set out to explore a part of Venice they hadn't been to yet. It was in an area that wasn't much frequented by tourists, or even by locals. As they went further on their way, they saw fewer and fewer people. They stopped in a quiet art gallery, then an old church with beautiful stained glass windows. It was very peaceful.

They crossed a bridge over a canal, then went into a walled garden. It was completely empty, except for some birds. They walked past a set of rose beds, then into a clearing surrounded by tall hedges, with a marble fountain in the middle. Fiona went to examine some carvings on the fountain.

"Freeze!" The voice came from behind him.

At the same instant, another man stepped out in front of him from a break in the hedges, with a gun drawn.

"I have a gun aimed right at your pretty girlfriend's head," said the man behind him. "Make one false move, and that's it for her. Now put up your hands. Both of you."

They raised their hands. Fiona's were trembling. A mixture of hot fury and cold fear made Justin's stomach lurch. He could hear that the man behind him wasn't close enough for him to whip around and disarm him before he shot her. He couldn't shift and then turn fast enough, either.

Then a familiar calmness washed over him. Despite the bad positioning, they were only two men. He could handle this. What's more, *he and Fiona* could handle this. He'd seen her under fire before. If her hands were shaking, it was because she was making them shake.

"Your pretty girlfriend," Justin thought. *He thinks I'm the only threat.*

He and Fiona could use that to their advantage. He glanced at her.

Right on cue, she cowered and said in a high, terrified voice, "Please don't hurt me! Here, take my wallet!"

She started to reach into her purse, but the man behind her yelled, "Freeze! One move, and you're dead!"

Fiona yanked back her hand and burst into tears. She was not only noisily sobbing, but real tears ran down her face. Justin was impressed. He couldn't have done that in a million years. His confidence grew. Sure, having a gunman behind him made the situation much more difficult, but—

A third man stepped out in front of them, also with a gun aimed at them. Justin had never seen the first one and hadn't recognized the voice of the man behind him, but this one he knew.

"McConnell," Justin said. "Fancy meeting you here."

McConnell didn't rise to the bait. Coldly, he said, "Make your girlfriend shut up."

"Anne," Justin said. "Annie, baby. Please stop crying. It's okay. I won't let anyone hurt you."

Fiona went on sobbing.

"Shut up, or I'll blow your head off," McConnell said.

She gulped loudly, sniffed hard, then pressed her hands over her mouth. Her sobs subsided, though her tears continued to flow.

How the hell does she do that? Justin wondered. Even in this dangerous situation, he was warmed by his pride in her. She could build robot dogs and blow up Apex bases and cry on cue. When they got out of this mess and back to somewhere with an oven, he was going to bake her all the cakes in the world.

"Who is he, Andy?" she asked in a shaky voice. "You—You know him?"

"Tell your pretty girlfriend," McConnell sneered.

"They're terrorists," Justin said. "Homegrown variety. White supremacists."

"We're freedom fighters," McConnell spat out. "Protecting our homeland."

"I don't understand," Fiona said, sniffling. "Andy, what do you have to do with terrorists?"

McConnell gave a short, humorless laugh. "Your boyfriend's not who you think. He used to be a government agent. Black ops. An assassin."

"What?" Fiona squeaked. Her voice rose, no doubt hoping to attract attention, as she said, "An assassin!"

"Shut up. One more word out of your pretty mouth—one single exclamation—and it'll be the last one you ever say," said McConnell.

Justin was only surprised he'd let her get away with being that loud for as long as he had. McConnell's gun had a silencer, as did the gun held by his buddy. For that matter, so did Justin's and Fiona's.

"Go on," McConnell said. "Tell that precious lady of yours why I'm here."

"Like I said." Justin put a sarcastic edge in his voice. He didn't know much about McConnell, but in his experience, terrorists never took well to being mocked. "They're terrorists. This asshole's father was their leader. He was planning to blow up a couple buildings to make a point, and who cares how many people were in them? The agency I worked for sent me to kill him, so I did. They figured once the leader was gone, the rest of them would scatter like the roaches they are. Looks like they were half right. I mean about them being roaches."

"Shut up," snarled McConnell.

"You're the one who told me to talk," Justin said with a shrug. "Did you shoot at me in New York?"

McConnell took a step closer to Justin. "Yes, I did."

"Your aim is for shit," Justin sneered. "Or did you get one of the losers here to do the actual shooting?"

He hoped that if he pissed off the man behind him, he'd move his gun off Fiona and on to him. They knew Justin couldn't see where that gun was pointed, so it didn't actually need to be aimed at her. Just the threat would be enough.

"I'm glad we missed in New York," McConnell snarled. "A bullet in the head is too good for you. I want to see you beg for a quick death."

Justin laughed. "From you? You don't scare me. You couldn't scare a little girl. I bet you hit like one, too."

McConnell went red with fury. He stepped in, still holding his gun on Justin, and raised his fist.

"Now!" Justin shouted.

In the blink of an eye, Fiona was gone. A snow leopard leaped for the man beside McConnell, sending his gun flying. At the same instant, Justin snatched McConnell's gun out of his hand and shot him. Before he'd even fallen, Justin whipped around to take out the man behind him.

But there wasn't one man behind him. There were two.

Justin fired, and saw one man hit the ground. But the other was standing farther away, and ducked behind a tree just as Justin fired again. The bullet smashed into the trunk, sending splinters flying and leaving the last enemy unharmed.

Justin dropped and rolled. He heard the soft pop of a silenced gun, and a bullet sent up a spray of dirt two inches from his cheek. He rolled again. But unlike his enemy, he had no cover. If he shifted, he'd just present a bigger target.

A snow leopard leaped down from the branches of a nearby tree.

There was another soft pop in the split second before the big cat landed on the enemy.

Justin scrambled to his feet and ran to help her. But it was already over. The last terrorist lay dead with a broken neck. Fiona's leopard crouched over him, snarling.

Relief flooded him. She was all right. The battle was over, and—

The big cat stepped away from her prey. She'd leaped with deadly grace, but now she was oddly clumsy. When she turned toward him, he saw a rapidly widening patch of red staining her white fur at the shoulder.

Justin's heart almost stopped. Then his years of combat experience kicked in. He snatched a pressure bandage from his jacket pocket. Keeping his voice calm, he said, "Fiona, you can shift back now."

The snow leopard took a step forward instead. When her left paw touched the ground, she drew it back and hissed. A stream of blood flowed from her paw and began to pool on the ground.

Cold fear crept down his spine. She was bleeding badly, his pressure bandage wouldn't stick on fur, and even with silencers, someone had to have heard suspicious noises and called the police. They had to get out of there, and fast.

"The fight's over, Fiona. You don't need to be a leopard any more. Shift."

She let out an eerie, high-pitched keen. If anyone had managed to miss the yelling and the pop of gunfire, that would catch their attention for sure. And why wasn't she shifting? Something was very wrong.

Any idea what's going on? Justin asked his own snow leopard.

His inner cat gave a confused growl, then said, *She sounded frightened.*

Justin had figured that part out already. But was she unable to shift because she was afraid, or was she afraid because she couldn't shift?

His own leopard was no help. But Justin's ten years as a PJ had given him a lot of experience with tending to wounded people in dangerous situations. He'd treated panicked civilians and uncooperative soldiers who didn't want to leave the field while their buddies were still fighting.

In a soothing tone, he said, "You're bleeding a lot. I need to stop it. I'm going to put my hand on your shoulder, all right? It's going to hurt, but I have to do it."

Moving slowly so she could see what he was doing, he reached out and pressed hard on her shoulder, stopping the bleeding. The leopard hissed in pain, but let him do it.

Lick her wound and make it better, hissed his own snow leopard.

Good idea, Justin replied. *Well. Sort of.*

With his free hand, he stroked the soft fur of her head. If she was unable to shift because she was in too much pain to focus, she should be able to once he got her to relax. If it was because there was some chemical on the bullet that was preventing her, they were both screwed. And he couldn't even begin to think of how to explain any of this to the police—especially since the only person who could speak Italian was currently a snow leopard.

But rushing her was only likely to make things worse. So he leaned his head against hers and spoke softly into her ear, keeping his voice and body as relaxed as if they had all the time in the world. "I'm here with you. I'll take care of you. Once you shift back, I'll carry you out and give you painkillers and tea. Or chicken soup, if you'd rather. If you want, I'll even do my best to bake you cupcakes on the hot plate. You can lie in bed and watch and laugh at me. Film it on your phone and put it on YouTube. I bet it'd get a million hits."

Justin nearly lost his balance as the snow leopard vanished and Fiona appeared in its place, naked and trembling, the blood very bright against her pale skin.

He quickly applied the pressure bandage to the gunshot wound in her shoulder, then checked her pulse and breathing. To his relief, both were within normal ranges. He ripped the shirt off the nearest terrorist and used it to wipe the blood off her and him. Then he started to pull his own shirt off, figuring she'd rather wear his clothes than a white supremacist's.

"I have a dress in my purse," she said. Her voice was shaky but clear.

"Okay, great." He opened it and unrolled the dress, then helped her into it. It was black and loose, with long sleeves and a zipper all the way down the back—perfect for hiding bandages and bloodstains, and easy to get on even with one arm out of commission. Which was undoubtedly why she'd picked it, in addition to being thin enough to roll up and cram into a purse.

"My shoes," Fiona said. "Put one of them on me, and the other in my purse. Anyone who sees me being carried with one shoe off will think

I twisted my ankle."

"Good plan."

Justin buckled on one shoe, stuffed the other in her purse along with the shredded remains of her dress, and wiped his fingerprints off McConnell's gun. With any luck the police would assume the terrorists had attacked each other. Then he gently lifted her and carried her out of the garden as fast as he could while still looking more-or-less casual.

His heart pounded as he emerged from the garden, but the narrow alley was empty. He retraced their path along the canals and across the bridges. Fiona lay silent in his arms. He could feel how much pain she was in from the tension in her body and her audible attempts to control her breathing. But he didn't have to imagine it from signs: he knew what getting shot felt like.

Justin felt a phantom ache in his own scar. The bullet she'd taken saving him had gone through her left shoulder. A few inches lower, and it would have struck her heart. And then no amount of first aid or shifter healing would have done any good. Her courage and wit, her beautiful eyes and soft lips, the heat of her body and the kindness of her heart: all of it would have been gone forever.

The thought of it hit him like a punch in the gut. For all that he'd tried to keep his distance, both literally and emotionally, he'd failed to do so in the most important way. He'd let his soul get intertwined with hers. Losing her would be like having his own heart cut out.

I see, purred his snow leopard, smug as could be. *You have a soul now. You have a heart.*

Justin remembered all the furious silent arguments he'd had with his inner cat, insisting that Apex had destroyed his heart and soul. *I'm nothing but an empty shell,* he'd said. *I'm just a machine that breathes.*

His snow leopard—the voice of his own hope—had forced him to keep going when he'd wanted to give up. But it had been Fiona who'd shown him that he was capable of more than just survival. She'd trusted him, and so he'd learned to trust again. She'd offered him beauty and sweetness, laughter and touch: everything that made life not merely worth living, but a wonderful and precious gift. Like Dorothy blown into Oz, he'd been transported from a bleak gray world to one of dazzling color. And Fiona was the one who'd taken his hand and led him there.

Most of all, she'd taught him to love again.

Love. The word had come so naturally to his mind. And looking down at the woman in his arms, he could no longer deny it. He loved her. He would always love her.

"If we were different people with different lives, we'd get together and it would be great," she'd said. *"But we're the people we are, with the lives we have. And it's not happening."*

If he couldn't be her lover, he'd be her partner, her protector, her knight in battered armor. She'd given him his heart back. If being together yet apart broke it anew every day of his life, it would still be worth the price.

CHAPTER SEVEN
Fiona

Fiona's shoulder burned like she'd been stabbed with a red-hot poker. Her skin prickled with cold sweat, and she felt sick and dizzy. So this was what it felt like to get shot. It was even worse than she'd imagined. She knew she should be coming up with some story or plan in case the police stopped them, but she couldn't concentrate on anything but how badly her shoulder hurt. And worse than that, on how the shock and pain had made her lose control of her ability to shift, and trapped her in the body of an animal.

For what must have only been a few minutes but had felt like an eternity, she'd thought she'd never be able to become a woman again. It had been her worst nightmare turned into a terrifying reality. She'd almost felt the slippery ice under her paws, heard the echo of a furious voice…

And then another voice had cut through her panic. With every reason to be as frantic as she was, Justin had remained calm and confident. She'd clung to the sound of his voice and the comforting touch of his hands as if she was lost in a blizzard, and he was the ranger come to rescue her.

He'd saved her. Not just by treating her wound, but by using nothing but his voice and hands to rescue her from a fate worse than death. Without him, she could have lost her humanity forever.

"Thank you," she whispered. "You saved my life."

"Thank *you*," he replied softly. "You saved mine. Took a bullet for me. You're not supposed to do that. That's supposed to be my job."

He had been walking smoothly and carefully, but his foot came down on a loose cobblestone, jolting him forward. The shock ripped through her entire body. She choked back a cry of pain.

"Sorry," Justin murmured. "I know how much it hurts. We're not far now. What can you feel under your hands?"

Surprised by the question, she had to concentrate even to figure that out. She had her arms draped around his neck. "Your shirt." She moved her hand a little. "Your skin." It was smooth and warm, good to touch. "Your hair."

"Try rubbing some of my hair between your fingers. Pay attention to how it feels."

She obeyed. It was silky, almost hot from the sun. The pain faded from her awareness as she tried to feel the individual strands, how they slipped through her fingers…

…and then they were in cool shade, going up a flight of stairs. They'd reached the apartment, she realized. They were safe. Home.

Justin laid her gently down on the bed, locked the door, got out the medical kit he'd packed in his duffel bag, and examined her. She lay still, watching him. His sharp features were taut with worry, but they relaxed by the time he was done.

"No broken bones," he said. "No shock. It's painful and you lost some blood, but it's not a serious injury. At least, not for a shifter. If you rest today and tomorrow, you should be up and about the day after."

"Perfect timing." The day after tomorrow was Carnival.

"No pressure. If you're not up to it by then, I can tackle Bianchi myself."

"No—I won't let you go alone—" She tried to grab his arm, but sharp pain lanced through her shoulder. She couldn't repress a moan.

"Easy. Nobody's going anywhere right now. Let me get you something for the pain." He filled a syringe and gave her a shot. "Take a deep breath. Again. One more. How do you feel now?"

Just like that, the pain was gone. So was the sick dizzy feeling, along with the inability to focus. Fiona could hardly believe it. "That was fast."

"Let me know when you need more. This should hold you for tonight, though. I'm going to change the bandage now. Close your eyes if you're squeamish."

"It's my body," Fiona pointed out, and kept her eyes open.

Despite the circumstances, she liked watching him work. His hands moved so deftly, and he was so quick and confident. It was only a few minutes before he was done, and he pulled the blankets over her.

"Do you want to sit up or lie down?" he asked.

"Sit up."

He put his arms around her and helped her sit up, stuffing pillows behind her back. "How's that? Comfortable?"

"Yes, thanks."

"I'll make you some tea. It'll help with the blood loss."

Now I know what he was like before Apex got him, Fiona thought as she watched him make the tea.

"Your patients must have loved you," she said.

"My patients had usually just gotten shot in Afghanistan, so they would've loved anyone who was trying to help them instead of trying to kill them."

She looked at him. "You can't tell me that's all there was to it. If you ran into some crying civilians, who'd be better at calming them down, you or Shane?"

"You'd be surprised how comforting Shane can be when he puts his mind to it. But yeah, it comes a bit more naturally to me."

"Would you want to be a medic again?" she asked.

He looked up from pouring tea into a mug, his dark eyes thoughtful. "I don't know. I hadn't thought about it. I hadn't... Nah, I shouldn't talk about this now. You're hurt, you need to rest."

"I am resting. What were you going to say?"

"I'll tell you while you drink your tea." He sat down beside her, blew on the tea, then held it out to her. "Careful. It might feel a bit heavy."

She took the mug, but as he'd warned her, it felt heavier than it should. Justin caught her hand and helped her support the mug before it could spill.

"Go on," she prompted him. His hands stayed where they were, keeping hers steady, as she drank her tea.

"I hadn't expected to survive taking down Apex," he said quietly. "And I didn't much care. I guess you might've figured that out."

Despite the heat of the tea, his words made her feel cold. "I wondered."

"But now…" He looked away, as if he couldn't bear to meet her eyes. "I found something worth living for."

Fiona also looked away. The rush of relief she felt was making her eyes burn, which was strange. Crying was a weakness. She could make her tears flow as part of a role she was playing, but she hadn't cried for real since she was nine years old. But though no tears came, when she spoke her voice came out as thick as if her throat was clogged with them.

"I'm so glad, Justin. I thought you'd changed your mind, since we came here. But if you hadn't, I was going to stop you. I had no intention of letting you just throw your life away."

"Seriously?" Now *he* sounded choked up. "Don't worry about that. I won't. I promise."

"Good."

He cleared his throat. When he spoke again, his voice was back to normal. "So, back to your question, I hadn't thought about what I was going to do in the future because I hadn't thought I had one. Now that I do, I still can't go back to the Air Force. There's no way I'm getting that close to the government again. So yeah, once all this is over, maybe I would like to be a paramedic. Though it might be a bit… slow… after being a PJ."

Fiona nearly bit her tongue on the suggestion that leaped to her mind. Was it too soon? Or perfect timing? Mentally crossing her fingers, she said, "You could join Protection, Inc. It's got all the excitement you could possibly want. And you'd get to do medical stuff sometimes."

Justin didn't react badly, but he didn't jump up and down for joy, either. He merely said, "Shane invited me too."

"I know."

"I told him I'd think about it."

"And?"

"I'm still thinking about it. Here…"

He tilted the mug so she could get the last drops of tea. In that gesture, like when he'd bandaged her shoulder or helped her sit up, she could feel his caring as strongly as if it was transmitted through the palms of his hands. He was like that with all his patients, she was sure. No wonder they'd loved him. Having all that concern and attention directed at her was comforting, but something about it brought back that burning in her eyes.

Because he loves you so much, purred her snow leopard. *It fills your heart until it overflows.*

Because he doesn't *love me,* Fiona corrected her. *Because none of this is personal. He'd be like this with everyone. And I want it to be just for me.*

I see, the big cat purred. *So it's like that, huh?*

Fiona realized that in her annoyance at her snow leopard's complete misreading of the situation, she'd said things she'd normally keep to herself. Things she'd normally keep *from* herself. She wished she hadn't. Her eyes burned more than ever.

To her great relief, Justin got up to wash and put away the cup. That gave her time to collect herself.

I'm the snow queen, she told herself. *I don't cry. Tears are hot liquid. Everything inside me is ice.*

She pictured that ice closing around her heart in a glassy shield. The burning subsided. When he returned, she was back to her regular cool self.

"Do you want to sleep in what you're wearing?" he asked. "Or shall I get you your nightgown?"

The last thing she wanted was to get into that hot, scratchy granny-gown she'd bought at the airport in the hope of discouraging lustful thoughts (both his and hers). But she never slept in her clothes. On the other hand, tonight was the one night that she could strip naked, if she liked, and neither she nor Justin would be tempted to make a move.

"Could you bring me the nightgown I wore in the Ritz?" she asked.

He brought her the short satin nightgown and laid it on the bed. In a matter-of-fact tone, he said, "I can help you get into it."

She tried to raise her left arm, winced, and said, "Thanks."

He put on a professional manner as he helped her out of the black dress and into the nightie, keeping his eyes fixed on her face the entire time. His face flushed a faint pink in the few seconds she was naked, but he neither said nor did anything that would have been out of place from a doctor to a patient. A minute later, he'd tucked the blankets back around her.

Her gaze went toward the bathroom as she recalled the sleeping arrangements of the night before. Following it, Justin said, "You're not sleeping in the bathtub tonight."

Fiona wasn't sure she was even capable of getting out of bed, but she had to put up at least a token resistance. "If you're on the floor—"

"If you want me to, I'll share the bed."

She blinked, startled by how easily he'd given in. "You will?"

"Do you want me to?"

"Yes."

"Then I will."

She must have still looked confused, because he gently brushed a lock of hair away from her face and said, "I left Shane when he was hurt and needed me, and I'll regret it for the rest of my life. I won't leave you now. Not even to go as far as the floor, if you want me closer."

"I want you closer."

"Then I'm here." He pulled off his shirt, giving her a tempting view of his shoulders and chest. Also of his treasure trail, which he hadn't dyed to match his hair. It drew a bright copper line down the groove between his abs before vanishing at his belt buckle. "Do you mind if I just sleep in my boxers? That's what I normally do, but…"

She snickered. "You can lay off the vomit-colored pajamas."

"I was thinking of them as fungus-colored, myself. But close enough."

He stripped down to his boxers, then got into bed with her and clicked off the light. Moonlight shone through the window, giving his hair a gloss like a raven's wing. With a hopeless longing, she wished she could stroke it. Not because it would make her feel better, though she was sure it would. Just because she wanted to.

Quietly, Justin said, "You've never been wounded before, have you?"

"No. I've gotten some cuts and bruises. Nothing serious. But you said this wasn't serious either."

"Medically, it's not. But it's a bullet wound and it's not that far from your heart. Three inches lower and you could have died."

"This is a cheery conversation to have right before I go to sleep," Fiona said, uncomfortable. She didn't know where he was going with it, and she wasn't sure she'd like where he ended up.

"I'm talking about it because it's the kind of thing shakes people up. If you wake up in the night and need anything—another shot of painkiller, some water—or if you want me to hold you—just say my name. I don't want you lying there suffering and embarrassed to say so. If you need a little help, that's nothing to be ashamed of."

Yes, it is, Fiona thought. Then she reconsidered. Justin had sounded like he was speaking from personal experience.

In all the time they'd been together, she'd never asked him about the scar on his chest. Nor had he pressed her for any details of her past. It was as if they'd both decided to treat their time together as if it had neither a past nor a future, but existed only in a beautiful and temporary bubble of present time.

But he was so close, nearly touching, that it felt as if she'd been given permission to get more intimate.

"You've been wounded," she said.

He swallowed. "Yes."

"Did it shake you up?"

"Yes."

It wasn't like him to answer in monosyllables. She knew she was pushing him and hoped it wasn't too far. But there was something she wanted to know.

"Did you need help?"

"I—" Justin fell silent. Just as she opened her mouth to tell him to forget it, he burst out with, "I can't talk about it, I'm sorry, I just—"

"No, *I'm* sorry," she interrupted. "Forget about it. I shouldn't have asked."

He took a deep breath. When he spoke again, he sounded calmer. "Don't worry about it. Now go to sleep. You need your rest."

"Good night, then."

"Good night." He brushed his fingers over her uninjured shoulder, light as a feather, then turned over to face away from her.

She closed her eyes. The pain was gone, and she felt nothing but an overwhelming sleepiness. Despite what Justin had said, she doubted she'd wake him up with demands for water or painkillers, let alone for him to hold her. She couldn't imagine asking for such a thing. Talk about needy!

Not expecting to wake till morning, she fell fast asleep.

She awoke in an unlit room flooded by silvery moonlight. Her shoulder didn't hurt, but it felt stiff and heavy. For a moment, she was confused, first unsure where she was, then puzzled by why she was in the bed rather than the bathtub. Then memory flooded back, along with the knowledge of what must have woken her.

Justin lay rigid on the bed beside her, his hands clenched into the pillow, every muscle tensed. Though the room was cool, sweat beaded on his forehead. His hair was wet with it. He muttered something Fiona couldn't catch, then made a choked sound as if someone was strangling him.

"Justin?"

He awoke with a gasp, black eyes opening wide and unseeing, and flung off the covers, shouting, "No! Stop!"

"Justin," Fiona said, keeping her voice calm and low. "You're safe. You were dreaming. You're here with me now."

He rolled over, still breathing hard, and raised himself on one elbow to look at her. She watched his expression shift from fear to confusion, and then to concern.

"Do you need another shot?" he asked. "I'll get my kit."

"My shoulder's fine. I woke up because you were having a nightmare."

"Oh." Justin lay back down, but he didn't relax. His whole body was shaking as if he had a fever.

Cautiously, unsure if her touch would be welcome, she laid a hand on his shoulder. As if he'd only been waiting for that permission, he threw an arm around her and clutched her like a drowning man snatching at a rope, pressing his cheek against hers. She could feel his chest heaving in wrenching breaths like sobs, but she couldn't tell if the wetness on her skin was sweat or tears.

Fiona held him tight, stroking his hair and back. She couldn't tell him it was all right—it clearly wasn't—so she said again, "You're safe. You're safe now. I've got you."

Gradually, his shaking subsided to occasional tremors, and his breathing evened out. He said something, but it was too muffled for her to understand.

"Sorry, I didn't..." she began.

Raising his head, he said, "They strapped me to a table. The metal was so cold. I fought and fought, but I couldn't break loose. A doctor bent over me. He..." Justin broke off, shuddering.

Tear out his throat, hissed her snow leopard. *He hurt our mate.*

"I'll kill him for you," Fiona said, quiet but certain. "Just tell me his name."

Justin managed a faint smile. "That's sweet of you. But you're too late. Shane already did."

"Then the next time I see Shane, I'll thank him with a box of chocolates."

He let out a huff of breath in surprised amusement. "Put a ribbon on it."

"Oh, absolutely. A big red one. In a bow."

Justin gave a deep sigh, and she felt a little of his tension ease. "You do that."

He lay quietly for a while, his breath warm on her throat. Then he said, "Fiona?"

"Yes?"

Seconds ticked by before he replied. "This is something I've never told anyone. I remember the first time I jumped out of a plane. Once my chute opened, it was fun. But that first moment that I looked down, the moment before I jumped, I was fucking terrified. And my first time in combat, same thing. I was fine once it started. But that moment before…"

"Justin, I'm sure everyone's like that. Do you really think you're the only person to be afraid for a few seconds before you risk your life?"

"Nobody says so."

"*You* didn't say so," Fiona replied. "Look, being afraid doesn't make you less brave. It makes you more brave. There's nothing special about doing something you're *not* afraid to do."

"Yeah, well, that's the problem. There's something I'm scared of, and I'd actually rather not do it."

"What is it?"

"I know we agreed to keep our hands off each other." His muscles began to tense again as he went on, "But I'm scared that if you stop touching me, and if I fall asleep like that, I'll… I'll…"

He didn't need to finish. She knew what he was thinking. He'd be right back there on the cold metal table.

Tightening her grip around him, she said, "I'm not letting go of you, Justin. I…"

She wanted to say, *I'll never let you go.*

But he didn't want that. He didn't want *her*. Not as a mate, anyway.

"You're my friend," she said instead, trying to keep her voice steady. She didn't want him to know that she was holding back tears. "Go to sleep. I'll hold on to you."

Justin let out a long, fluttering sigh. Then she felt him relax. When he spoke, his voice was calmer than it had been since he'd woken up. "Thanks. I'll get your box of chocolates later."

"With a red ribbon?"

He shook his head. "Green. To match your eyes."

Justin settled himself against her, and she felt him yawn. Then, with his head on her chest and his soft hair caressing her throat, he lay still. Within minutes, his deep breathing told her that he was fast asleep.

Fiona lay awake longer, holding him close. She knew it made no difference whether she slept or not—it wasn't as if she could scare nightmares away—but she felt like she needed to stay awake to guard his sleep.

His words came back to her as vividly as if he was whispering in her ear: *They strapped me to the table. I fought and fought.*

She shuddered. Justin stirred in his sleep, his fingers flexing against her back.

"I'm here," she murmured, stroking his hair. "I won't let you go."

He gave a soft sigh and turned his head into her touch. Now his lips were pressed against her throat. Fiona shivered, though not from cold. Then weariness overcame her, and she too slept.

She awoke to golden morning light.

Justin lay nestled into her side, with one arm thrown over her waist. He was fast asleep. A bar of sunlight fell across his face, turning his eyelashes to tiny fans of flame.

Fiona eased herself up, bracing herself on her right hand, to get a better look at him. She expected him to wake up the instant she moved, ready for danger, but he slept on.

When she'd watched over him at the Ritz, he'd looked pale and worn down, his bones sharp beneath the skin and his body tense, as if even sleep brought him no true rest. But the sun of Venice had given him a warm tan, and the meals he'd cooked had filled out his body. He was no longer painfully thin, but as lithely muscled as the leopard he could become.

Normally, even when he seemed happy, there was an underlying wariness to him, as if he was forever waiting for the other shoe to drop. It clung to him even in sleep. But now, for the first time since she'd known him, he looked at peace.

Fiona felt a tremendous rush of tenderness toward him. She wanted to protect him and heal his wounds, fight by his side and hold him all night.

I love him.

The realization was terrifying, but undeniable. She loved him like she'd never loved any man before. Like she'd never love any other man. And though he was right there with her, even touching her, she could never have him the way she wanted to have him. He was willing to be her friend, but nothing more.

Her eyes burned as she thought, *This is what happens when you lose control of your feelings. If I can be content with being Justin's buddy, then I'll be happy that I've gained a friend. If I keep wishing I could be his mate, then I'll be frustrated and lonely and feel like I've lost out on something I never had to begin with.*

Her snow leopard gave an annoyed hiss. *You* are *his mate.*

Tell him that, Fiona retorted.

The big cat gave a feline shrug. *Our mate has been badly wounded. He is in too much pain to see clearly. Once he feels better, he will come to his senses.*

Fiona doubted that very much. Sure, once he recovered more, he'd be ready for a relationship with *someone*. But no amount of emotional healing on his part could change who Fiona was, any more than everything she'd done since she'd joined Protection, Inc. could erase her past.

But there was no point dwelling on what couldn't be changed. She'd made her choices, and now she had to live with the consequences. That was all there was to it.

The burning in her eyes increased until a tear overflowed. It fell to Justin's cheek with a tiny splash.

Fiona jerked back, horrified, as he opened his eyes. The movement jarred her shoulder, and she winced.

Justin sat up, his eyes widening with alarm as he took in the tears that ran down her face. "You should've woken me up! Let me get my kit, I'll give you—"

"No, no," she said hurriedly. "My shoulder's fine. It aches a bit, that's all. I don't need anything for it."

Justin, who had already swung his legs over the edge of the bed, stopped still, frowning. "You're crying. If it's not your shoulder, what is it? Did *you* have a nightmare?"

She could give him that excuse, and save herself the hideous embarrassment of confessing her unrequited love. It would be so easy to convince him. He'd already half-convinced himself. "Yes," she could say. "I had a terrible nightmare. I dreamed I was bleeding to death. I feel all shaken up, just like you said." He'd hold her and comfort her and tell her it was normal after being wounded in combat. And that would be it.

It was incredibly tempting. She knew he'd believe her. And if she told the truth, it would make their relationship much more awkward, and make her seem pathetic. And needy.

No, hissed her snow leopard. *Do not lie to your mate!*

Fiona gritted her teeth. The idea of telling Justin the truth was so much scarier than facing armed terrorists had been.

"Fiona?" Justin laid his hand over hers. "If you don't want to talk about it…"

And there he went, giving her an easy out. She wouldn't even need to lie. She could honestly say, "I don't want to talk about it." He'd make the wrong assumption, of course, but wasn't that really on him?

No! Fiona told herself. *It's too late for me, but I'm not going to lie to him now. Justin deserves better.*

"I didn't have a nightmare." To her horror, she once again dissolved into tears as she went on, "I was crying because—because I'm in love with you—and you're not in love with me."

For a moment, Justin simply stared at her in utter astonishment. Then a brilliant smile broke over his face, bright as the rising sun. "But I am."

He leaned in and kissed away her tears. His lips were warm against her skin, his touch gentle. He stroked her back as if she was a cat, and like a cat, she arched her back into his hand. And then his lips met hers, and his passion proved his feelings better than words ever could. A part of her that had been frozen for years melted like frost under a summer sun.

He does *love me,* she thought, almost too dazed to respond. *Maybe I don't deserve it. Maybe I'll lose it once I he knows my secret. But right here, right now, Justin loves me.*

"Should I stop?" Justin asked suddenly.

"What? Why?"

"Your shoulder."

She had completely forgotten about it. Now that he'd brought it to her attention, she noticed that it did ache. But she had absolutely no wish to stop.

"Just don't throw me up against the wall," she said.

"I'll save that for later," Justin said with a grin. "And speaking of safety…"

"You don't need to run out for condoms. I have an IUD."

"Just as well," he remarked. "No idea how to ask for them in Italian. I'd probably come back with an eggplant. Or—"

She interrupted him with a kiss. Their tongues met with equal passion, sending delicious tingles of pleasure up and down her spine. His strong arms closed around her back, making her feel safe and protected. His hands slipped under the short hem of her nightgown, stealing their way up her thighs until she gasped into his mouth. His attention was on *her*, for her, and burning with desire.

Justin carefully lifted off her nightgown, slowly working it over her injured shoulder. He set it aside, then sat back and looked at her naked body. The heat in his eyes was like black fire. She felt herself get wetter just from watching him watch her, as if she was the most desirable woman in the world. As if he'd die of longing if he couldn't have her, right now.

"You're so gorgeous." His voice was husky. "I've got the most beautiful thing in the most beautiful city in the world, right here in this room."

"What about the Grand Canal?"

Justin shook his head, smiling. "Not even close. It isn't warm. It doesn't breathe."

Fiona reached up and tugged at his boxers. They slipped off, leaving him naked. Then she too got to feast her eyes. He was perfectly proportioned, tall and leanly muscled, with long legs and broad shoulders. She found herself fascinated by different parts of his body in turn, now that she finally had permission to look her fill. His fingers were long and graceful, his collarbones and the hollows of his pelvis beautifully sculptured, his nipples pink nubs that she couldn't wait to tease with her fingers and mouth.

His rock-hard erection showed her just how much he wanted her, not just with his heart and mind but with his body. A glistening drop of liquid beaded at the tip. She sat up and licked at it, enjoying its slippery sweetness. Justin groaned at the touch of her tongue, his body stiffening and his fists clenching at his sides.

Then he moved back. "Better save that for later. I haven't made love in three years. At least. And I only get one shot."

"Oh, I'm sure you can go more than once." Teasingly, she added, "Maybe you're no spring chicken anymore, but you're not *that* old."

He looked at her with such tenderness that it made her heart ache. "But there's only one first time with you."

And so when he started to crouch down on the bed, she pulled him back up. "You're right. For me too. So let's be face-to-face. I'm ready now."

He lowered her down until she was reclining with her back propped up by the pillows. "I think this'll be the least jarring position for you. But stop me if it hurts."

She couldn't imagine that she'd notice if it did, but she nodded. Her anticipation was so intense that she was trembling with it, her breath shuddering in her throat, her heart pounding. Justin too was breathing hard, his hands shaking. She had the sense that he was barely holding himself in check.

He knelt over her thighs. Even that contact was enough to make her gasp. His steel-hard erection touched her mound, sending a shock of pleasure through her body. She instinctively thrust up at him, making him whisper, "Easy. Let me do the work."

He bent to kiss her. Eagerly, she kissed him back. Their lips locked together as she stroked his fine hair, his rough stubble, the smooth muscles of his back. He slowly pushed through her slick folds until they were fully joined, then began to gently rock inside her rather than thrust. She'd never felt anything like it. Every movement sent waves of pleasure through her entire body, building and building until she could hardly bear it.

She forced herself to open her eyes, which had fallen closed. She wanted to see Justin's face. His eyes were open, gazing at her with so much love that she felt like her heart would break. Or maybe it had already been broken, and what she felt now was the ache of healing.

The waves crested and broke over her in a crescendo of ecstasy. For a brief but eternal moment, she didn't know where she started and Justin left off. They were one being, joined together in a timeless joy.

As she lay contented in his arms, toying with his silky hair, Justin suddenly chuckled, his chest vibrating against hers.

"What's so funny?" she asked.

"You," he said. "You slept in a bathtub for an entire week, when we could've been doing this instead."

"People who sleep on the floor shouldn't throw stones," she retorted. Then, curious, she asked, "Why did you?"

"I'm guessing the same reason you were in the tub. I thought you weren't in love with me. Well, and also I figured I'd be dead in six months, max. And even if I wasn't, I thought you deserved someone who wasn't so damaged. I didn't want to tie you down."

"You don't." Her fingers interlaced with his, then closed tight. "You lift me up."

But she couldn't help thinking of her other reason for denying their bond. What would happen if Justin learned the truth about her past— the truth about *her?*

Nothing, purred her snow leopard. *Except bring you closer together.*

Fiona doubted that very much. The thought of telling him felt like running naked into a snowstorm. But as she'd told him, there was nothing brave about doing something that *didn't* scare you.

"I've been keeping something from you," she admitted. "But I don't want there to be any more secrets between us."

Justin clasped her hand, running his thumb in little circles over the back of it. "You don't have to tell me anything until you're ready."

She swallowed. Her heart was beating quick as a rabbit's. "I'm as ready as I'll ever be. Let me just get it over with. And then you can think… whatever you'll think."

He didn't so much as blink. His dark eyes, that could look so cold and hard, now seemed soft as velvet. "It's not exactly shocking that some bad things happened to you. You never talk about your past. It's like you sprang full-grown from the Protection, Inc. office. So I already know something happened. I just don't know what. But whatever it is, it won't make me think less of you. And—"

"You can't know that!" Fiona burst out.

As if she hadn't spoken, he went steadily on, "And it won't make me love you any less. Because nothing could."

CHAPTER EIGHT
Fiona's Story

I loved my father.

My mother died having me, so Dad raised me. He was a mechanic. When I was a little kid, I used to hang around his shop. At first I'd just pass him his tools. It was our game. He'd hold out his hand and say, "Torque wrench," and I'd hand it to him, like he was a surgeon and I was a nurse. The people who brought in their cars thought it was hilarious. By the time I was seven, he was teaching me how to do basic repairs. For my ninth birthday, he bought me my own tool kit, with tools small enough to fit my hands. I wish I still had it…

That was the year he died. A drunk driver hit his car while I was in school. Dad was killed instantly. The driver was barely scratched. He was a rich guy and could afford a good lawyer, and he used it to get probation. Never served a day in jail.

Mom and Dad didn't have any family. We were it. So I was placed with a foster family. I said I didn't want them, but they told me it wasn't about what I wanted, it was about what I needed. I said I didn't need anyone. They didn't listen, of course. So every time they took their eyes off me, I smashed everything in sight. They finally couldn't take it any more, and sent me back to the social workers.

Right away, another couple wanted me. I guess I was a cute kid. But the man made the mistake of telling me I could call him Daddy. Two sets of replaced china later, I was sent to a group home. And I stayed there.

It wasn't a terrible life. I definitely liked it better than foster parents trying to get me to love them. The food was institutional and my clothes were cheap and I didn't get any luxuries, but luckily it was near a public school with a good science and technology program. It had an electronics lab where I could tinker to my heart's content. It also had a computer lab, and a teacher who used to work for Google. I ended up getting a scholarship to study computer science.

College was fine. I did well. My professors liked me. I didn't make any friends, but I hadn't in school or the group home, either. It didn't bother me. I told myself I didn't need anyone. I wanted to learn everything I could. Not just about computers, but finance, too. I had a goal in mind, and it wasn't to be the top of my class.

When I was nine, I'd made a promise to myself. It was to get revenge on the man who killed my father.

So I kept tabs on him. For thirteen years. It was easy; I was still in the same city, and he was all over the internet. His name was Jared Kelly, and he owned a pharmaceuticals company that was infamous for jacking up the price of medications that people needed to live. He'd killed my father and gotten away with it, and people were dying when they could've lived if he hadn't decided to charge them seven hundred dollars per pill.

By the time I graduated from college, I'd come up with a plan and learned enough that I thought I could do it. I bought myself a few outfits that looked pricier than they really were, plus a cell phone that I made a couple little adjustments to. And I went to a club where Kelly liked to get drunk and hit on pretty blonde women who were young enough to be his daughter.

It was so easy. That was what amazed me. I'd spent years planning contingincies for everything that could possibly go wrong, but nothing did.

I let Kelly get a look down my shirt, and next thing I knew, he was driving me to his home. I told him how famous and brilliant and rich and handsome he was, and he ate it up. When we got to his house, I told him how great *that* was, and he showed me the entire place, bragging all the way. He had a laptop lying right there on the living room table.

He asked if he could get me a drink, and I said I just loved fancy cocktails and I bet he knew how to make some really special ones. He said he could make me the best cocktail I'd ever had, but it would take a couple minutes. I said to go right ahead, and I'd wait in the living room so I could be surprised by it. I'd read about his super-special cocktail in an interview with him in some online magazine for wealthy creeps, and I knew it took about fifteen minutes to make.

While he was in the kitchen making it, I hacked into his laptop. Once I was done, I made my own phone ring. I pretended my sister had an accident and was in the hospital. Kelly didn't want to drive me there, but once I said I'd told my mom whose house I was at, he called me a cab. It dropped me off at the hospital, I walked in, I waited a while, I called another cab, and I went back to my crummy motel room, linked my laptop with Kelly's, and started looking through his finances.

I'd figured there was no way a man like him wasn't doing all sorts of dishonest things. And I was right. I'd figured he was cheating on his taxes, and he was, but it turned out he was also committing stock market fraud. And probably other crimes that were so complicated I couldn't even tell what they were. So I downloaded all the data and sent it anonymously to the IRS and the FBI.

But there was one thing I did before I did that. And it wasn't part of my plan. Originally, I'd just wanted Kelly to go to jail. But when I was in his house, looking at all the nice stuff he had, I'd thought, *Why should a man like Kelly live like this, when a man like my father had to work so hard to get so little?*

And when I was looking at his bank account, which had more zeroes than I'd seen in my entire life, I thought, *I can't give Dad any of this. He's gone. But if I gave some of it to myself, maybe that'd be the next best thing.*

So I transferred some of his money to my own account, erased the record of it, and *then* turned him in.

I was right: he'd been committing financial crimes I hadn't even noticed. But the FBI figured out what they were. And the IRS thought he'd hidden some of his money so well that even they couldn't find it. I'd taken it, of course, but since he actually was hiding money to evade taxes, they didn't believe him.

You can kill a little girl's father and walk away free if you have enough money. And it's not illegal to raise prices on medicine until sick people can't afford to live. But the one thing you can't get away with is cheating on your taxes. That's why Al Capone went to jail. And so did Jared Kelly.

I'd been planning my revenge ever since I was nine. It had kept me going all those years. Now it was done. I thought I'd feel satisfied, but I didn't. I felt lost. I didn't know what to do with myself. I'd only learned about finances and computers so I could ruin Kelly's life, not so I could have a career playing the stock market or doing other people's taxes.

But when I'd been flirting with Kelly, and getting him to make that stupid complicated drink and think it was his own idea, and hacking his laptop, and taking the fake call from my non-existent sister… I'd enjoyed that. It'd been dangerous and tense and I'd had to use all my skills. It made me feel alive. Like my whole life between the day Dad died and the night I'd strolled into that bar had just been marking time.

When I'd been researching Kelly, I'd come across a whole lot of other scummy rich men just like him. The world seemed full of them. Who would it hurt, really, if I siphoned off some of the money they'd cheated off other people? Why not get a little of my own back at their expense?

So I used his money to buy some more fancy outfits, and I started looking for wealthy creeps. It was easy. I just flirted and smiled and flattered them until they left me alone with their phone or laptop, and then I drained their bank accounts and disappeared.

And that's how it started. At first I only stole from men who were scum of the earth. Then I branched out to men who were only moderately scummy. Then men who were just very rich. There was never a moment when I decided to stop being a thief who only stole from people who deserved it and became a thief who only stole from people who could afford it. But it happened. And I just kept going.

It didn't take long before I had plenty of money. I could have invested it, lived off it, and never stolen again. But I'd gotten to like the lifestyle. It was exciting. And somewhere in the back of my mind, I was afraid of what would happen if I gave it up. When you stay on a merry-go-round long enough, you fall over when you jump off. What if I quit stealing, and never felt alive again?

Maybe if I hadn't been stopped, I'd have woken up some morning and thought, "What am I doing with my life? Is this the person I really want to be?" But that's not what happened.

I targeted a tech billionaire, Carter Howe. He was just a rich playboy, not a criminal or a terrible person as far as I knew. So I wasn't expecting to run into any trouble.

I should explain that none of the men I stole from ever got anything more from me than a kiss, and most of them didn't even get that. Once they started pressuring me for sex, if I hadn't managed to hack into their accounts by then, I'd make an excuse to leave, then disappear and move on. So if I couldn't get to them by one or two dates, that was usually it.

But Carter was different. When I told him I wanted to wait, he said that was fine instead of getting pushy. He didn't leave his phone or laptop lying around, his office door was always locked, and he never left me alone long enough for me to pick the lock. So instead of seeing him once or twice, we dated, sort of, for a couple months. In retrospect, I guess we saw each other as a challenge. He wanted to get into my pants, and I wanted to get into his laptop.

I was overconfident and careless. I'd forgotten why he was a billionaire. He hadn't inherited his money, like most of the men I scammed. He'd earned it, and he'd earned it in computers. He had the same sorts of skills that I did. I'm sure that's how he caught me. He must have checked out my fake identity, found something that didn't add up, and gotten suspicious.

I showed up for a date at his house. We were supposed to go to the opera, and I was wearing high heels and a strapless, floor-length, red satin gown. He told me how beautiful I looked, and then he apologized and said he had to make a business call and it'd take about fifteen minutes. I smiled and said I'd brought a book.

He went into his bedroom and closed the door, and I took out the other thing I'd brought, which was a set of lockpicks, and opened his office. There was his computer. I broke into it pretty fast—too fast, which should have tipped me off—set up remote access so I could get into it from my laptop, turned it off, locked the door behind me, and sat down on his sofa to read my book.

I remember how smart I felt. Right up to the point where he walked in holding a monitor. He turned it around, and there was a full-color, high-definition video of me breaking into his office, complete with close-ups of his computer screen showing exactly what I'd done there. I'd checked the office for hidden cameras, of course, but I obviously hadn't checked well enough. Like I said, he was a tech billionaire and he knew his stuff.

I couldn't deny what I'd done, so I bluffed. I said, "I'm an FBI agent and you're under investigation for securities fraud."

"Bullshit!" he said.

I said, "I'll prove it. I'll call my home office and put them on the line."

I reached for my purse. I was going to go for my pepper spray. All those years ripping people off, and that was the first time I'd have to used it.

But I never got the chance. Carter moved faster than I'd ever seen anyone move before. He grabbed my purse before I could get to it and threw it across the room. He was so angry, it scared me.

I said, "Harming a federal agent is a capital offense. And keeping me here against my will is kidnapping. Just let me go, and that'll be the end of this."

I started toward the front door. He stepped in front of it. And he said, "Stop lying to me. I know what you are. You're a predator. I should show you what that really means."

I thought he was going to kill me. I panicked and bolted for the kitchen. I was going to grab a knife to try to fend him off, then run out the back door. But I'd never tried to run in heels and a long dress before. I tripped and went flying. My head slammed into his marble countertop, and everything went black.

I woke up freezing cold. My head ached. When I opened my eyes, I couldn't see anything but white. Just flecks of white, whirling around me in an icy wind, and more white beneath me.

It was snow. I was in a snowfield, in the middle of a blizzard. Even when I remembered what had happened, I had no idea where I was or how I'd gotten there. Carter lived in Las Vegas. It didn't snow like that there.

I yelled for help, but I could tell that even if someone was there, they couldn't hear me over the wind. So I got up and started walking. I was still in my high heels and satin gown. As far as protecting me from the cold went, I might as well have been naked. My shoes kept slipping in the snow, but I was afraid I'd get frostbite if I took them off. I was wearing a lot of pricey jewelry—a diamond choker, emerald earrings, and an emerald bracelet—but it was so cold that the metal burned my skin. I finally took them off and dropped them in the snow.

When I took off the bracelet, I noticed that my left hand was bleeding a little. I had a few puncture wounds, not very deep. I couldn't think what they were from. I finally decided I'd stabbed my hand on a fork or something when I'd fallen. After a few minutes, the blood froze.

I thought, *Maybe I died when I hit my head. Maybe this is Hell.*

I wasn't even sure I believed in Hell, but once that had occurred to me, I couldn't stop thinking it. I was a thief. I was selfish and greedy. I took and took and never gave anything to anyone. Maybe I'd been sent to this place because I belonged there—because my heart was cold as ice.

I don't know how long I'd been walking before I heard a voice. A low hissing voice inside my head. It said, *Let me take over.*

I thought I was so hypothermic that I was hallucinating. At least, I hoped it was a hallucination and not a demon. I ignored it and kept stumbling on through the blizzard in my high heels and opera gown. Every now and then I'd slip on ice or trip over a rock buried in the snow, and fall. Every time I did, I'd get snow down my dress and in my hair, and I'd get even colder and wetter. The voice kept on hissing, demanding that I let it take over. It scared me. I felt like I was losing my mind.

Finally I tripped, fell, and couldn't get up. I was too weak, and my arms and legs were too numb. I lay there in the snow, and I thought, *This is it. I'm going to die here. If I'm not dead already.*

The voice hissed, *Let me take over, or you'll* definitely *die! I can survive the cold. You can't.*

By then I was so desperate that even a hallucination seemed better than nothing. I said, "Do it."

Then the voice became more than just a voice. I felt this… presence… inside my head. It was fierce and feral and angry, and it would do *anything* to survive. And it was me. I could feel that.

It hissed, *Let go of being human. Be me.*

I focused on what I'd felt from that presence: rage and pride, ruthlessness and cunning, and above all, the will to survive. I pushed away the part of me that was Fiona, and I tried to fall into that other part of me.

My body seemed to stretch out. And then I was something else. I wasn't cold any more. I was crouched on all fours in the remains of my dress, with my tail lashing. I could see through the blizzard that I was on a mountain peak. And I could smell that there was prey nearby.

I let that other me guide me. I stalked my prey through the snow, found it shivering in a shallow cave, and then I pounced. It was a small deer. It felt so good to pull it down and eat it up. Then I curled up in the cave and slept.

When I woke up, the blizzard had stopped. But I was still a snow leopard. And I stayed that way for a long, long time.

For months, I hunted and stalked on that mountain. I kept trying to shift back, but I never could. I was trapped inside the leopard. There was just enough of me left to realize that whether this was Hell or real, it was my punishment. Carter had been right: I was a predator. And now I'd become one for real.

With every day that went by, the leopard got stronger and I got weaker. I could feel myself wearing away, and I knew that eventually nothing would be left of me. I'd be a snow leopard who didn't even remember that she used to be a woman.

Every now and then, I'd see a hiker or two. When I did, I tried to go to them and ask for help. Only I couldn't speak, and all they saw was a snow leopard hissing at them. They ran for their lives. It felt like they were seeing what I really was: a monster. I finally stopped trying.

Then one day I smelled something strange on the wind. It was an animal, but not one I could identify. I climbed a tree to lie in wait and see what it was. Eventually it came into view. It was a huge, shaggy grizzly bear. And it was carrying a backpack in its mouth.

That was so strange that I pushed back my snow leopard's instincts to climb higher, and climbed a little lower down. The bear sniffed the air, then looked up at me with these huge hazel eyes. It dropped the backpack. There was a shimmer in the air, and the bear was gone. A big naked man stood in the snow where he'd been.

He opened the backpack, took out some clothes, and got dressed like the whole thing was completely normal. I was fascinated, and I climbed a little lower.

I thought, *He's like me. He's a person* and *an animal.*

When I thought that, I realized that it had been a long time before I'd been human enough to think in words. That scared me.

The man looked up at me and called, "My name's Hal Brennan. I'm a bear shifter, like you saw. I'm guessing you're a shifter too, and you're stuck the way you are. Is that right?"

I didn't know how to answer him, but he said, "If you're stuck, come down exactly one branch more."

I jumped down another branch and sat there.

He said, "I thought so. Some stories about a snow leopard approaching people here got back to the shifter community. There's no leopards in Wyoming. Sooner or later, someone's going to either decide you're getting too close to people and need to be captured or shot, or you're a rare specimen of an albino mountain lion and ought to be in a zoo. I'd like to get you out of here before that happens."

I tried to say, "Yes, please get me out." But all that came out was a long hiss.

Hal said, "I think I can help you shift back. But you're going to have to come down. I won't hurt you, I promise."

My snow leopard didn't want to do it. *She* didn't trust him. To be honest, I didn't really either. But at that point, I didn't care. If he could help me become a woman again, great. And if he killed me, that would be better than being trapped like this forever.

I jumped out of the tree and walked up to him.

He said, "Great. I'll talk you through it. I promise, this is much easier when you have help. Now lie down. I'm going to sit next to you."

I lay down and let him sit by my side. Hal told me later that he'd never tried to talk down a stuck shifter before, and he'd had no idea if he could do it or not. But I never guessed. He sounded completely confident, and that gave me hope.

He put his hand on my head and scratched me behind the ears. I twitched a little. It had been so long since I'd been touched. But it felt good. Calming.

"I'm going to ask you a few questions," he said. "Just nod or shake your head. Were you born a shifter?"

I shook my head.

"I thought so," Hal said. "So I'm guessing someone bit you. Is that right?"

At first I wasn't sure. Then I remembered those puncture wounds in my hand. I nodded.

This may sound weird, but it was the first time that I realized that Carter must have done this to me. When I was bitten, I hadn't even known shifters existed. And then I nearly froze to death, and then my snow leopard took me over. I had no context for anything, and I wasn't in any condition to think clearly. But once Hal suggested that someone had bitten me, I remembered what Carter had said about making me a predator for real.

He did this to me, I thought, and snarled.

Hal didn't so much as flinch. He just said, "I'm guessing that wasn't something you wanted."

I shook my head and snarled again.

Rip his throat out, came that hissing voice. *He hurt us.*

Hal went on, "Had you even heard of shifters before someone made you one?"

I shook my head.

"Okay," he said. "Let me tell you about them. Us."

Hal sat there in the snow for something like an hour, stroking my fur and talking about shifters. He explained that the voice inside me was my snow leopard, and that it was the part of me that was raw emotion and animal instinct and the will to survive.

"It's taken control of you because you needed it to," Hal explained. "You would have died without it. But it's safe to be a woman now. Once you shift back, I'll give you some clothes, we'll hike down to my car, and I'll get you a good meal of human food, whatever you like. And then I'll take you to stay with some shifters who can teach you the ropes. How's that sound?"

It sounded great. I felt this weird rumbling in my chest, and my body started vibrating. A moment later, I realized that I was purring.

Very casually, Hal said, "So here's how you shift back. Think of something that only a human can do. Something you've done a lot, so you can picture how it looks and feels and smells and sounds. I used to be in the Navy, so I might picture cleaning my gun. The way the metal feels in my hands. The weight of it. The smell of the oil. The sound of the parts clicking together. You got anything like that?"

I didn't even have to think about it. When Hal had mentioned metal and oil, something popped right into my mind. It was fixing a car engine, like I used to do with Dad. I could smell the engine oil, and feel the weight of the wrench in my hand…

And just like that, I was a woman again, stretched out in the snow with Hal's big hand resting between my shoulderblades.

He helped me to my feet, and took off his long coat and put it over me. Then he picked me up, since he hadn't brought any shoes that fit me, and carried me to his car. We had a long drive ahead of us—we were in Wyoming, and he lived in California. I had no money, of course, so he paid for everything, even my clothes.

I wasn't very good company. I was ashamed to tell him exactly what had happened, so all I said was that a man had turned me against my will and I didn't want to say who it was. Mostly I stared out the window and vowed to never go back to being that predator. I didn't like who I was. But I didn't know who else to be.

When we hit the California border, Hal offered me a choice. He said he could drop me off with his family of bear shifters. He said they were back-to-nature, salt-of-the-earth types who lived in a little rural town and didn't like the modern world. He said they'd be kind to me, but they were nosy and wouldn't take "I don't want to talk about it" for an answer. Or he could take me to the city where he lived and introduce me to a friend of his, a tiger shifter who used to have trouble controlling her power too. He said she was friendly but would respect my privacy.

Needless to say, I picked the friend. That turned out to be Destiny Ford, one of the bodyguards at Protection, Inc. Back then there were just three of them, Hal and Rafa and Destiny. She let me crash at her apartment and coached me on shifting until I could do it easily. And since I was unemployed and had nothing to do, she took me to the office and showed me around.

When she did, I saw that their security system was lousy and their computer system was worse. So I fixed all that for them, and taught them some computer skills while I was at it. In return, they taught me to shoot and fight. Turned out, I had a knack for it. Eventually Hal offered me a job.

I took it thinking I needed something to do, so I wouldn't go back to stealing just because I was bored. I didn't expect to get attached to my teammates. But I did. They're the only friends I have, and they still don't know what I am.

    I know I should have told you earlier. I just couldn't face it. You rescued people and saved their lives. I lied to them and stole their money.

    At least I'm not lying anymore.

CHAPTER NINE
Justin

Fiona looked him in the eyes, her chin raised and her jaw set, as if she was facing a firing squad and intended to die bravely.

She thinks I'm going to judge her, Justin realized. Then, with a pang like he'd been stabbed in the heart, he thought, *No, it's worse than that. She thinks I despise her.*

"I love you," he said.

Her clear green eyes widened and her lips trembled, as if she wanted to believe him but was afraid to. As if the only thing more painful than knowing the worst was to think it might not be true, and then have your hope snatched away from you. Justin knew all about that.

He pulled her into his arms, hoping his touch would convince her more than his words. She was stiff as a mannequin, not warm and melting into him like she had before. But he held her close and kissed her cheeks and throat and lips until she softened against him.

"I love you," he repeated. "Did you think this would change how I feel? All it does is make me love you even more. You loved your father and you got justice for him. You had the endurance and tenacity to survive absolute hell. Your entire life got smashed to bits, but you didn't give up—you picked yourself up and built a totally new life. In fact, you did it twice, and the first time, you were *nine*. Fiona, you're amazing."

She looked at him like he'd lost his mind. "I was a thief. A criminal."

"So what? That Kelly guy—I heard of him. Your father wasn't the only person he killed. People died because he was greedy. You did the world a favor when you put him away."

"Kelly, sure," she said. "I've never regretted what I did to him. But the others…"

"What, like that guy who bit you and dumped you on a mountaintop—in a blizzard?!" A wave of hot fury made his fists clench. "That son of a bitch! Is he still in Vegas? As soon as we're done with Bianchi, he's next. I'll make him pay for what he did to you."

Her hair brushed against his chin as she shook her head. "Too late. He's dead. He had a little private plane he liked to fly—that must've been how he got me to Wyoming—and it went down somewhere in the Pacific."

Disappointed, Justin muttered, "I hope he had time to know what was happening. I hope he was just as scared in those last few minutes as you were when you woke up on that mountain."

Fiona spread her hands in a "who knows" gesture. "I do too, to be honest. But we'll never know. The black box is at the bottom of the ocean. Anyway, he's gone."

"Good riddance," Justin said. "You shouldn't feel guilty about trying to rip him off. He deserved a lot worse. Sure, stealing is wrong. But it's not like you ruined anyone's life. They had plenty of money to spare. They probably lost more than you took from them in an average day at the stock market."

"It's not about whether the guys I stole from deserved it or not, or could afford it or not. It's that I didn't care about anything but my next score and my next thrill. Once I was forced to take a break and think about who I was, I really didn't like myself." She lowered her head, letting her hair fall forward to hide her face. Softly, she said, "My father was an honest man. I can't imagine he'd have been proud of the woman I became."

"I bet he'd have been proud of the woman you are now."

She looked up, startled.

"You protect people," Justin said. "You put away criminals. Your whole career is about making the world a better place. You're brilliant and beautiful and kind. And you build little robot dogs. What Dad wouldn't want that in a daughter?"

"He'd definitely have liked the robots," she said, and smiled a little. "I hadn't thought of that before. Thanks for saying so."

"You could've gone right back to being a thief, if you'd wanted. You didn't. Yeah, there's things in your past that you regret. Things you're ashamed of. But you can't change the past. What matters is what you're doing now."

Fiona looked him steadily in the eyes. "That's right, Justin. Now *is* what matters. For you, too."

His first impulse was to deny it, to argue, to say that it was different for him. But was it? Sure, no one had died because of her. But she'd gone through hell. And she'd walked out the other side. He'd gone through hell too, though of a different sort.

And you walked out, purred his snow leopard. *Here you are, on the other side.*

"Maybe you're right." His voice came out in a whisper.

"You know I am." She yawned. "Sorry. I'm really tired, all of a sudden."

"You should go back to sleep. You need rest to heal."

"All right." She let him help her lie down, then pulled him down beside her. "Same to you. Keep me company. I won't let you go."

Holding each other tight, they fell into a deep and healing sleep.

Fiona spent the rest of that day and the next resting. When she woke, he made sure she ate and drank, and then they lay together kissing and talking; when she slept, he made sure she lay safe and warm in his arms. And as long as she held him, he slept peacefully and unafraid. Maybe all he'd ever needed was to know that if he did have one, he wouldn't wake up alone.

For those two days and nights, Justin was happier than he'd been in his entire life. Fiona had trusted him enough to tell him the darkest secret of her life. Now that she had, he could see that a weight had been lifted from her. The shadow behind her eyes, which he'd perceived without knowing what it was, had vanished. If he'd never done anything else to help anyone in his life, he'd have been content just with that.

And she loved him. Whenever he looked down at her as she slept, her platinum hair fanning out over the pillow and her rose-pink lips slightly parted, he'd think, *She loves me.* Every time, the thought filled him with astonished joy.

Fiona had seen how damaged he was, even if she didn't know all the details, and she *still* loved him. He'd never thought he'd ever consider himself lucky again… but he felt lucky.

I told you so, purred his snow leopard.

Yeah, yeah, you're smarter than me, Justin replied. *Don't let it go to your head.*

They got up at dawn on the morning of Carnival, to get their costumes before the streets filled up with costumed revelers and make sure that they caught Bianchi on his way out. The morning air was very cold, and Fiona pulled her coat tight around her body.

At the shop, Mr. Toscani handed them a bag containing their wrapped packages, along with a flood of Italian. Justin and Fiona smiled and nodded.

"Any idea what he was saying?" Justin asked once they were outside.

"Not much," Fiona admitted. "Well, I did get that the black packages are for you and the white ones are for me."

He made a face at her. "He handed the black ones to me and the white ones to you. No points for that. Did you get any idea of what they actually are?"

"Absolutely none," she admitted.

"I remember you telling him we were like Cirque du Soleil. I saw them once. I hope he didn't take that literally, or you'll be a clown and I'll be a polka-dotted earthworm."

"Guess we'll find out," she said cheerfully.

"If I can't move or see in this thing, I'm going as a snow leopard," he warned her. "You can tell everyone I'm on all fours and wearing a fur rug."

Her clear laugh echoed in the empty streets.

When they returned to the apartment, she suggested, "Let's surprise each other and change separately."

"Sure. Dazzle me with your beauty. Even more than you normally do, I mean."

Scooping up his packages, he went into the bathroom and closed the door. As he turned to put down the packages, his reflection in the mirror caught his eye. Instinctively, he started to turn away. Then he made himself look.

Ever since Apex had taken him, he'd hated to see his own reflection. Living underground had paled his skin, and his handlers had dyed his hair. His skin and hair could change, of course. But his eyes wouldn't. Before he'd been forced to undergo the Ultimate Predator process, they'd been a deep, intense green. Afterward, he'd watched them slowly darken. At first he'd thought he was imagining it. But within three months, they were black as engine oil. For weeks he'd stared and stared, trying to see the man he was within those fragments of black ice. He never could. Finally, he'd stopped trying.

Apex had kept him in good physical condition, more or less. They fed him nutritous meals, assigned him an exercise program, and made sure none of their "experiments" caused any permanent physical damage. They'd carefully monitored when and how long he was invincible, and always gave him plenty of recovery time afterward. But since he didn't sleep well even when he wasn't invincible and tranquilizers didn't work on him, he always looked tired and worn. By the end of the first year, there were new lines in his face. Whenever his hair started to grow out between dye jobs, he saw strands of premature white.

Every time he'd caught a glimpse of himself in the mirror, he'd thought, *That's not me.* It had bothered him so much that he'd eventually hung a towel over the mirror in his bathroom.

After he'd escaped, he'd tried going back to his natural hair color, but that lasted all of a week. Then the turned heads and stares had made him too edgy, and he'd dyed it again. With no one to stop him from becoming invincible, he'd stayed that way more and more, and for longer and longer, until he lost so much weight that the shape of his face changed. Whenever he saw his reflection, in the window of a shop or in the rear-view mirror, a stranger gazed back at him.

But now, Justin stopped to look at himself. He'd regained a lot of the weight he'd lost, and the winter sunlight had given him a light tan. His hair and eyes were still the wrong color. But when he looked into his own eyes, he could see himself in those inky depths.

I look so different, he thought. Then, *I look like me.*

Justin stood transfixed at the mirror until clattering from the other room pulled him back to his task at hand. He unwrapped the larger package without giving the costume a close look, his mind still on that realization. Then he unwrapped the mask.

The sight of it brought him back down to earth. It was a half-mask, covering the upper part of his face, made of soft leather painted in stark blacks and whites with one eye-catching splash of color. The left side was painted black, with delicate lines to indicate laughter. The right side was painted white, with lines of sorrow and, just below the hole cut for the eye, a single scarlet tear.

Unsettled, Justin thought, *No wonder Mr. Toscani is famous. I guess a true artist can see things without being told.*

Only then did he look at his costume. As Mr. Toscani had promised, it was easy to move in. It consisted of polished black boots, black pants, a white shirt, a black jacket, and a long black coat. The buttons on the coat and jacket were silver, and there was white piping on the jacket. It was beautifully made and perfectly tailored, and it looked nothing like a Cirque du Soleil costume. What it did look like was a military uniform for a formal occasion.

He put on the shirt and pants and boots, then his shoulder holster. Slowly, he buttoned the jacket so that the only white showing was his shirt collar.

Dress blacks, he thought. *Like my Air Force dress blues.*

He put on the black coat. The hem swirled around his calves. It would look very dramatic when he walked, but wouldn't hinder his movements. If necessary, he could shrug out of it in an instant.

Now that he was in a sort of uniform, he looked more like his old self than ever. His hair was even starting to grow out, giving him a band of brilliant copper at the hairline. Cut it short and close his eyes to hide the black, and he could be the man they'd called Red, who'd gotten in that helo with Shane and Mason and the others for what he'd thought would be just another mission.

Red had gotten everyone but Shane killed. He'd put Shane through hell and given him scars he'd bear for the rest of his life.

He couldn't risk that happening to Fiona.

She's wounded, he thought. *Vulnerable. The man she needs now is Subject Seven.*

No! The snarl inside his head was loud and frantic, almost a scream.

Don't—

Justin closed his eyes and summoned the ice. His snow leopard kept on shrieking at him until the ice reached his heart. Then the scream cut off. Justin was alone in the silent dark.

He opened his eyes, put on the mask, and went back into the bedroom. Fiona now wore a knee-length dress and a half-mask. She twirled around, making the skirt flare out.

"Good," Justin said. "You won't have any trouble moving in that."

Fiona stopped dead. "What have you done?"

"What do you mean?"

"You're using that power of yours. Aren't you." It wasn't a question.

"Invincibility. Yes, I am."

"Take it off," she demanded.

Justin shook his head.

"Why not?"

"You were wounded recently," he reminded her. "I need more of an edge to make up for that."

"Exactly how does turning yourself into a robot make up for me having a sore shoulder?"

Patiently, he explained, "When I'm invincible, I can't feel pain or shock. If I get shot, I can still keep on—"

"I know that!" Fiona's voice rose. "You already told me. So let me tell *you* something I've already told *you:* if you get shot, we've got bigger problems than whether you collapse on the spot or half an hour later. Take it off."

"No." He checked his watch. "We need to go."

"I know. Take it off, and then we can leave."

"I won't." He tried to read her body language. She was angry, obviously; her arms were folded across her chest, and her face was bright pink. She seemed unlikely to drop the matter. "All right. You stay here. I'll go by myself."

Her mouth fell open. "What? No!"

"Either we go together, or I'll go alone. Either way, I'm going as I am."

Fiona's flush went from pink to red. "Fine. There's obviously no point trying to talk to you when you're like this. But we will once you take it off."

Justin shrugged. That made no difference to him. "Sure. Let's go."

They set out in silence. But they'd already thoroughly reviewed their plan, so there was no need to discuss it again.

They reached their chosen lookout with a view of Bianchi's house. The guards were still there. Justin and Fiona settled in to wait. As time passed, more people began to appear. Many of them were in masks and costumes. As Fiona had predicted, a number of those found good spots to see and be seen, and stayed in them. No doubt Justin and Fiona would be assumed to be doing the same thing, if anyone noticed them at all. He didn't think their costumes were spectacular enough to attract much attention, which was good.

By 8:00 AM, the streets were crowded.

At 9:14, Bianchi appeared. He was dressed as a king, with a gold robe and crown and half-mask, and accompanied by four men dressed as courtiers, who were presumably guards. He began to slowly walk down the street, clearly enjoying the attention of passersby. Justin waited to him to pass the alley he and Fiona were in. They would then wait for him to get a little farther away, then start following him.

He instead turned to go into the alley. Justin briefly considered jumping him and his men right there… but no, they were too close to the house and all the other guards. Even the slightest error that allowed one to yell would bring all the others running. They'd have to just let Bianchi and his guards pass by.

But when he did pass, it was possible that he might recognize Justin from his body or the bottom half of his face or even from his eyes, if he got close enough—and it was a narrow alley, so he could easily get that close. Justin had to hide his face.

He turned to Fiona. She'd obviously had the exact same thought, because as Justin stepped to turn his back to Bianchi, she stepped to face him. She clasped him around the waist, he wrapped his arms around her back, and he pressed his lips to hers. They stayed like that, pretending to kiss, until Justin heard their footsteps pass by, then fade in the distance.

He straightened up and said softly, "Let's give them a count of ten, then follow."

Fiona's face was red again. In a low, thick voice, she said, "It's too bad you can't feel pain right now, because I would love to slap you and make you snap out of it."

"That's not how it works."

"I know that," Fiona whispered angrily. "I just—never mind. Let's go after them."

They slipped out of the alley and followed Bianchi and his courtier-guards at a distance through the streets of Venice, waiting for a chance to ambush them. If they didn't get one, they had a plan ready to lure them into an empty building, or even for Fiona to talk Bianchi into their apartment. But forty minutes later, they got their chance. Bianchi looked at a crowded bridge over a canal, then beckoned his men to cut through an empty alley instead.

Justin waited till they were halfway down, then nodded at Fiona. Holding hands and laughing, they ran into the alley, then broke apart and struck. Justin punched the two guards on the left, knocking them out, then slammed an elbow into Bianchi's solar plexus as he opened his mouth to scream. Bianchi sank to the ground, gasping like a fish. Justin glanced to the side. The other two guards also lay unconscious on the ground with Fiona standing over them.

They had no time to lose. They hauled the guards into doorways and set them up in sitting positions, so it looked like they were drunk or snoozing.

Justin bent over Bianchi and pulled his own mask off. "Remember me?"

From the way the gasping man's eyes bulged, he did. Justin replaced the mask.

"Remember my power?" Justin grabbed him by the throat, getting his imprint. "Now I can track you anywhere in the world."

Over Bianchi's shoulder, Justin watched Fiona delicately pat him down. Bianchi, distracted by Justin's threats, didn't seem to notice she was doing it. Nor did he so much as blink when Fiona extracted his cell phone, then slipped it down the front of her blouse.

"Now stand up." Justin hauled him to his feet. "You're coming with me. Make any indication that anything's wrong, and I'll break your neck."

Bianchi nodded frantically. Justin strolled out of the alley with him, with Fiona following. They walked around until Justin spotted another empty alley where they could talk without the possibility of someone noticing the knocked-out guards. Justin led him into it. Fiona walked silently behind them. With any luck, Bianchi had no idea she was there; with lots of luck, he'd never seen her at all.

Justin leaned casually against the alley and indicated to Bianchi to do the same, like they were friends having a chat. Fiona stood behind him, quietly working on his cell phone.

"Where's the Apex base?" Justin demanded.

"Um… There is no Apex base. You blew it up."

Justin again pushed up his mask and let Bianchi get a good look into his eyes. The arms dealer flinched back.

"Where's the Apex base?" Justin repeated.

"If I tell you, then you'll have gotten what you wanted, and then you'll kill me!" Bianchi babbled.

"I didn't kill Dr. Attanasio," Justin said. Over Bianchi's shoulder, he saw Fiona hold up the cell phone, then nod at him. Justin suddenly grabbed Bianchi by the shoulders. He jumped and squealed. As he did so, Fiona smoothly replaced the cell phone, then turned and walked silently out of the alley.

"That's because he told me what I needed to know," Justin went on. "So it's up to you. Tell me where it is and live, or don't tell me and die. What'll it be?"

Bianchi whimpered and sniffled, then said, "It's in the Bitterroot Mountains, in Montana. There's a dirt road off Lost Trail Pass. The sign says 'Fire Hazard' and there's some graffiti scribbles on the bottom right corner. Follow it twelve miles. The entrance is concealed by some boulders on the right-hand side."

"That better be true," Justin said. "Because if it isn't, I'm coming back for you."

"It's true, it's true, I swear!"

"And don't tip them off that I'm coming."

"I won't!'

"Fine. Now go back home. I don't want to see your face again." Justin gave him a shove in the direction away from Fiona. Bianchi didn't need more encouragement. He bolted.

A minute later, Fiona joined him. "Did he spill it?"

Justin shrugged. "He gave me some directions. Might be real, might be a trap. You got his cell phone, right?"

"Hacked and bugged," she replied. "Let's see if he says anything interesting."

They put in their earbuds, concealed them with the ribbons of their masks, and stood waiting with their arms around each other. If anyone walked by, they should look like lovers enjoying a private moment away from the crowds.

It was barely ten minutes before Bianchi's frantic voice came over the earbuds. "I just got attacked by Subject Seven! He took out my guards and threatened me! Demanded that I tell him where our base is!"

A cold woman's voice answered. Justin recognized it as Dr. Mortenson. "Did you tell him?"

"No!" Bianchi's voice came out in a squeal high enough to make Fiona wince. "I gave him the directions for the Bitterroot Mountains, just like you said. But you have to make sure you get him when he shows up. Otherwise he's going to kill me! He put his hand on my throat! He has my imprint!"

"We'll get him," Dr. Mortenson said. "I'll be there myself, to make sure it's done right. Since he's immune to tranquilizers, we'll do it old-school."

"What do you mean?"

She gave a humorless chuckle. "You said the entrance was by the boulders, right? We'll set up a bunch of modified bear traps all around them. Padded, so we don't break his ankle. Then a few guards go in with bomb squad-level armor, confiscate his weapons, cuff and manacle him, and we're done."

"All right. Just keep me posted." Bianchi hung up.

Justin removed his earbuds. Fiona did the same.

"We're done," she said. "The invincibility. Take it off now."

Justin considered it, then shook his head. "Not yet."

Her lips pressed together in a white line. "Why not? Danger's over."

"If we go straight to the airport, we can be in Montana to ambush Dr. Mortenson in another day or so. I'll need it then. I can take it off afterward."

She looked at him for a long time without replying. Then she said, "Let me ask you something. Don't answer me immediately. I want you to think about it first. Dr. Mortenson's the one who waterboarded you. How do you feel about getting revenge on her?"

He thought about it, then said, "She's a sadist. She did that to me because she got a kick out of it. Saying it was an experiment was just an excuse. She'll hurt more people if I don't take her down."

"I said how did you *feel*, not..." Fiona folded her arms across her chest. "I want you to remember what it felt like when she did it. Do it, Justin."

He didn't see any reason not to. He remembered Dr. Mortenson pouring water over his face until it filled his lungs. He'd been sure he was dying when he'd finally passed out, but he'd woken up still strapped to that cold table. His first thought had been to regret that he hadn't died, because being alive meant she'd do it again. But it was just a memory. He could recall that he'd felt pain and suffocation, panic and shame at being panicked, but none of it meant anything to him now.

"I remember it. It doesn't bother me. I know it would if I wasn't invincible. But I am, so..." He shrugged.

Fiona took off her mask. Her eyes were glistening. Wet. A tear slid down her cheek.

Something stirred in his chest. Not pain, he couldn't feel that, but the sense that the pain was there whether it hurt or not. That was how it felt when you were given morphine. The pain didn't actually go away. It just stopped bothering you.

"What's the matter?" Justin asked.

"I don't know how to reach you. I suppose I could wait a week until you hit your limit and have to take it off or die, but..." Her fists clenched at her sides, then opened. She clasped both his hands in hers. "Do you love me?"

"Yes," he said automatically. He knew he did. He just couldn't feel it. Like that phantom pain, he could tell that his love existed, but was beyond his ability to perceive.

"Then take it off now. Do it as a favor to me. I know you don't want to. But do it anyway. Do it because you love me, and I'm asking you."

That sense of feelings just outside of his grasp increased. He caught himself trying to lift his hand to press it against the scar over his chest. As if it hurt, even though it couldn't hurt. Or maybe it was his heart that almost hurt. His reason for wanting to stay invincible was part and parcel of that knot of not-quite feeling. Like the reason he was with Fiona at all. And he'd never understand it unless he did what she was asking.

"All right," he said. And, knowing it was true even though he couldn't feel it, "Because I love you."

Justin closed his eyes and opened his heart.

CHAPTER TEN
Justin

Even before he opened his eyes, the memory of the last few hours came flooding back, only now with emotions attached.

How he'd pressed his lips against Fiona's in a cold mockery of a kiss, without a trace of love or passion or desire. No wonder she'd been furious.

How once he was invincible, he didn't see any reason not to stay that way. He'd known it could kill him, and he simply hadn't cared.

In a rush of horror and shame, he remembered how he'd made Fiona cry. He loved her. How could he have done something so cruel to someone he loved?

Love!

He'd been unable to love Fiona. He'd literally forgotten what love felt like.

Justin felt the blood drain from his face. "Oh, God."

Strong fingers dug into his upper arms. "Justin!"

He opened his eyes. Fiona was holding him, her face still streaked with tears. He could see her beauty now, but more importantly, he could see *her*. She'd been desperately trying to save him from himself. And he'd fought her.

"I'm sorry," he said. "I'm so sorry."

"Sorry doesn't cut it," she hissed, her voice choked and angry. "Promise me you'll never do it again."

He hesitated. Part of him was protesting, *But I need it!* Another part was shouting, *It hurts Fiona!* His snow leopard was snarling furiously, *Look what it makes you do! Look what it does to your mate!*

His first inclination was to tell his snow leopard to shut up. But that had been how this entire mess had started. Just because his leopard had been forced on him didn't mean he had to try to push him down and ignore him. His snow leopard was the voice of his own deepest instincts and emotions. Maybe he was worth listening to.

Justin waited patiently as his snow leopard ran through his usual, frantic snarls and shrieks of *Don't do it! It's bad for you! It'll kill us both!* But he calmed down as he realized that for once, Justin was listening.

You have to tell your mate why you think you need it, his snow leopard hissed. *You have to tell her what happened at Apex.*

Justin flinched. He wanted to say, *I can't.*

But when he looked at Fiona and felt his love for her, like a fire burning in his heart, he knew that he could. It was his choice, just like turning over a new leaf had been her choice. Just like telling him her story, which had obviously terrified her.

"I can't make that promise until I know you understand what it means," he said. "But it's a long story, and people could walk in on us at any second. Let's go back. I'll tell you as soon as we're alone."

He'd expected her to be angry that he wouldn't immediately agree. But instead, she took his hand. "I appreciate it. I know this is hard. I'm still scared to tell my teammates my story. But I'm going to anyway. I feel a lot better since I told you. And since you didn't blame me, it makes me think maybe they won't either."

"Shane won't," Justin said. "I know him, and there's no way. From what you told me about Hal, I can't imagine that he would either. And Nick, I just met briefly and not really under great circumstances, but he said a couple things that made me think he'd committed some crimes himself."

"Nick's an ex-gangster. I gave him hell for it when he first joined. Looking back now, I didn't want him around because he reminded me of what I used to be. But it was unfair of me. I owe him an apology."

"It's never too late."

"It really isn't." She squeezed his hand, then said, "Now that you can appreciate it, let's try again. What do you think of my costume?"

Fiona lifted his hand over her head and twirled beneath it like a ballet dancer. Her skirt flared out, showing off her slim but muscled thighs. Now he could admire her costume, and the woman in it. Her dress was white satin embroidered with clear crystals, like a field of snow flecked with ice. The tight top offered a tempting view of her luscious cleavage. White ballet slippers covered her dainty feet.

She wore an elaborate tiara of silver, white feathers, and sparkling clear jewels. Her half-mask was made of white lace decorated with the same clear crystals that were on her dress. A sapphire crystal shaped like a teardrop was placed beneath her eye, and a series of smaller sapphire teardrops made a trail down the mask. The blue crystal trail continued across the shoulder of her dress and made an asymmetrical pattern across the bodice and skirt, until it encircled the bottom of the skirt in a rippled pattern, like the sea.

Mr. Toscani had seen into Fiona's heart, just as he'd seen into Justin's: he'd dressed her as a snow queen whose tears were melting the ice.

"It's beautiful," Justin said. "*You're* beautiful. I'm sorry as hell I couldn't see it before."

"You can now. That's the important thing."

He took a second look. Her shoulders and arms were bare, and so were her legs. "Aren't you freezing?"

She shrugged, then gave him a wry smile. "You have to suffer for beauty."

Justin put his arm around her and held her close, sharing his warmth. "No, you don't."

They walked out of the alley. It was mid-morning now, and Carnival was in full swing. The narrow streets were full of people in elaborate costumes and masks. Living gargoyles peered from windows, kings and queens were rowed along the canals by gondoliers, and masked lovers in elaborate costumes waltzed in the squares.

It was beautiful. More than beautiful—it was magical. Justin felt as if he'd stepped out of reality, and into the sort of dream he used to have, the kind he was sorry to wake up from. He couldn't believe that he'd seen all this earlier and barely even registered it, let alone appreciated it.

He'd expected to be filled with dread for the entire walk back to the apartment, now that he'd agreed to tell her his story. But instead, he felt strangely light. He could feel again. He could perceive beauty and experience love and enjoy the warm grip of Fiona's hand in his.

Unexpectedly, joy had entered his heart, filling it to the brim if it was making up for lost time.

A huge crowd had gathered in St. Mark's Square. To the accompaniment of wild cheers, a young woman dressed as an angel leaped from a high tower and floated down on an invisible wire, scattering confetti over the crowd.

Justin flicked one of Fiona's braids. "You have confetti in your hair."

"So do you. It suits you. You should wear it all the time."

"Maybe I can hire that angel to follow me around and sprinkle it from a height."

Fiona laughed. The clear sound filled his heart, and he bent to kiss her.

The touch of her lips was a shock as intense as if he'd stuck his finger in an electric socket, but a jolt of pleasure rather than pain. She swayed against him, her body seeming to melt into his. He was instantly hard as a rock, aching with desire. After that long morning of numb emptiness, the rush of love and lust made his head swim. If they hadn't been in public, he'd have ripped her clothes off then and there.

Her eyes were burning with an emerald fire, and her nails bit into his shoulders. She was breathing as hard as if she'd just finished a marathon. She lowered her head and gave a sudden nip at his throat that sent a bolt of desire straight down his spine.

"Come on." His voice came out in a rough growl, like his leopard's.

They pushed through the crowd, dodging costumed revelers as they ran through the narrow streets. His boots clacked against the cobblestones; her leather slippers made no sound. He only knew his feet were touching the ground by the noise they made. It felt like he was flying.

It seemed like both forever and no time at all before they reached their apartment. Justin was shaking from the intensity of his desire; he dropped the key the first time he tried to unlock the door. Fiona snatched it up, but fumbled as she tried to unlock it. Her hands were trembling too. When they finally got the door open, Justin kicked it shut behind them and shoved the bolt in place with the heel of his hand. Then they stumbled up the stairs together and into the bedroom.

Before they even reached the bed, they were in each other's arms, kissing passionately. He was vaguely aware that they were both still wearing their half-masks, but his was made of thin leather and hers of lace; they didn't interfere. Taking them off would require lifting his hands away from the soft skin of her bare shoulders, and he couldn't bear to do it.

In a moment, he thought vaguely.

Fiona had pulled up his shirt and was caressing his chest. Her hands slid over the gunshot scars on his chest and back, but it didn't bother him. If anything, her touch made him realize that they were only scars now. The wounds had healed. And then he forgot about them entirely, because her hands had dropped down to tug at his belt buckle. He helped her undo it, then pulled it off and tossed it aside.

The bed was right there in front of them, but his blood was running too hot and his pulse pounding too fast to take the time to lie down. Nor could he imagine taking the time to get undressed. He needed to be in her now, merging their bodies until all barriers between them melted away.

Fiona gave him a nudge forward, and his back met the wall. In a voice low and husky with arousal, she said, "I can't wait."

"Me neither."

She pushed his pants down to his hips, and slid her palm along him as she went. He groaned, thrusting into her hand. His whole body felt like it was on fire. His hands were once again shaking as he reached up her skirt, feeling the heat of her thighs, and pulled down her panties. They fell around her ankles. Fiona stepped out of them, then kicked them away.

He put his hand under her skirt and slipped a finger into her slick folds. She cried out aloud at just that brief caress, and he knew she was as close to the edge as he was.

"Come on," she whispered. "Just like this."

She stood on her tiptoes, pressing herself against him. Justin put his hands under her thighs and lifted her. She gripped his shoulders and kissed him hard as he slid into her like a key into a lock.

He gasped at the intensity of the sensation. She was so hot and wet and tight inside, gripping him from within. Fiona too gasped, her eyes opening wide. As he began to thrust, she kissed his lips, his throat, his cheeks, his eyelids. As his pleasure built within him, his love for her burned hotter and hotter until it exploded in an ecstatic white-heat, like the heart of a sun.

Justin leaned against the wall, holding Fiona in his arms. She lay as boneless and content as a cat in the sun, her head resting on his shoulder. He felt like he could stay like that forever.

After a while, she lifted her head and nudged him. "Aren't you getting tired?"

"Never." Then he admitted, "But my feet might be starting to fall asleep."

She laughed. "Let's take a shower."

He carried her to the bathroom, where they took off their masks and undressed. Fiona unpinned her braids and Justin helped her unravel them, her hair sliding through his fingers like silk, before they stepped into the shower. The hot water washed away his sweat and made her hair seem to flow like liquid. She might have been a water spirit risen to pull him into the depths, not to drown but to find a new life in a strange new world.

When they left the shower and dressed again in their regular clothes, Justin sat down on the bed.

You're not brave if you're not scared, he thought. *It only feels like telling this story will hurt so much that it'll actually kill me.*

He still felt exactly like he had that first time he'd stood at 13,000 feet above ground with a parachute strapped to his back. But he beckoned to Fiona. "Come here. I've got a story for you."

She curled up beside him and put her arms around him. Stroking his back, she said quietly, "We haven't really talked about it, but I do know what you've done. Way back in New York City, you told me Apex forced you to become an assassin. But that wasn't your choice. I didn't blame you for it then, and learning the details isn't going to make me blame you now."

"That's not what I'm going to tell you. Like you said, I didn't just up and decide to become a hit man. I'd never have done it if I'd had a choice, but it's not what's keeping me awake at night."

"Then what is?"

As he began to speak, he hoped her love would be his parachute.

CHAPTER ELEVEN
Justin's Story

There were eight of us on the mission where we got captured by Apex. There was a team of four PJs, me and Shane and two other guys, and the crew of the helicopter that was transporting us.

I hadn't met the helo crew before, but it was a pretty long flight and I'm a chatty guy—at least, I was then—so I knew them a bit by the end of it. Not that we were best friends or anything, but we talked some about movies and some about their families and some about sports. Me and Elizabeth, who was one of the door gunners, made a bet on the World Series. She seriously thought the Cubs were going to win it this time.

I already knew the other PJs. I'd worked with Armando a couple times, just enough that I liked him and trusted him to have my back. Mason was a buddy of mine. I'd baked one of his kids *Hunger Games* cupcakes for her last birthday. They had white chocolate arrows and raspberry jam blood splatters. Her mom thought they were way too gory, but Mikayla loved them.

Other than me, Shane wasn't close to anyone on the mission. He doesn't get close to many people. He's choosy. If you're his friend, that's a big deal for him. He'll be loyal to you forever. I don't know if he ever mentioned his own nickname. It's Comeback. It's from this old cowboy movie called *Shane* that a bunch of us watched on the base. It was mostly a joke about this one part where this kid starts screaming, "Come back, Shane! Come back!" But there was also a part that wasn't a joke, which was that Shane would always come back for you.

The details of the mission aren't important. All you need to know is that we were in combat and I was hit. It felt like someone had taken a swing at my chest with a baseball bat. It didn't hurt at first, it was just this tremendous impact that knocked me down. I knew I had to get the hell out of the line of fire, but I couldn't get up.

Shane ran out and dragged me to the nearest cover, and that separated us from everyone else. At first I didn't realize how bad it was. I was wearing body armor, so I thought I'd just had the wind knocked out of me. But it was an armor-piercing bullet. By the time he got my body armor off to take a look, a pool of blood had already started spreading out beneath me.

That was about the first time I'd ever seen Shane look scared. And that scared me as much as the blood did. My chest started to hurt, and it got worse and worse. He gave me a shot of morphine, which helped with the pain, but he couldn't get the bleeding to stop.

Shane had been trying to keep an eye out for the enemy at the same time he was helping me. But he finally put down his gun, put his palms on my chest, and leaned his whole weight on them. He was telling me I'd be all right and to stay with him, but I'm a paramedic too. I knew he was getting desperate, and that if I didn't get medevaced ASAP I'd bleed to death.

Then Shane collapsed on top of me. I thought he'd been shot too. It was about the worst moment of my entire life. Then I saw this little black dart sticking out of his hand. I was just barely conscious at that point, so I didn't understand what it meant until later. Then I passed out too. I don't even think they had to tranquilize me.

I woke up in a hospital and saw everyone, and I thought we'd been rescued and we were back on the base. It was a while before I realized what was really going on. Shane told me later that at first I was in such bad shape that nobody wanted to stress me, and then when they did try, I was so out of it that I just said, "Uh-huh, uh-huh," and fell asleep and then didn't remember anything about it. That one armor-piercing bullet did a hell of a lot of damage. It was weeks before I could even sit up in bed.

What had happened was that Apex had taken advantage of Shane being distracted by taking care of me and everyone else being distracted by being in combat, shot us all with tranquilizer darts, and imprisoned us in an underground lab.

I was in an intensive care unit, and everyone else was put in barracks attached to that. They were allowed to visit me as long as they didn't make any trouble. Shane moved in with me. He slept on the floor until they put in another bed so they could stop tripping over him. Doctors and nurses and scientists could come in and out, but whenever they were in our rooms, a bunch of guards with dart guns were too. There were more guards outside the doors, and the doors were always locked.

They'd captured us as test subjects for a process called Ultimate Predator. It was supposed to make you into a super-soldier, but mostly it just killed you. By the time I'd recovered enough to understand what was going on, Elizabeth and Neil, the helo co-pilot, were already dead.

Shane knew I was afraid—afraid I'd die of my wounds, afraid Apex would decide I was too much trouble to keep alive anymore, afraid of being helpless and alone. He kept telling me anyone who wanted to hurt me would have to go through him first, and he'd never leave me. But that was the problem. The reason Apex was keeping us all together was so they could use me as a hostage. As long as no one was willing to leave me, none of us could escape.

I told them to go anyway. I said once they were gone, they could get help and come back and rescue me. But I only said that to talk them into leaving, not because I thought they really could. I thought my only value to Apex was as a hostage. There was no point in experimenting on me when there wasn't even a chance that I'd survive it. If everyone else got away, Apex would probably just kill me.

Shane said, "You're right, someone has to go for help. But not me. I'm not leaving you."

They came up with a plan for some of them to fight and distract the guards while some of them tried to escape. Shane was one of the fighters, of course. If I could've gotten out of bed and fought, even if I knew it would kill me, I would have. But all I could do was lie there and watch.

The plan failed. They knocked out a few guards, and then everyone got tranquilized. After that, Apex increased the security.

They kept taking people to the lab. Putting them through the Ultimate Predator process. Every time, the doctors said they'd learned so much and they were improving the process and the next time would work.

It never did. Everyone died.

Everyone.

Finally Shane and I were the only ones left. I'd recovered a lot, in the sense that I could get up and walk slowly around the room. But I couldn't run. I couldn't fight. If Shane and I tried to escape, he'd have to carry me, and then *he* couldn't fight. I told him to leave me. I *begged* him. I told him I'd rather die than live with knowing that he'd thrown his life away to save someone who couldn't be saved, and I meant it. But he wouldn't leave me.

I thought for sure they'd take Shane next and save me for last. But they didn't. They took me. I was glad. At least I wouldn't have to die alone. And then I felt terrible for thinking that, because it meant Shane would.

Shane went berserk when they came for me. But it didn't make a difference. They shot him with a dart gun, and that was that. It was a two-step process: first they made you into a shifter, and then they used Ultimate Predator to try to give you powers. I didn't realize until I became a shifter why they did that first. I hadn't known shifters had healing powers. But once I was one, I started getting much better, much faster.

I realized that Apex could have done that any time, but they'd let me suffer to keep everyone else in line. But I was so happy to be strong and healthy again, I didn't brood too much about that. Shane and I planned to jump the guards and fight for our lives when they came in to do Ultimate Predator, which was the part that killed you.

Only Apex was too smart for that. They didn't send guards in at all. They drugged our food instead. I woke up in the lab, and it was already done.

I felt fine. The doctors were all excited. They thought they'd finally gotten it right. They put me back in with Shane, who was glad as hell to see me walk in. And then, all of a sudden, I was on the floor with Shane holding me. I couldn't breathe. I thought that was it for me, that the process had killed me after all.

But it hadn't, quite. Just nearly. I woke up in another ICU. Apparently I'd been there for weeks, and I'd barely pulled through.

I was alone. I thought that meant Shane was dead. But the doctors said they'd finally perfected Ultimate Predator on him. They said he'd come out fine, he'd gotten powers, and he'd used them to escape. At first I didn't believe it. But they described how he'd done it, and it sure sounded like a Shane type of plan. So I thought, 'He finally took my advice. He escaped, and he'll get help and come back for me. I just need to stall for a couple days. A week, max. And then we'll both be free.'

Only he didn't come back. I thought, 'Well, maybe he's run into some trouble. *I'll* escape and go looking for him.' I was under tight security, but they obviously wanted me to do things for them, so they had to let me out sooner or later. I figured the moment they did, I'd slip whatever leash they had on me and go looking for Shane.

It turned out that they had one hell of a leash. My version of Ultimate Predator—the flawed one, the one that had nearly killed me—made it so you needed to do a treatment every ten days or so, or you died a slow, horrible, painful death. I didn't believe the doctors when they told me that, so they said to feel free to not do the treatments and see what happened. It was horrible and painful, all right. I gave in and asked for the treatment before I got to the 'death' part.

And then they had me. If I escaped, I'd die. But they said they'd improved it after me, so that wouldn't happen to Shane. He didn't have to come back unless he wanted to. And he didn't.

Time passed. I finally realized that he wasn't coming back. After that, I pretty much stopped caring about anything.

Of course, it was all a trick. They'd had Shane all along, in a different base. They told him I'd died and they told me he'd abandoned me, so we wouldn't go looking for each other. They'd lied about Shane not needing the treatment, too. When he finally did escape, he almost died of it. I thought he'd abandoned me, when he'd actually given up his own chance at freedom to stay with me. He didn't hold it against me, but it's hard to forgive myself.

It's hard to forgive myself for any of it.

CHAPTER TWELVE
Fiona

When Justin had started his story, Fiona hadn't thought he'd be able to get through it. He'd choked up every time he said the names of the men and women who'd died, and every time he told her how Shane had refused to leave him. By the time he finished, he was shaking and drenched in sweat.

But he did finish. And Fiona loved him for it. Stroking his wet hair away from his face, she said, "I know a lot of brave people. But you're the bravest man I've ever met."

"I didn't do anything brave. Shane and Mason and Elizabeth and…" He shook his head, unable to get the rest of the names out. "They fought like hell. I just lay there."

"You 'just lay there' because you'd been shot in the chest," Fiona pointed out. "Same as Shane did when he got shot. It's not like you were having a fit of the vapors because a bat got tangled in your hair!"

Justin let out an amused huff of breath. "That's certainly a vivid image."

"So, was it easy for you to tell everyone to save themselves and leave you behind? Was it easy for you to tell Shane to leave you imprisoned by the enemy, wounded and helpless and alone? And how about telling me this story now—was *that* easy?"

"No." He spoke so softly that Fiona could only hear him because they were pressed so close together. "No, none of that was easy. If you're defining courage by how much something scares you, then yeah, it took some."

It took a lot, Fiona thought. She couldn't imagine doing what he'd done. She'd have begged them *not* to leave her. But she kept quiet. It had been hard enough for Justin to admit to even that much.

He went on, "I've wondered whether the Ultimate Predator powers we got were influenced by who we were and what we wanted. Shane was always kind of intimidating and stealthy, and he got that turned up as far as it could go. Catalina loved cats, and she got the agility of one."

"Catalina used to have a hard time getting men to take her seriously," Fiona said. "And her other power is super-strength. Hard to sneer at a woman who can throw you across the room with one hand."

"Right. And as for what I wanted, it was to get up from that fucking hospital bed and stop holding everyone up, even if I dropped dead as soon as I got outside. And that's what invincibility would have let me do."

"It also takes the pain away," Fiona said quietly. "I imagine you wanted that, too."

"Yeah." He sighed. "I know that's mostly why I've been using it. But that's not why I can't promise to never use it again. As long as I'm invincible, I never have to be a burden for anyone. And nobody else will ever die because they had to take care of me."

"Oh, Justin…" The hurt in his voice was so raw, Fiona couldn't imagine anything to do or say to make it better. All she could do was hold him tight. But he relaxed in her arms, so maybe she had done something.

Then her thoughts returned to what he'd said. She'd been so caught up in how painful it was for him that she hadn't considered whether it was actually true. But the more she considered it, examining it with the same objective eye she'd bring to bear on a broken machine she needed to repair, the less convincing it seemed.

"If I'd been invincible when I was hit on the mission, I'd have kept on fighting," he said. "And then Shane wouldn't have been distracted by me, and Apex wouldn't have been able to sneak up on him."

Like that, Fiona thought. *That can't be right.*

"What would've happened if you'd been invincible, and you'd kept fighting?" she asked.

He sounded baffled by her question. "I just told you. Shane wouldn't have been captured. Maybe none of us would have."

"No, I mean literally, what would've happened? Talk me through it. You were all fighting, Apex agents were sneaking up on you with tranquilizer rifles, you were hit with an armor-piercing bullet, and your wound was bad enough that you ended up flat on your back for weeks. What would've happened if you'd been invincible at the time?"

She could see from his expression that he'd never thought past, *If I'd been invincible, none of the rest would have happened.*

Slowly, he said, "I would've kept fighting. So I would've kept bleeding. And running around would have made it worse. I'd have been dead in about ten minutes. Maybe less."

"What do you think Apex would've done then?"

"Probably exactly what they did do, only Shane would've been giving me CPR." Justin frowned. "Okay, I see what you mean. But the important part is what happened at Apex. That was when I really would have needed invincibility. If I hadn't been laid up, we all would've been out of there. And then nobody would've died."

"Except you!"

"Well..." He trailed off as if he wanted to disagree with her but couldn't figure out how.

"You're the medical expert, not me. What would've happened if you'd had the same injuries, but you'd been able to get up and run around and fight anyway?"

Justin took a moment to think about it, then reluctantly said, "I'd have died. But I was willing—"

"Yeah, *you* were willing. How about Shane? He's a paramedic too. He'd have known what would happen. Even if you'd had your invincibility, would he have let you use it like that?"

"Umm." Even more reluctantly, Justin admitted, "I actually did try to get out of bed a couple times. He held me down. Threatened to tell the doctors to strap me down if I tried it again."

Fiona stared at him, her eyebrows raised, letting his own words sink in.

"I hadn't remembered that till you reminded me just now," he said slowly. "You know... Maybe it wouldn't have even made a difference if I'd never been shot in the first place. Shane was distracted and I was out for the count, but the others weren't. Apex still got all of us. So if

I hadn't been wounded, they probably wouldn't have kept us together or they'd have had higher security from the get-go. Once they made us into shifters but before they'd put us through Ultimate Predator, they chained us to the walls. They could've done that from the start."

"They *chained you to the walls?*" Fiona repeated. The fact that he'd said it like it was a minor detail that hadn't been important enough to mention before made it even more horrifying.

"Yeah. That's pretty bad, huh?"

"I'll say!" She squeezed his hand.

He lifted her hand to his lips and kissed it. "I'm glad I told you. When I was keeping it all bottled up inside me, I had no perspective. I was so sure the only thing stopping us from escaping was me."

"What was stopping you from escaping was Apex. Everything that happened was their fault and their choice. Not yours."

For a long time, he was silent, looking thoughtful. "You're right about the invincibility. It's cutting my own heart out, and for what? An extra five minutes to do something that won't change anything, at the cost of my life? No. I can't do that anymore. I *won't*."

Fiona hugged him. "You don't need to, anyway. You were alone before. Now you've got me. Don't forget, I'm a bodyguard. Wherever you go, I'll be there to watch your back."

"Same to you," he said promptly. Then his gaze turned away from her and to the bright light from the window. "Do you want to go out again? We have the whole rest of the day. And Carnival comes but once a year."

"Absolutely. I don't think we'd be able to get a flight out before tomorrow, anyway. Let Dr. Mortenson cool her feet in Montana."

She offered her hand to Justin, but he didn't move. His brow wrinkled as it he was trying to remember something, and then he said abruptly, "We can't go to Montana. It's a set-up. She knew I was listening in. If we show up, she won't have a couple of men with bear traps, she'll have a lot of men with something she thinks can take me down. Nets, maybe. Tranquilizer darts don't work on me anymore. It was one of the Ultimate Predator side effects."

She trusted his judgment, but didn't understand how he'd figured it out. "What makes you think it's a trap?"

"Dr. Mortenson had this tone she always got when she was lying about something to fuck me over. I didn't realize it at the time because I was invincible. I guess because I can't feel emotions, it's harder for me to pick up on them. I only realized when I thought back on the call just now." He gave an ironic chuckle. "You were right that invincibility is bad news. If I'd kept it on all the way to Montana, she'd have gotten us for sure."

She hesitated over bringing up the obvious solution. He'd shot it down before… but things had changed. *They'd* changed, and so had their relationship. They'd stripped each other down to the naked truth, and neither had flinched at what they'd seen. She didn't have to hold back with him anymore.

"We can still ambush her," she said. "We just need reinforcements. Let's bring in my team."

For the first time, Justin didn't flinch at the suggestion. "Yeah. You're right. It's time."

"Are you okay with seeing Shane?"

His lips quirked in a half-amused, half-sad smile, making her think of the mask Mr. Toscani had made for him. "We've been best friends for ten years. He's saved my life more times than I can count. I *want* to see him. It's just that I felt guilty over getting shot and him not leaving me and me thinking he'd left me and then *me* leaving *him*… Stop me before I talk myself out of this."

"Would it help if I told you that Shane feels guilty over believing that you were dead and leaving you?"

"Not really. But I'll survive. And I want to say hi to Catalina. And see Nick—I always like seeing patients of mine after they're recovered. And I'm curious about your other teammates. They must be great."

"They are," Fiona assured him. "You'll love them. Except—"

"What?" Justin asked suspiciously.

"They're very protective. So any time someone comes in with a mate…"

"They go all big brother, huh? 'You break her heart, I break your legs?'"

Fiona tried and failed to think of a way to explain the Protection, Inc. mate hazing rituals that didn't make them—which included her—sound like a bunch of lunatics. "Something like that."

Justin smiled. "Don't look so nervous. I have no intention of breaking your heart, so my legs are safe."

She gave up. Probably they wouldn't do it to him, anyway. Shane certainly wouldn't, Catalina already knew Justin, and Nick owed him one. And all the previous mates had been civilians. It was natural to be concerned that a delicate princess or a purple-haired stage manager might not have the steely will and death-defying courage that one's teammate needed and deserved. But Justin was a PJ. His will and courage had already been proven beyond a shadow of a doubt.

He took her hand. "Come on. Let's say good-bye to the confetti angel before we go."

CHAPTER THIRTEEN
Justin

As Fiona and Justin drove to the Protection, Inc. office, she said, "About that hazing thing I mentioned…"

"It'll be fine," Justin said absently. He patted her hand where it rested on the steering wheel. "I just want to tell Shane I'm sorry."

She shot him an odd glance, then smiled. "He'll be over the moon to see you."

At Justin's request, she had texted Shane to make sure he was at office, but hadn't said anything other than that she was coming in. He'd texted back, *The gang's all here, having lunch. If you hurry there might be some sandwiches left.*

They parked in an underground lot, where Justin gave an appreciative glance to the several beautiful sports cars, and also to a tank-like armored car. "Someone's got a need for speed. Several someones, looks like."

"The Dodge Viper belongs to Nick, the Porsche Carrera belongs to Lucas, and the Ferrari belongs to Grace. And the armored car is Hal's. His previous car got blown up, so he got a bit obsessed with durability."

"I can see how that could happen," he allowed.

They walked into the lobby, where he glanced at the hardwood floors, black leather sofa, and animal photos on the walls. There was a wolf in a forest, a panther lying in wait on a tree branch, a snow leopard caught in mid-leap from one icy crag to the next…

"Ah-ha," said Justin. "Nice shot of you. Where was that taken?"

"Destiny dragged me on a ski trip to Mammoth," Fiona said. "She thought it'd be fun for me to be in my natural environment, and I couldn't figure out how to say it wouldn't without telling her stuff I didn't want to get into. It's a great photo, but that was the last time I ever let anyone take me somewhere where the snow's the main attraction."

"For our anniversary, I'll take you to Death Valley," he offered. "Hottest place on Earth. Good hiking, too."

"That's right, we have an anniversary now. And it's in the winter. Nix on Death Valley. I vote for Tahiti." She took out her cell phone. "Let me get you and Shane a moment before everyone pounces on you."

Peering over her shoulder, Justin read the text, *Come into the lobby. Alone.*

"That doesn't sound at all suspicious," he remarked.

Shane came in. The door swung shut behind him as he stopped still and stared.

All the words Justin had meant to say melted away. He knew in that moment that there was no need for apologies, and that he had nothing to apologize for. Shane was the friend he'd lost and found and found again, this time for good.

"Hey, Comeback," said Justin. "Long time no see."

"About time, Red." Shane pulled him into a bone-cracking embrace.

For a moment, Justin was too startled to respond. In his experience, Shane was not the hugging type. Then he threw his arms around his buddy. If there had ever been a man who deserved a hug, it was Shane.

"Do *I* get a hug?" Catalina inquired from the doorway.

Justin and Shane broke apart, grinning.

"Sure you wouldn't rather get your ears scritched?" Justin asked, then lifted her off her feet and swung her around.

"You want one too?" Shane asked Fiona sardonically.

She held up a hand to stop him, looking mildly horrified. "Thanks, but I'll pass."

"You look good, Justin," Catalina said, inspecting him. "Much better than when I saw you last."

Shane gave him and Fiona a sharp glance. "How did you two find each other?"

"Well..." Fiona began.

Before she could go on, a whole crowd piled into the lobby. Justin recognized Ellie, the blonde paramedic who'd been caring for Shane after he'd been shot, and who was now visibly pregnant. But the rest were strangers.

A chorus of exclamations and questions arose from the crowd, half addressed to Fiona and half to him. He felt a little dazed. He'd only just gotten used to having conversations with anybody at all, and he hadn't been the center of this sort of attention for years.

A young man in a black leather jacket slapped him on the back. "Thanks, man. Don't think I remembered to say that before."

"Yes, thank you very much," said an elegantly dressed woman with flowing silver hair and silver tattoos winding down one arm. "I owe you a great debt."

It was only then that Justin recognized the pair. The last time he'd seen them, she'd been in tattered and bloodstained dancing clothes, crouched in a dark alley and holding the man, who'd been naked, badly wounded, and pale with shock.

"You must be Nick," Justin said. "How's your leg?"

"It's fine," Nick said, flipping his hand dismissively. "Completely healed. So what're you doing here? Visiting Shane?"

Before Justin could answer, Fiona's clear voice cut through the chatter. "Everyone, this is Justin Kovac. Also known as Red. He and Shane were PJs together. He's a snow leopard shifter. And he's my mate."

The room instantly split into two factions. Shane, Catalina, Nick, and the silver-haired woman looked delighted and started congratulating him and Fiona. And everyone else—not just Fiona's teammates, but the women who must be their mates—fell silent, staring at him suspiciously.

A handsome man with a lot of shiny black hair switched out the glare for a charming smile as he offered Justin his hand. "I'm Rafa Flores. Pleased to meet you. It'll be nice for Shane to have another Chairborne Ranger to talk shop with."

Justin had heard that one before, along with jokes about the Chair Force, and had a retort ready. "Our chairs travel at Mach 3." Then, remembering Fiona saying Rafa was a Navy SEAL, he added, "I hear the surf's great in Santa Martina. We should go some time. I'll bring a floatie for you."

Rafa chuckled, and when he stepped back into the crowd, his smile stayed.

A big man shook Justin's hand and said in a very deep voice, "Great to see Fiona paired up. You probably know her better than we do now. You can see this gang loves teasing, but we've never been able to get any dirt on her. She's so cool and collected. But I bet she lets down her hair around *you*."

Feeling awkward, Justin said, "Well…"

A young man with a golden chain wrapped around his throat chimed in, "Yes, Justin, tell us something we can tease her about. Only in fun."

"Like an embarrassing story from when she was a kid," the big man went on. "Go on. Spill the beans on the ice queen."

In fact, Fiona had told him a few stories that were exactly the sort of thing that buddies would tease each other about. But she *was* private. If her teammates didn't already know those stories, then Justin had no right to repeat them. In a tone designed to squelch the entire subject, he said, "If Fiona wants you to know something about her, she can tell you herself."

He expected the men to try again—the type of guy who'd pry for dirt on a woman, even with harmless intentions, wasn't the type to drop it at the first refusal—and to accuse Justin of being uptight and no fun. Instead, they looked at each other and smiled.

"You're a good man," said the big man, in an entirely different tone.

"Very honorable," said the man with the gold chain, sounding like he sincerely approved. "Fiona deserves no less."

Shane shot them both an exasperated glance, "You guys, this is *Justin*. Of course he's honorable."

In a frigid tone, Fiona said to the men, "Have you had enough of testing my mate? Because I certainly have had enough of you doing it."

"Oh," Justin said, enlightened. "That was the thing you warned me about. I was expecting something a bit less subtle. Like, 'See this shovel? It's what I'll bury you with if you hurt her.'"

He eyed the men with new appreciation. They'd not only been looking out for Fiona, they'd known her well enough to check for something that actually could hurt her. Of course she shouldn't be with a man who wouldn't keep her secrets, even seemingly inconsequential ones, or respect her right to have them!

"Maybe *I'll* get a shovel," Fiona said icily, glaring at them.

Justin patted her shoulder. "It's fine, Fiona. No harm done."

"Hal Brennan," said the big man, offering Justin his hand.

Justin blinked, his perception of the man shifting. So *that* was Fiona's boss—the one who'd sat with her in the snow, patiently talking her back to humanity. No wonder he hadn't introduced himself till afterward. His little trick would never have worked if Justin had known who he was.

"Pleased to meet you," Justin said, and meant it.

"I am Lucas," said the man with the golden chain. After enough of a pause that Justin wasn't expecting a surname, he added, "Dragomir."

His hand, when Justin shook it, was oddly hot.

Except for Fiona, the women of Protection, Inc. had clustered together. Ellie and Catalina stood in a group with the silver-haired woman, a curvy black woman with short braids, a purple-haired woman in a ruffled pink dress and combat boots, and a redhead wearing casual clothing and very expensive-looking jewelry. The women who didn't know Justin were openly staring at him.

"Hi," he said, offering his hand to whoever felt like taking it.

The woman with braids introduced herself as Destiny, Fiona's teammate. The redhead introduced herself as Lucas's mate Journey, and the silver-haired woman as Nick's mate Raluca.

The purple haired woman took his hand. "Hi. I'm Grace Chang, Rafa's mate. Your hair, wow. Very retro. But you know, if you're going for a 90s grunge look, you really ought to be wearing a plaid flannel shirt and black-and-white high-top Converse sneakers. Your jeans are okay, but you need to rip them up a bit."

"A Pearl Jam T-shirt would work too," the redhead suggested.

"And your hair should be bleached, not black," Destiny said, examining it critically.

Instantly self-conscious, Justin lifted his hand to his hairline. "It's not supposed to look like this. I'll cut off the dyed part as soon as it grows out a bit more."

The women all murmured sympathetically.

Grace rummaged around in her purse, which was shaped like a Hello Kitty with safety pins through its ears, and pulled out a slip of paper. "Got it! Oh, this'll be perfect. Take it, Justin. Fiona was the maid of honor at my wedding. I'd be honored for her mate to have it."

The other women leaned over to look at the paper, muttering softly amongst themselves and blocking his view.

"What...?" Justin began.

"Excellent," said the silver-haired woman, straightening up. "Fiona deserves a mate she can be proud to take to *any* occasion."

"And you'll enjoy it, Justin," said Catalina, grinning. "It's very relaxing. Just what you need."

"But what is it?"

"A Groupon for a luxury makeover!" Destiny held it up and read aloud, "'Includes a haircut and coloring, a mani-pedi, full-face threading with shaping, eyebrow microblading, and mink eyelash extensions.' But the best part is the manscaping!"

He had no idea what any of that was other than the haircut, but it all sounded deeply alarming. "What's manscaping?"

Gleefully, Grace said, "That's when they shave off ALL your hair!"

"Or shave it into shapes!" said Journey.

"Like a landing strip!" said Catalina. "Which is perfect for you, right? Since you were in the Air Force..."

Ellie made a graphic gesture with an imaginary razor.

"This is a luxury spa," Raluca said reprovingly. "They will not shave your hair, Justin. They will use hot wax, followed by a laser."

Justin's face felt as hot as if the wax and laser had already been applied. He looked desperately around for an escape route.

And then the penny dropped. Finally.

He took the coupon from Destiny and pocketed it. Keeping his voice and expression as sincere as he could manage, he said, "Thanks, ladies. You're right, I need it. Especially the manscaping. It's like the Amazon jungle down there. Only red instead of green. Maybe for Christmas I could have the manscapers dye most of it green, and just leave some of the red as trim."

For the briefest of instants, they stared at him in very satisfactory horror. Then they burst out laughing.

"Are you all *quite* done?" Fiona inquired, her hands on her hips. "Has my mate run the gauntlet to your satisfaction?"

"Yeah," Ellie said, her cheeks bright pink. "Yeah, we're never doing that again."

"Did not need that image in my head," muttered Catalina.

"Just visualize it manscaped into an Air Force landing strip," Justin suggested. "With some sequins woven in to represent the runway lights."

"Stop!" She put her hands over her ears.

"You started it," he pointed out.

Shane laughed and patted Catalina's arm. "If you'd been in the PJs with him, you'd have known not to try that."

"I was with him for two weeks, and he never even cracked a smile," Catalina protested.

"That wasn't representative," Shane said. "This is what Red's really like."

His words struck Justin like a thunderbolt. He'd spent years in despair, believing that he'd lost everything he valued—most of all, himself. He'd thought that the man who'd played and joked and enjoyed life had died, and all that was left of him was a sort of living ghost. But here he was again, alive and laughing.

"Yeah," he said in wonder. "This *is* what I'm like."

Fiona put her arm around his waist and held him close. They didn't need to exchange words for him to know she'd understood what he'd meant. "Come on. I seem to recall Shane saying something about sandwiches."

As they headed for the breakroom, Fiona nudged Destiny. "You're next."

She shook her head, sending her braids flying. "Nah. I'm going to hold down the happy single slot."

"So you and Ethan aren't…?"

The briefest flash of sadness passed over Destiny's face before she snorted. "Pfft! That never-here Marine and I are just pals. Come on, I've known him for over a year now. Don't you think I'd have noticed if we were mates?"

Justin had no idea who Ethan was, but given that he and Fiona had been forced to sleep on the floor and in a bathtub to keep their hands off each other, he found it hard to imagine that mates could have been pals for a year without noticing.

Fiona shrugged non-committally, then said, "Well, there'll be someone. And whoever he is, I'm going to make him blush harder than Justin did when you explained manscaping."

"If you do, I'll make *you* blush harder than Ellie did when Justin made us all visualize his Christmas-colored junk jungle," Destiny retorted.

In the breakroom, they all sat down to eat some impressively good sandwiches. Fiona and Justin told the story of how they'd met, but ground to an awkward halt when they got to the part where they agreed to go to Venice together. Both of them glanced first at Shane and then at each other.

"That's on me," Justin said. "She wanted to tell you. I wouldn't let her."

"It's all right, Fiona," said Shane. "Red gave me the slip three times. No one's ever been able to get him to do anything till *he* decides he wants to."

"This time, *I* want to stay," Justin said, and went on with the story.

When they'd finished their account, the team immediately volunteered to help them ambush Dr. Mortenson's ambush. They worked out a solid plan for doing so, and decided to all fly out to Montana first thing the next morning.

Justin was impressed with how well Hal led them, getting everyone's input, Justin's included, while still providing strong leadership. He was equally impressed with how well everyone worked together, as smoothly and confidently as a PJ team. He loved seeing Fiona in her element, and to get the chance to once again plan out a mission with Shane. It made him feel like he was in the Air Force again, an essential part of something bigger than himself.

Shane and Fiona had both asked him to join Protection, Inc., but now that he'd actually met the team, he knew it wasn't up to them. It was Hal's call. No doubt Hal would want to observe him on this mission, see how well he performed and how he meshed with the others, and then—

"Justin?" said Hal. "How'd you like to join the team here at Protection, Inc.?"

"I'd love to," Justin said, startled. "But don't I need to try out? Or at least do a job interview?"

"You already did." Hal leaned across the table to shake his hand. "Welcome aboard."

Shane said, "Welcome home."

CHAPTER FOURTEEN
Fiona

Fiona had completely forgotten what her apartment was like until she saw Justin's expression when she unlocked the door.

"Should I take my shoes off?" he asked. She could tell he was completely serious.

She looked with new eyes at the expanse of spotless white carpet, the carefully selected pieces of minimalist furniture, and the single blue vase on a pedestal. The open kitchen had under-floor heating and granite countertops. Everything was flawlessly tasteful, absolutely perfect, and polished until it looked like no human being had ever touched it, let alone lived there.

"Don't bother," she replied as she pulled him inside, shoes and all. "I'm going to redo the carpets. In fact, if you move in, I'll redo the entire place. With input from you."

Justin looked horrified. "You don't want my input. You haven't seen the places I've lived in. The closets are so full of old sports equipment, there's hardly any room for my clothes. The kitchens have everything piled up on the counters. In my perfect home, there'd be a doggy bed in the middle of the floor."

"For you? Shouldn't that be a kitty bed?" Fiona teased.

"For the dog I've always wanted if I ever got a job that didn't involve leaving the country at a moment's notice for up to six months at a time. When I was a kid I had my heart set on a yellow Lab. But now I think I'll just go to the pound and rescue whoever needs rescuing."

"That'll be all of them. You're going to be the canine version of Catalina."

"She has three cats, right? Three dogs isn't that many. I'd just need a big backyard. But we don't need to live together. We could have separate homes and stay over a lot. I don't want to cramp your style." He waved his hand in a wide sweep, taking in everything from the white carpet to the delicate orchids to the modern art glass sculpture.

Fiona considered the ways that Justin might cramp her style if they lived together. His three dogs would shed on the furniture and leave squeaky rubber balls on the floor. Her closets would fill up with baseball bats and rock climbing shoes. Her kitchen would no longer be spotless, because unlike her, he'd actually use it, baking cupcakes for kids (and Grace, and her teammates) and cooking delicious meals for her.

That life sounded like the opposite of cramped. If anything, he'd free her style.

"If we moved into a house with a big backyard, would you mind if I kept a couple rooms that the dogs aren't allowed into?" she asked.

"Of course not." His smile told her that he hadn't really wanted to live separately. "Your glass jellyfish will have a safe home."

With dignity, she replied, "For your information, that is not a jellyfish. It's an abstract sculpture called Polychrome Anguish Twelve."

"Treat yourself to Polychrome Anguish One through Eleven, then. I'll keep the dogs out."

"You're on," she said. "You know, when I was a little girl, I wanted a dog too. But we never lived in an apartment where the landlord would allow them."

"Me neither. Was there a particular one you wanted?"

"A Siberian husky. They have beautiful eyes."

"They do. Almost as pretty as yours." He touched her cheek, sending a pleasant shiver through her body.

Just then, her phone buzzed with a text message. Much as she'd have liked to ignore it, very few people had that number and a message from any of them was likely to be urgent.

"Hang on," she said. "I have to check this."

The text read, *Hey Annie its yr old friend Julie. I have boyfriend news! Call me NOW for all the dirty dirty details.*

She groaned. "Great timing."

"What is it?"

Fiona turned the phone to show him the text. "It's Elson. He's got something urgent to tell me. The 'dirty dirty details' is in case you see the text, to give me an excuse to talk privately."

"Do you think you should call him?"

"Yeah, I'd better. I'm still hoping to get enough evidence to throw him in jail. If I drop off the map, he might send goons to see if I took his money and ran."

She closed her eyes, putting on her spy persona, then made the call.

For the first time in her experience, Elson sounded worried. "Are you alone?"

"Yes. We can talk now."

"Oh, good." He sounded relieved. "Where are you?"

"Santa Martina."

"Perfect. I've got a friend there who you need to meet."

Fiona let her real wariness come through as she asked, "What's going on?"

"I've found some information about your boyfriend. I'm sorry to say that he's bad news. It's time to end the relationship. You need to meet my friend right now. He can tell you how to break up safely."

Fiona thought fast, then said, "All right. Give me his address."

Elson gave it to her, then hung up.

She turned to Justin. "Well, this is a complication."

"What is it?"

"I have to murder you."

He stared at her, then let out an incredulous laugh. "Seriously?"

"Seriously. It looks like Elson found out who you are and thinks you're too hot to handle. He wants me to come pick up the murder weapon. Poison, I assume."

"Wow. That *is* a complication. What do you want to do about it? How can I help?"

A warm rush of love suffused Fiona for his trust in her abilities, willingness to let her make her own decisions, and steadfast determination to stand by her side.

"Elson threatened to have you murdered before, and I can testify to that," she said. "But if he actually orders me to do it and hands me a murder weapon, that'll make a much stronger case against him. And if I don't do it tonight, I'll miss my chance. Who knows how long we'll be in Montana, or where we'll go after that. If I stall Elson for days, he'll figure I'm getting cold feet. Or worse. So I'd better go collect the poison."

"And…?"

"And then I turn in the murder weapon and everything I've learned so far to the FBI," she said with a shrug. "I wanted to get more on him, but hopefully this will be good enough. Since I'm not actually planning to put cyanide in your coffee, that's the end of this mission."

Justin smiled. "Good plan. But I meant, 'And how do you want me to guard you?' I assume I'll have to watch from a distance, but can I listen in? Will you wear a wire?"

She shook her head. "I can't risk it. Elson had me searched every time I met with him. He does it to everyone who gets near him. Vision only."

Fiona texted Hal to let him know what had happened and pass on the address.

He responded, *Do you need backup?*

I have backup, she replied. Justin, leaning over her shoulder, added a snow leopard emoji.

They drove to the meeting point with Justin crouched out of sight in the passenger well. It was in an industrial part of town that was eerie and deserted at night. She parked in the shadows behind an abandoned building whose roof would have a good view into her meeting place, then got out and walked to the warehouse where the meeting would take place.

Fiona didn't expect anything to go wrong, but it felt good to have Justin watching her back. She'd had backup on undercover missions before, of course, and if he hadn't been there, she'd have called in one of her teammates. But this was the first time that she'd truly felt that she wasn't alone.

She rapped on the warehouse door.

"Come in," a man's voice called.

Fiona stepped inside. The warehouse was dimly lit and cluttered with old industrial equipment, but she immediately spotted the man who had spoken to her.

"Hands out," he said. "I need to pat you down. Are you armed?"

"I have a pistol in a thigh holster," she replied.

"I'll have to unload that. Just procedure."

"No problem." Fiona had expected that. Elson's guards always did the same thing when she visited him.

The man unloaded her pistol and returned it to her, then gave her a thorough but professional patdown, checking closely for wires. Then he offered her a tiny plastic bag of white powder.

"It's tasteless and odorless, and dissolves in hot liquid." He smiled unpleasantly. "It'll give you a great night's sleep."

Fiona pocketed it. "Thanks. I'll let Mr. Elson know how it works. It might be a couple days before I get a chance to try it."

"That's fine."

She turned around and started for the door. And then froze at the unmistakable clicks of guns being cocked.

Brilliant white light flooded the warehouse. As she blinked, dazzled, ten men stepped out from behind the machinery, all aiming guns at her head. They were followed by a middle-aged woman in a white doctor's coat.

"What...?" Fiona began, shocked and baffled. "Who...?"

The most sadistic smile Fiona had seen in her entire life spread across the woman's face. She turned to the windows and held up a big paper sign. It read:

SUBJECT SEVEN
COME IN UNARMED
OR SHE DIES

Despite the guns aimed at her, Fiona didn't think twice. She lunged at the woman. A tiny pain like a needle prick stung her back. Her legs went numb, and she pitched to the floor. Fiona struggled frantically to get up, but she couldn't move her legs at all. All she could do was prop herself up on her elbows.

The man who'd given her the packet of white powder—probably cake flour, she thought bitterly—bent over her. Fiona lashed out with a ridge-hand strike that Shane had taught her, breaking his nose. She had one second of satisfaction before she was dogpiled by more of the guards. They wrestled her into submission, confiscated her empty pistol, and cuffed her hands behind her back.

Furious and frightened—more for Justin than for herself—she shouted at the top of her lungs, "JUSTIN! GET OUT OF HERE!"

Her effort left her ears ringing and her throat raw. But even as she'd yelled, she knew it was in vain. He'd never leave her.

The woman in the doctor's coat said, "It doesn't actually matter if Subject Seven comes in or not. We've staked out the building where he's hiding, so we'll get him either way. This is just my little experiment to determine the answers to two questions. One, does he care what happens to you? And two, does he care enough to sacrifice himself?"

"You have got to be Dr. Mortenson," Fiona said. Since the sadistic doctor obviously liked to show off how smart she was, she went on, "How in the world did you find us?"

"Mr. Elson told us," Dr. Mortenson explained. "He did some independent research, figured out who Seven was, and decided that he wouldn't make a trustworthy employee. So he contacted us and suggested a mutually beneficial deal: he turns over Seven to us, and we take him off the market and pay Mr. Elson for the privilege. Once we compared notes, it became obvious that you were more than just a spy. So we raised our offer, and got two for the price of… well, for the price of two, actually. But I think you're worth it."

"I don't know what you think I am…" Fiona began.

"You're a shifter." Smugly, the doctor went on, "I can tell by your response to the tranquilizer dart. One dose anesthetizes humans, but partially paralyzes shifters. It takes two darts to knock a shifter unconscious. But what will be really fascinating will be to see if—"

The door was kicked open.

"No!" Fiona screamed. "Justin, run!"

Justin stepped in, his hands raised above his head. His face was pale, his mouth set. But he'd come for her anyway, as she'd known he would.

"Subject Seven," said Dr. Mortenson. "Welcome home."

She gave a slight jerk of her head. A guard stepped into the doorway from outside, and squeezed the trigger of his dart gun.

Justin spun around and lunged for the man with the gun. He managed one step forward before he staggered, then crumpled to the floor.

"I thought so." Dr. Mortenson's voice practically oozed satisfaction. "It was impossible to know if it would work till I put it to the test, but our new formula was specially designed to overcome Subject Seven's resistance to tranquilizing agents."

Fiona wanted to murder her. She was talking about Justin like he was a lab rat.

Justin braced his palms on the floor and addressed Dr. Mortenson. "If you let her go, I'll cooperate with whatever you want from me. She's just a regular shifter, nothing special. You don't need her."

Dr. Mortenson made a "tch-tch" sound. "That's *why* I need her. You're right, she's nothing special. So the only reason I have to keep her alive is for leverage over you. Misbehave, and she dies. Or worse."

Justin's pale face flushed red. He struggled frantically, and with a grunt of effort, managed to force himself up to his hands and knees.

"As I hypothesized. His resistance is still slightly greater than that of an ordinary shifter. I expect he'll regain consciousness sooner, too." The doctor snapped her fingers. "Give him another dose."

The man with the dart gun fired again.

"No!" Justin yelled. "No! I'll kill—"

His eyes closed. He slumped down and lay still.

Fiona let her own head rest on the cold concrete floor, cursing herself. She shouldn't have let Justin come with her. She should have told Hal she wanted more backup—but with that big of an ambush, wouldn't whoever he'd sent just have gotten captured too? In that case, she shouldn't have come at all.

With an effort so hard that it felt tangible, Fiona pulled herself together. Blaming herself was a waste of time and a distraction from what needed to be done. She'd gotten out of bad situations before. She just needed to stay calm and keep her wits about her.

"Knock her out too," said Dr. Mortenson. "I don't want any trouble on the plane."

A sharp pain jabbed into Fiona's back. Just before the darkness took her, she thought, *We did want to know where the Apex base is. I guess we're about to find out.*

CHAPTER FIFTEEN
Fiona

Fiona woke up sitting in a chair. She opened her eyes with a gasp.

She was in a sterile white room. Her hands were cuffed behind her back and her ankles were cuffed to the chair, both with metal shackles to prevent her from shifting, and the chair was bolted to the floor. Apex was taking no chances.

Justin was also cuffed to a chair. He looked alert enough that he'd probably been awake for longer. Dr. Mortenson sat behind a heavy steel desk with a computer. Four guards, two armed with tranquilizer rifles and two with real guns, stood off to the side.

My team—our *team*—*will track us down*, Fiona told herself. *When we turn up missing, they'll know where we disappeared from and who was probably involved, and they'll find us. That's how we found Shane when Apex kidnapped him.*

But the comparison to Shane was less reassuring than she'd intended. It had taken them a long time to track him down, and in the meantime both he and Catalina had nearly died.

"Welcome back to the world of the waking," the doctor said. "We've been waiting for you, haven't we, Subject Seven?"

The glee in her voice made Fiona's skin crawl. Justin didn't reply, but his fists clenched.

"Remember how I said you were my leverage over Seven?" Dr. Mortenson went on. "I'm going to test that right now. We spent a lot of time, money, and effort on him, and we were very disappointed when he ran away. We want to make sure that will never happen again."

"It won't," Justin said.

He sounded scared. Fiona didn't blame him one bit. The contents of the room sent a chill down her spine: metal tables with straps, medical-looking devices and machines she couldn't identify, and—most horrifying of all—a wooden chair with a tangle of electrical wires attached to it.

An electric chair, she thought. *But not for executions. It's to hurt prisoners until they* wish *it would kill them.*

But Justin's eyes slid over the electric chair with barely a flinch. Instead, his gaze was captured by a metal table near an industrial sink with a bucket and a cloth sitting ready. Fiona didn't understand why that, of all things, was what frightened him. It was the most innocent-looking thing in the entire room. Then she remembered how Dr. Mortenson had waterboarded him until he could hardly stand to have a sheet of damp paper put over his face, and she felt physically ill.

Trying to keep her voice calm, she said, "Justin, remember that promise you made not to use your invincibility? Forget it. If she tries to torture you, do it so you can't feel pain."

"A reasonable plan," said Dr. Mortenson. "However, it won't work. Seven, tell her why not."

Justin let out a long, shaky sigh. "It turns off automatically if I pass out. I need a minute or two to concentrate to turn it back on, and I can't do it if I'm too stressed. Tranquilizers don't work on me—I mean, back then they didn't—so if they wanted me to stop being invincible and I wasn't cooperating, they had to cut off my oxygen." He jerked his head at the table by the sink. "That's how that got started."

"And, of course, your friend Subject Ten—" Dr. Mortenson indicated Fiona. "—can also feel pain."

"Don't hurt her!" Justin sounded frantic. "I told you, I'll cooperate."

"I'm going to need some proof of that," replied the doctor.

Dr. Mortenson snapped her fingers at the guards. The ones with real guns leveled theirs at Fiona, and the ones with tranquilizer guns aimed theirs at Justin.

"Remember, she's expendable," warned the doctor. Then she walked to his chair and unlocked his bonds. She indicated the table by the sink. "Go lie down on that."

Justin went white. "I'll do it…"

"No!" Fiona burst out. "Don't do this for me!"

He ignored her, his gaze fixed on Dr. Mortenson. "On two conditions. One. Take her away. I don't want her to see it. Two. Put me in with her afterward, so I know she's all right."

"Agreed," said the doctor.

Justin stood up.

"Justin, no!" Fiona shouted. Then, realizing she could never persuade him, she too turned to Dr. Mortenson. "Torture me instead. I won't fight either."

"Hmm. What would I gain by that?"

"New data," Fiona suggested. "I've never had it done before. My reactions might be more interesting than his."

"This isn't about science," Justin said to Dr. Mortenson. "You just want to punish me for running away. Fine. Do it. Just leave her out of it."

He walked to the table and lay down on it.

"No!" Fiona yelled, frantic. "Do it to me instead!"

"Get her out of here," Justin said quietly. "Now."

Dr. Mortenson was clearly enjoying the entire scene. With a dramatic sigh, she said, "Oh, all right. Just remember, Seven, how long the deal lasts is entirely up to you."

"I know." He reached out and pulled the straps across his own chest.

Inside Fiona's head, her snow leopard let out a long, wordless shriek of pure rage.

A scarlet haze came across Fiona's eyes. Though she knew it was useless, she threw herself against her bonds, intent on killing the doctor before she could hurt her mate.

"I'll go harder on him if you don't stop fighting," Dr. Mortenson said sharply. "Every minute you struggle is an extra minute he'll spend in here."

Fiona went limp. She let the guards unlock her from the chair and escort her out. The electronic door slid shut behind them.

Rip out her throat, hissed her snow leopard.

I will, Fiona vowed.

As the guards escorted her along a corridor and then locked her into a small room with two cots, she tried not to imagine what was happening to Justin. What he was willingly suffering to protect her. She couldn't bear to think about it, but she could think of nothing else.

It felt like an eternity before the door opened. Two guards supported Justin between them. His eyes were open but his head hung down and his feet dragged on the floor. When Fiona reached out for him, four more guards leveled their tranquilizer rifles at her.

"I'm not going to attack you." She tried to keep her voice calm, even though she felt anything but. "Just let me have him, all right?"

"You better not try anything," a guard warned her. "No sudden movements."

Moving slowly, Fiona put Justin's arm over her shoulder and her arm around his waist. He couldn't seem to support his own weight at all. As she laid him down on one of the cots, the guards backed out. The door shut behind them.

She knelt on the floor beside the cot. His hair was dripping wet, his face was ashen, and he was shaking like a leaf in a high wind. When she touched his cheek, his skin felt cold. She pulled the blanket over him, then fetched the blanket from the other cot and draped that over him too. Finally, she pushed the narrow cots together so she could lie in the other one and hold him.

"You shouldn't have done it," she said. "It should've been me."

His voice was so soft that even lying with her arms around him, she had to strain to hear. "I couldn't let her hurt you. You know that. Besides, I had to finish the demonstration."

Fiona wondered if he was delirious. Nervously, she said, "What demonstration?"

"That I'm too scared and weak and broken-down to risk making a break for it."

Relieved that he was making sense, she asked, "What's your plan? Jump her the next time she hauls us into the lab?"

He shook his head. "Jump the guards the next time they come in. It'll be the last thing anyone will expect."

Doubtfully, she said, "Can you?"

"I think so. They don't have clocks here to keep us disoriented, but one of the guards dragging me was wearing a watch. I sneaked a look at it. It's 1:00 AM. They'll shove some breakfast in around 9:00. That gives me eight hours to recover."

Fiona didn't want to throw cold water on his plans, but there was a very obvious problem with it. "You really think the two of us can take out six guards without either of us getting nailed by a dart?"

"No." Then, to her amazement, he smiled. "But I think I can take out six guards by myself if it doesn't matter if I get hit."

"But—"

"The darts don't affect me."

"They don't?"

"When you got ambushed at the warehouse, I couldn't rescue you and I couldn't go for help. My only chance was to get myself taken along with you. I didn't have a plan for getting free afterward until they shot me with a dart. They know tranquilizers don't work on me, so they'd only do that if they thought they had one that did. And I know how they usually work. So I faked it."

"Wow." For the first time since they'd been captured, Fiona felt hopeful. Admiringly, she said, "You're sneaky."

"Thanks. I learned it from you. Seriously. I remembered what I'd seen you do, and I tried to do it like that. Though I couldn't figure out how to cry on cue. How do you do that?"

"Do you ever cry at movies?"

"Never," he declared. "Well… *The Shawshank Redemption* gets me a bit misty-eyed if I'm watching it alone."

Fiona translated this from guy-ese as *Never come home unexpectedly when I'm watching it because you'll catch me crying like a baby.*

Trying not to laugh, she said, "If you ever want to cry, picture the most moving scene in it and say the dialogue to yourself. Are there any lines you remember?"

"Sure. 'Remember, Red, hope is a good thing, maybe the best of things, and no good thing ever dies.'" Justin's eyes welled up as he quoted the line.

Fiona had forgotten that he shared a nickname with one of the characters. That must have felt as if those words had been spoken directly to him. *Hope never dies.* No wonder that got to him.

"Whoa. It works." He wiped his eyes. "What's yours?"

"*The Lion King*. When Simba's father dies." She was relieved when he didn't point out the parallel with her life, but merely squeezed her hand, letting her know he understood without making her talk about it.

His eyes fluttered shut, and it was a moment before he opened them again. He'd stopped trembling and his skin felt warmer, but Fiona could tell he was still exhausted and shaken.

She kissed his cheek. "Go to sleep. You'll need your shifter healing. You've got a big day ahead of you."

Justin nodded and closed his eyes. He seemed to drop off immediately, but Fiona stayed awake longer.

Once in her life, she'd had everything and still wanted more. More designer clothes, more expensive trips, more nights out on the town. She'd gotten everything she'd longed for when she'd been a teenager in the group home, living on hand-me-downs and store-brand cereal with powdered milk. But it hadn't made her happy. The more she had, the emptier she'd felt.

Now, as she held Justin close, she no longer felt empty, but she wanted something more desperately than she'd ever wanted anything before.

I want Justin to get out of here safely and never have to worry about Apex again, she thought. *I want him to get his house with the big backyard and the three dogs. And me. I want him to get the happily ever after he deserves.*

She hoped she wasn't tempting fate.

CHAPTER SIXTEEN
Justin

Justin lay on the cot, eyes closed, waiting for the guards to enter the cell. He'd slept deeply and felt much stronger, but his heart was beating rapidly. Once the guards found out he was still immune to their tranquilizers, they'd never use them on him again. He'd only get this one shot.

The loud click of the door opening almost made him start, but he made himself lie still. He heard footsteps coming in.

"Hey, Justin, they brought food..." Fiona said, shaking him lightly. "Justin?"

She shook him harder. He let himself flop limply.

"Justin?" Her voice was sharp with alarm. "He's not breathing!"

More footsteps, hurrying. Fiona exclaimed, "Hey!"

That was the signal: all the guards were inside.

As a male hand came roughly down on his throat, feeling for a pulse, Justin shifted. His big paws lashed out at the guards bending over him, sending them flying into the walls. Out of the corner of his eye, he saw Fiona whip around to punch the nearest guard in the jaw just as he reached for his walkie-talkie, then snatch his ID. He lunged to put his body between her and the guards as she whirled to close the door.

A sharp pain stung Justin's side, then his neck. He ignored it and pounced on the guard who was firing at him, slamming him into the floor. The man's head bounced off the concrete, and he lay still.

Justin looked up. Fiona had grabbed a tranquilizer rifle and was methodically firing darts at all the downed guards, making sure they were out for the count. The first guard he had attacked, who had just staggered to his feet, dropped down again and lay still.

There was silence in the cell. All the guards lay unconscious on the floor.

Justin shifted back. He took a quick look at Fiona to make sure she was unharmed, and plucked two darts out of his body. Then he dressed in the uniform and shoes of the guard who was closest in size to him, and took the guard's ID and tranquilizer rifle. Fiona did the same.

"You were great," Justin said.

"You too."

They exchanged a quick kiss, then opened the door a crack. The corridor was empty. They stepped out and used an ID to close and lock the door, then set out. When they turned the corner, they nearly ran into four guards who were just exiting a room. Justin's pulse thundered in his ears, but Fiona nodded pleasantly at them. The guards nodded back. One of them locked the door behind him, and then they headed off in the opposite direction. Justin was immensely relieved.

The door the guards had just locked bore a small plaque that read SUBJECT NINE.

"That's right," Justin muttered. "Shane was Subject Eight, and Dr. Mortenson called you Subject Ten. They've got someone imprisoned here. We need to let them out."

"Let's go in," said Fiona. "I don't want to try to explain everything standing in the corridor."

Justin used his ID card to unlock the cell, and they slipped inside and locked the door behind them.

A man was sitting on the floor with his knees up and his face buried in his arms. An untouched meal tray was on the floor beside him. He must have heard them come in, but he didn't move a muscle.

Justin's heart went out to him. How many hours had he spent at Apex in that exact position? He crouched down in front of the prisoner, out of easy striking reach in case the man lashed out in panic or rage. Speaking softly and gently, he said, "Hey. We're not with Apex. We're prisoners who just escaped. And we want to take you with us."

The man's head jerked up. He looked at Justin, startled and suspicious.

"*You!*" Fiona's exclamation was filled with shock and fury.

Justin scrambled to his feet. The prisoner was staring at Fiona like he'd seen a ghost, and she looked ready to kill him.

"Who is he?" Justin asked.

"Carter Howe," Fiona spat out. "The man who bit me and left me to die in the cold."

Red rage engulfed Justin. He moved faster than thought, yanking the prisoner to his feet and punching him in the face. Carter staggered back against the wall, bleeding from a cut lip. Justin drew back his fist to hit him again...

...and only then realized that the man wasn't trying to fight back. He wasn't even defending himself. He stood still, arms at his sides and hands open.

Justin stopped, angry and frustrated. "Put up your fists!"

For the first time, Carter spoke. But it wasn't to Justin. His gaze was fixed on Fiona. "I'm sorry for what I did to you. It was wrong."

"Sorry doesn't cut it!" she snapped.

"I know. Go ahead and kill me. I deserve it. And I don't care." Carter tilted his head back, exposing his throat.

Justin glanced at Fiona. She looked as unsettled as he felt. He took her hand as they both backed away from the man.

"What do you want to do with him?" Justin asked her.

"I *was* going to help you beat the living daylights out of him," she replied. "But now I'm not so sure. Unless this is some kind of trick."

"I don't think so." Justin recognized the prisoner's blank, bleak gaze; he'd seen it in the mirror. To Carter, he said, "How long have you been here?"

"I don't know."

"Supposedly his plane went down over the Pacific," Fiona said. "If that's when they took him, it'd be over a year."

Carter looked neither surprised nor unsurprised. He seemed lost in his own private hell.

"Serves you right!" Justin burst out. "You bit Fiona against her will. You left her to freeze to death!"

"No." Once again, Carter spoke to Fiona rather than to Justin. "I bit you, yes. But I didn't leave you to die. I was watching out of sight to make sure you didn't freeze or fall off a cliff. When I saw you shift, I left. I thought you'd spend a night on the mountain regretting all your life choices and deciding to turn over a new leaf, then walk back to civilization."

"That's not what happened," she said.

"I know," Carter replied. "I eventually heard through the shifter grapevine that some grizzly bear shifter had gone to that mountain and rescued a woman who'd been stuck as a snow leopard. I realized it had to be you. I swear, I'd had no idea you were still there. I hadn't known getting trapped like that was even possible."

"That's not an excuse," Justin said furiously. "You're the one who bit her! Everything that happened because of that was your fault."

For the first time, Carter spoke to Justin. "I know. Believe me, I know."

"Why did you do it?" Fiona asked. "And don't you dare say you were in love with me. I know you weren't."

"No, I wasn't," Carter replied. "But I liked you a lot. When I found out that you didn't care about me at all—that you were just using me—I felt betrayed. I was angry and I wanted to teach you a lesson. Well, I'm the one who got taught. I put an animal into you against your will. Want to hear about some poetic justice? Apex did the same thing to me."

"Apex made you a shifter before you even met me?" she asked.

"No, no. I was born with my leopard. Apex took him away. He's gone." The bleak look in his eyes deepened. "And they put something else in."

"They did?" Justin said, baffled. He'd had no idea that was possible. "What is it?"

"A... a *thing*. I don't even know what to call it." Carter shuddered. "Never mind. Go on, take your revenge. I won't put up a fight."

Justin looked at Fiona. Carter had wronged her; what to do with him was her call.

She folded her arms across her chest. "Talk is cheap. But action means something. If you really want to make it up to me, you can tell us everything you know about this base and how to get out of it. You must've picked up *something* in a year. We don't even know where we are."

"Alaska. The base is northeast of Fairbanks." Carter gave them directions to the airstrip, then added, "Are you just trying to escape, or are you trying to blow up the base?"

"I wish I could, but it's not like I brought explosives with me," Fiona said.

"You don't need them. The base has a self-destruct mechanism. They do evacuation drills—that's how I know where the airstrip is. You could probably set off the self-destruct command from the computer in Dr. Mortenson's lab." Carter flinched as he said her name, making Justin unwillingly sympathize with him. "If you're willing to risk it."

"We are." Justin and Fiona spoke simultaneously, then grinned at each other.

She gave him directions to their cell, then tossed him an ID badge. "We drugged the guards and locked them inside. Take a uniform and a tranquilizer rifle, then steal a vehicle and get out of here."

Carter caught the ID automatically, then stood staring at her. "You're letting me go?"

"I'm hardly going to trap you here while we blow up the place. Look, I wasn't the nicest person to you either. So this is how I'm making it up to you. And now that I know what this place can do to you…" Fiona shrugged. "To be honest, I think you've been punished enough."

Justin had been thinking along the same lines. In fact, he was tempted to say more. But Carter had harmed Fiona; Justin had no right to offer to help the man.

She seemed to know what he'd been thinking, though, because she said, "Justin, if there's anything you want to tell him, it's fine with me. But only if you want to."

"I don't *want* to. What I *want* is to kill this guy for what he did to you. But yeah, I think it's the right thing to do." Justin turned to Carter, who had been listening with visible bewilderment. "You're not the only one who's been hurt by Apex. It doesn't have to be the end of your life. You can get through it. I promise. And if you ever need to hear me say that again, you can call me at Protection, Inc. in Santa Martina."

For the first time, some life came into Carter's eyes. "Thanks."

He opened the door and went out. It clicked shut behind him, leaving Justin and Fiona alone.

"I can't believe I offered to let that guy cry on my shoulder," Justin muttered. "Ever since you told me about him, I've wanted to toss him out a plane without a parachute. I kind of still do."

"I've wanted to get revenge on him for much longer than that," Fiona said. "But seeing him here now, like that… I'm not sure if I forgive him. But I'm not angry anymore."

There was a peace in her grass-green eyes that he hadn't seen before. If it took meeting her old enemy again to put it there, then he was glad she'd gotten the chance.

"On to the lab?" she asked.

He nodded. "Wish I'd managed to get an imprint off Dr. Mortenson. She was too careful, though. Maybe if you'd given me crying lessons earlier, I could've lured her in closer."

She chuckled.

They slipped out of the cell and headed for the lab. Justin hoped the doctor would be there. *He* wasn't going to come to any kind of understanding with his enemy. He just wanted to make sure she didn't escape.

Fiona stood back when he opened the door, in case any dart-wielding guards were inside. But the lab was dark and empty. He beckoned her forward as he flipped on the lights.

A harsh white glare illuminated the electric chair with its tangle of wires. The steel tables with their straps to hold him down. The industrial sink. The cloth for his face. The bucket of water.

Water filling his lungs. Pain knifing through his chest. His snow leopard shrieking in terror and agony. He was drowning on dry land, helpless, dying—

"Justin."

Fiona's voice and touch brought him back to reality. Her warm arm was around his shoulders, steadying him.

He forced himself to step into the lab and close the door behind him. "I'm all right."

And he was. He hated being in the lab with the torture equipment and the memories, but he could stand it. Apex had hurt him, but it hadn't broken him.

"Anything I can do?"

"You can help me blow this hellhole sky-high." He gave her a nudge toward the computer. "Go do your genius hacker thing."

She kissed him, then settled down behind it. He went to guard the door, taking a position where he could see the door and Fiona, but not the torture equipment. It felt like he stood there for ages, the room silent except for the hum of the electrical equipment and the tapping of her fingers on the keys.

"Got it!" Fiona exclaimed. She beckoned him over and indicated a key. "Want to do the honors?"

"I couldn't deprive you of the pleasure."

"I blew up the last base," she pointed out. "This one is all yours."

"Since you put it that way..." He hit the key.

A loud automated recording began to play. "Warning! The self-destruct sequence has been initialized. All personnel, exit the premises immediately. This is not a drill. The base will self-destruct in fifteen minutes."

"How's it feel?" Fiona asked, grinning.

"Very satisfying." He turned to take a good long look at the table and the sink and the bucket. They didn't bother him half as much now that he knew they'd be vaporized in the next fifteen minutes.

He heard running footsteps in the corridor outside, along with a lot of yelling. Justin kept an eye on the door, but no one tried to come inside. It seemed like everyone was too busy getting the hell out of there.

"Looks like there's some closed-circuit cameras," Fiona said, peering at the screen. "Here's some footage from outside our cell... The guards we knocked out are getting hauled out... Ah-ha, and here's the airstrip. It's got some snowmobiles, but no one's taking them. They're all piling into a couple of little planes."

"You see Dr. Mortenson anywhere?"

"Not yet. Let me keep looking."

The recording played again. "Warning! The self-destruct sequence has been initialized. All personnel, exit the premises immediately. This is not a drill. The base will self-destruct in fourteen minutes."

Justin heard a commotion outside the door. He moved closer to it, tranquilizer rifle at the ready. It was only because he was listening so carefully that he heard the faint hiss of an automatic door behind him. He spun around.

A hidden door had opened in the wall behind Fiona's desk. Absorbed in her work, she hadn't noticed. Dr. Mortenson stood in the doorway, her face twisted with fury and a pistol in her hand. She glanced at Justin, then, with a sadistic smile, swung the pistol toward Fiona.

He knew what that smile meant. Dr. Mortenson wasn't going to take any more hostages. He'd destroyed her life's work, and she was going to take revenge by killing the woman he valued more than his own life.

He didn't have time to shout a warning or bring his own rifle to bear. Instead, he leaped forward to shield Fiona with his own body.

The crack of a gunshot filled the air as a hard impact slammed into his side.

Like getting hit with a baseball bat, he thought. *I remember that.*

He landed in a sprawl against the wall, with a metal table and the electric chair partly on top of him. Fiona hit the wall so hard that the tranquilizer rifle she'd slung over her shoulder flew off and skidded across the floor. As she lunged for it, Justin saw Dr. Mortenson peer out from behind an overturned metal table.

"Left!" he yelled.

Fiona dove to her left just as the doctor fired. The bullet smashed into the wall, and Fiona ducked down behind the heavy steel desk. Justin shoved the table and chair off him, keeping the table on its side so he could use it as cover. He reached for his own rifle, then realized that he'd dropped it when he'd jumped. Now he and Fiona were trapped apart from each other, and only the enemy was armed. Either of them could become a snow leopard and jump the doctor, but she could shoot them before she went down.

As if to rub that in, Dr. Mortenson fired again. He heard the distinctive ricochet of a bullet bouncing off metal and saw a dent appear in the table.

The automatic recording came on, startling him. "Warning! The self-destruct sequence has been initialized. All personnel, exit the premises immediately. This is not a drill. The base will self-destruct in thirteen minutes."

While it played, he took a closer look at Fiona. To his immense relief, she hadn't been hit. But she looked worried. She pointed to him, then pressed her hand to her left side.

He glanced down. His shirt was soaked through with blood at the side. He lifted it and examined the in-and-out wounds. They were both bleeding a lot, and far enough apart that he needed both hands to cover them. He applied pressure, wincing. But he was more worried by how weak and dizzy he felt. He could lie there and fire a gun, if he had a gun. But if he tried to shift and jump the doctor, he'd probably pass out mid-leap.

Cold fear squeezed a fist around his heart as he thought, *It's happening again. I'm hit, and I can't help the people depending on me. All I'm doing is distracting Fiona when she needs to focus on protecting herself.*

This is not then, hissed his snow leopard. *This is now. What is happening* now? *What can you do* now *to protect your mate?*

Justin could see a bit through the jumble of wiring from the electric chair, and he scanned his surroundings. Papers from the desk were scattered all over. The computer was smashed. The bucket Dr. Mortenson had waterboarded him with had been overturned, and a wide puddle of water was spread across the floor.

He could see the two tranquilizer rifles, but neither was close enough to grab without getting shot. Dr. Mortenson could probably see the rifles too, which meant she knew they were both unarmed. He wondered why she hadn't just walked up and shot them already... but no, she wouldn't risk coming that close to people who could turn into snow leopards.

"Warning!" blared the recording. "The self-destruct sequence has been initialized. All personnel, exit the premises immediately. This is not a drill. The base will self-destruct in twelve minutes."

If they waited, maybe Dr. Mortenson would take off rather than risk getting blown up with her lab. But he thought she was more likely to cross her fingers that she could shoot them dead before they could jump her, and get up and come kill them. In fact, it surprised him that she hadn't come for him already. He was wounded, unable to put up much of a fight...

Ah. She must not know he'd been hit.

Justin caught Fiona's eye. He took a hand off his side and pointed to the open floor between them and the doctor: *we need to lure her out.* Then he ran his finger from the corner of his eye down his cheek, tracing a line in blood that, he hoped, would look like tears.

Fiona nodded, then said sharply, "Justin? Justin! Don't pass out! Stay with me!"

He moaned in pain, which wasn't hard, then mumbled, "It hurts."

"Just hold on." Her voice had the forced calm of a woman on the verge of panic. "We can wait her out."

With perfect timing, the announcement played again. "Warning! The self-destruct sequence has been initialized. All personnel, exit the premises immediately. This is not a drill. The base will self-destruct in eleven minutes."

Remember, Red, hope is a good thing, maybe the best of things, and no good thing ever dies, Justin thought. He let the tears fill his eyes and clog his throat, then said, "I can't stop the bleeding. I'm scared."

"I know, Justin, I know," Fiona replied. "Just try to keep pressure on it, all right? I'll be with you as soon as I can."

Justin gritted his teeth. He *was* losing a lot of blood. But there was nothing he could do about it. He had to keep both hands free to be ready for when Dr. Mortenson walked into his trap.

Fiona went on talking in her trying-to-sound-soothing-while-actually-terrified tone. Meanwhile, Justin kept careful track of the sightlines. He and Fiona were on the same side of the room and could see each other. Fiona was behind a heavy steel desk and couldn't see the opposite side of the room, where Dr. Mortenson was.

Dr. Mortenson, who was hiding behind a steel table, couldn't see anything unless she peeked out. Even then, she'd just see the table and chair and jumble of electrical wiring attached to the chair that was hiding him, not Justin himself. However, he could see Dr. Mortenson's desk and the space between her and him through a peephole-sized break in the wiring.

Justin bet Dr. Mortenson had also figured out the sightlines. If she wanted to go kill him without getting jumped by Fiona, she'd have to wait till Justin wasn't looking, then move silently so Fiona didn't hear her.

He pointed sharply at Fiona: *Now.*

"Justin!" she cried out. "Wake up! Wake up, Justin! Justin!"

Fascinated, he watched Dr. Mortenson stand up, look straight at him, and smile that fucking sadistic smile of hers. When she stepped out from behind the table, he saw that she'd taken off her shoes. Her bare feet moved silently across the floor as she approached him.

Fiona was still calling to him, her voice increasingly frantic.

Dr. Mortenson glanced down at the wide puddle of water from the overturned waterboarding bucket that covered the floor between her and Justin. She stepped into it, very carefully so as not to make a splash.

Justin lunged out with a wire from the electric chair in his hand. He stuck the broken end into the puddle, and with his other hand, he flipped the switch.

A loud crackle sounded, and a white arc of electricity leaped up. Dr. Mortenson let out a long, piercing shriek of agony, then pitched forward. She lay still, her face in the water. A wisp of smoke rose up from her clothes.

"Warning! The self-destruct sequence has been initialized. All personnel, exit the premises immediately. This is not a drill. The base will self-destruct in ten minutes."

Justin turned off the switch and let go of the wire. He knew that they had to get out of there, and he told himself to get up. Instead, he found himself sagging against the overturned chair with black spots dancing before his eyes.

Fiona jumped up, but rather than run to him, she bolted for the medicine cabinets. He watched in a daze as she yanked out an entire drawer full of bandages and brought it to him. He fished out a pair of pressure bandages and applied them. To his relief, the bleeding stopped.

"Anything else you should do?" she asked.

Stay warm, lie down with my feet elevated, and start an IV, he thought. *Then medevac immediately.*

"Warning! The self-destruct sequence has been initialized. All personnel, exit the premises immediately. This is not a drill. The base will self-destruct in nine minutes."

"Yeah," he said. "Get the hell out of here."

"I can carry you," she offered.

He knew she was strong enough. But it would slow her down—maybe enough to get them both killed. "Just help me up. We'll see how fast I can go."

She wrapped her arm around his waist, he put his arm around her shoulders, and they stood up together. He was relieved to find that with her support, they could get down the empty corridors in an awkward, shambling run.

I'd be faster if I was invincible, he thought. *I wouldn't need her help at all.*

His snow leopard gave a warning growl.

But Justin wasn't seriously tempted. He could still move, and that was good enough. If he was invincible, he wouldn't notice if he started bleeding again. Worst of all, he wouldn't love Fiona.

If I don't make it, I want to die loving her, he thought.

She kicked open a door, and they stepped out into icy air and a field of white stretching out in all directions. Snow fell lightly from a gray-white sky. It took him a moment to realize that they were on the airstrip; the planes were gone. There were no cars, which made sense because there didn't seem to be any roads. Several weird-looking little vehicles like motorized sleds were parked under an overhang.

"Great," Fiona said with a distinct lack of enthusiasm. "There's the snowmobiles."

So that was what they were. Justin had heard of them, but never seen one before. "Do you know how to drive them?"

"Warning! The self-destruct sequence has been initialized. All personnel, exit the premises immediately. This is not a drill. The base will self-destruct in four minutes."

"Yeah." Fiona was already heading for the nearest one. "Destiny taught me. I'm just not big on snow-related stuff, that's all. Hop on."

She helped him on, then climbed on herself. "Hold tight."

He wrapped his arms around her, pressing his chest against her back. The key had been left in the ignition. She started it up, and began to skim across the snow. He was startled by how fast it went. From the looks of it, he'd expected something like a golf cart, and had been wondering if it would be better to run. But it was fast as a car. He relaxed. They were in no danger of being caught in the blast.

He counted off the seconds in his mind, and when he got to three and a half minutes, he nudged her. "Stop. I want to see it blow up."

She turned the snowmobile around, then brought it to a halt. The base loomed in the distance. A second later, it blew up with an earsplitting crack and rumble, followed by the slight push of the shockwave. Debris shot up into the sky, then fell down. And then there was nothing left but a heap of rubble.

It was over. Dr. Mortenson was dead. Apex was gone. Justin had finally accomplished what he'd sworn to do, all those years ago. But when he'd imagined it then, he'd always thought he'd die doing it. Then there would be no more pain, no more guilt, and no more trying. He'd be done with it all. He'd figured it would be a relief.

Justin's blood-soaked shirt was starting to freeze in the icy air. His side hurt so badly, it was making him break out in a cold sweat, and then *that* froze on his skin. Just sitting upright was unpleasant and difficult. If he'd known they'd had minutes to spare, he'd have given himself a shot of morphine and taken the equipment to start an IV line. He longed to lie down the way a man lost in a desert longs for water, and they hadn't even started their journey yet.

But Fiona's body was warm against his, and he no longer wanted to be done with anything. He had a team and friends to return to, and a mate to build a life with. He had dogs to adopt.

He must have said some of that out loud, because she said, "We'll go to the shelter as soon as you're better. I want to help pick them out."

"Of course. They're your dogs too. I hope they're not too much of a shock, after your robots. I hate to break it to you, but real dogs slobber."

"Everything's a tradeoff," she said with a shrug. "Robot dogs don't love you back."

"Yours might. Maybe that's why they haven't taken over the world yet."

"They're probably just biding their time."

Fiona bent over the snowmobile and programmed the GPS for Fairbanks, Alaska. She twisted around to kiss him, her lips warm on his chilled skin, and then they set out into the wilderness.

CHAPTER SEVENTEEN
Fiona

Fiona had never imagined she'd be so glad that Destiny had dragged her on that miserable ski trip where she'd learned to drive a snowmobile. Even if Justin had known how, doing so in his condition would have been hellish at best and impossible at worst. It had no power steering, so turning it meant physically wrestling it around by the handlebars, and on the rough terrain they were traveling on, she kept having to stand up and lean to one side to keep it from tipping over. Even with her shifter strength, it was tiring.

Justin hung grimly on, silent and stoic. At first she'd tried to talk to keep his spirits up, but the icy wind whipped the words from her mouth, and his efforts to shout replies were obviously wearing him out even more. Now she just followed the GPS and drove, weaving around trees and boulders. A couple more hours, and they'd reach Fairbanks. Justin would never agree to go to a hospital, but they could hole up in a motel where he could warm up and lie down, and she could call her team to fly in Dr. Bedford, the shifter doctor who'd treated some of her teammates before.

The snowmobile slammed into what felt like a brick wall. Fiona was flung forward. She automatically tucked and rolled, tumbling head over heels until she came to rest in a snowbank.

Jolted but unhurt, she leaped to her feet. "Justin!"

He lay nearby. At her words, he struggled to a sitting position. He didn't seem to have any new injuries, but his arm was pressed to his wounded side and he was obviously in pain. "I'm all right. You?"

"I'm fine."

She helped him up and they trudged through thigh-deep snow to the snowmobile. It had hit a big rock buried under the snow, then flipped over and slammed into a tree. The frame was askew, one of the skis was bent, and gasoline was streaming out from the engine. Even if Fiona had all her tools with her, she'd have written it off as totaled.

"Goddammit!" she burst out as she spotted the shattered pieces of the GPS.

"We don't need it," Justin assured her. "I can find the way."

She gave him a dubious glance. "Your power only finds people. Do you know anyone in Fairbanks?"

"No," he admitted. "But it's southwest of here. And so is Santa Martina. Hundreds of miles past Fairbanks, but still. If I track Shane, that should put us roughly in the right direction."

She kissed his cheek. "You're a genius."

He concentrated briefly, then pointed. "That way. How close to Fairbanks are we?"

"A couple hours. On snowmobile."

Justin frowned, undoubtedly tripling that to figure out how long their trek had to be.

"It won't be that bad," she promised him. "We'll do it as snow leopards. We'll make better time, and we'll be much warmer."

But he was shaking his head. "I can't. If I shift, it'll pull my bandages off."

She shuddered at a flash of memory. "Nick did that once. He nearly bled to death. Okay, forget it, then. We'll just walk the way we are."

"No," he replied firmly. "*You* have to shift. We're talking about a nine-hour trek in the snow. If we're both human, we'll both get hypothermic, and then we're done for. If one of us stays in reasonably good shape, then we'll have a chance."

Fiona hated the idea of being comfortable herself while he was freezing—especially when he was the one who was wounded and most needed the warmth. But she couldn't argue with his logic. No one knew where they were. If they sat down and waited to be rescued, they'd freeze to death. And she couldn't help him if she was incapacitated herself.

She pulled off her shirt and tossed it to him. "Put this on."

The cold wind knifed into her bare skin as she stripped. Justin was able to haul her shirt, which she'd taken from a male security guard, on over his. Then he wrapped her pants around his waist, tied her shoes around his neck by the laces, and stuffed her bra and panties into his pocket.

To leap and pounce…
To hunt in the snow…
To be one with the night…

The bitter cold was suddenly no more than pleasantly brisk. Justin staggered, then caught himself with his palm braced on her back. She nuzzled him, scenting both his natural scent and the sharp tang of blood, and he stroked her head.

They set off into the snow. Fiona kept a slow pace, making sure Justin could keep up. He had to stoop to lean on her, which had to be uncomfortable, but he never complained.

She tried to stay on level stretches of land, avoiding hills and valleys and rough areas, but he was the one leading the way. The terrain got rougher and rougher, covered with boulders and snowbanks and fallen trees, and the snow got deeper, going from knee-deep to thigh-deep. Her leopard's lithe form easily slipped through the snow, and her thick fur kept out the cold. But for Justin, it was like slogging through deep water. He braced himself on her with one hand and clutched his side with the other, shivering and panting, then gasping. She stopped to let him rest, nudging him to sit down.

"Go on," he said.

She didn't move, and nudged him again.

"If I sit down, I don't know if I can get up." His teeth were chattering, and his words came out in jagged bursts. "Better keep going."

Reluctantly, she went on, slower than before. The light snowfall slowed, then ended. At first she was relieved. She'd been afraid of a blizzard. But the temperature quickly began to plummet, until even she grew cold.

Justin's walking grew less and less coordinated, until he was stumbling even on level ground. His shivering changed to slow, whole-body shudders, then stopped. She knew what that meant: he'd gotten so cold that his body was starting to shut down to conserve energy. Fiona looked up, alarmed. His eyes were half-shut, his lips blue with cold, his face ashen. He tripped and didn't catch himself, falling bonelessly into the snow.

Her first thought was to shift and pick him up. But she needed to warm him up, and she could do that much better in the form she was in. So she lay down beside him, wrapping her legs around him to keep him from the icy ground and curling her body into him. In giving him her warmth, she was losing her own heat. But if she didn't, he could freeze to death.

With no way to tell time, she had no idea how long they lay there. But after a while, Justin began to shiver again, then opened his eyes.

He looked around, confused, then gave her a tired smile. "Oh. Thanks. Guess we didn't make very good time, huh?"

She shook her head.

He reached out a trembling hand to stroke her ears. "I'm so cold, my side's gone numb. No pain. Small blessings, I guess."

Fiona wasn't any kind of medic, but that didn't sound like a good sign to her.

"Yeah, I know," he said, as if she'd spoken aloud. "I don't think I can walk any more. My head's spinning. I think my only shot at getting back on my feet is to become invincible."

She nodded and flicked her paw at him: *Do it.*

Justin closed his eyes. When he opened them a minute later, they were black mirrors, uncaring and unfeeling. Though she agreed that he had to do it, seeing him like that struck a chill into her that was colder than the frigid air.

She stood up, giving him something to hang on to. He forced himself to his hands and knees, then put both his hand on her back and levered himself up.

As soon as he stood upright, he collapsed again. Fiona pawed him on to his back. His eyes were closed, but her leopard's hearing picked up the sound of his breathing.

A moment later, his eyes fluttered open. The cold hard stare was gone, and the man she loved was back.

Dreamily, he said, "Orthostatic hypotension. Hypothermia. Hypovolemic shock. Elevate feet, keep warm, give warmed fluids by mouth or IV, medevac immediately."

Alarmed, Fiona gave him a hard nudge with her head.

Justin blinked and seemed to force himself to focus. "Sorry. Thought I was back in medic training for a second. Let me translate. My blood pressure's dropped so low that I'll black out if I stand up, invincible or not. You were right. Invincibility really isn't good for much after all."

She nuzzled him: *It's all right.*

He pulled in a deep breath, and looked at her with so much love and resignation that she felt her heart shatter like ice. "Fiona… I'm not going to make it. There's no point in both of us dying. You need to leave me."

Anger flared up in her until her face felt hot enough to melt the snow. She was yelling almost before she finished shifting. "You actually think I'd leave you to die? If you give up now, *you're* the one who's leaving *me*. To hell with that! We live together, or we die together. ARE WE CLEAR?!"

Justin blinked, startled. "We're clear. Uh… You'd better put your clothes back on."

It was only then that she realized that she was kneeling naked in snow up to her waist. She retrieved her clothes and hauled them on. They barely eased the cold, but the time it took to get dressed also gave her time to calm down.

She pulled him into her arms, held him close, and said, "Remember, Red, hope is a good thing, maybe the best of things, and no good thing ever dies."

With their cheeks pressed together, she couldn't tell if the wetness that warmed and then froze on their skin was his tears or hers.

"Which way?" she asked.

He pointed. "That way. But…"

"Hal carried Shane out of Apex and me off the mountain," she said. "You carried me in Venice. I'll carry you now."

She wrestled him over her shoulders in a fireman's lift, then stood up and started walking. Even with her shifter's strength, it wasn't easy to walk through thigh-deep snow carrying a man who weighed more than she did.

"Stay with me, Justin," she said. "I need you."

She felt him draw in a breath. "I know. I won't leave you."

Fiona struggled through the snow. Her back and knees and chest burned with effort, and her skin burned with cold. She'd never been so exhausted in her entire life, and they probably had at least a six-hour hike ahead of them. But Justin needed her, she needed him, and she was the only one who could walk. She'd walk if it killed her.

Every few minutes, as best as she could estimate time, she asked him to point the way, mostly to make sure he was still conscious.

"Straight," he usually said, or occasionally, "Bit to the right."

Fiona stubbed her toe on a snow-buried rock or fallen tree and nearly fell on her face. She staggered, regained her balance, and carefully stepped over it.

"Which way?" she asked.

He didn't reply. A stab of fear pierced her heart. "Justin!"

"Sorry. I'm awake." He gave a weary, exasperated sigh. "This is just what we need. My power's gone haywire."

"What do you mean? Can't you find Shane?"

"Well, I *can*. But it's telling me he's..." Justin pointed at the sky. "...up there."

Too baffled to even be upset, Fiona stopped and stared upward. A bleak gray expanse met her eye... and then a spark of gold.

The sun's coming out, she thought with relief. *Finally. Maybe now we can stop and rest and warm up...*

The spark got bigger. It was coming nearer, spiraling down out of the sky.

"Hey," Justin said slowly. "Is that... What *is* that?"

Fiona's heart lifted as high as the clouds, as high as a dragon could fly. "It's Lucas!"

A moment later, Justin exclaimed, "It's Shane!"

The golden dragon landed in front of them. Fiona was so exhausted that the buffet of wind from his wings nearly knocked her over. Shane leaped off, ran up, and steadied her as she staggered.

"I've got you," Shane said to them both. Urgently, he added, "It was Apex, wasn't it? Are they following you?"

She shook her head. "We blew up their base."

"What, again?" To Justin, he said, "And you! I take my eyes off you for *one night*..."

Fiona felt Justin breathe out in a soft chuckle as Shane lifted him from her shoulders. Relieved of both weight and tension, Fiona's knees started to buckle.

Lucas, who had become a man when she wasn't looking, caught her. "Are you hurt?"

"Just tired. And cold." She saw that Shane was watching, concerned, and said, "Never mind me. Justin's been shot."

Shane shrugged off the backpack he was wearing, pulled out a tarp, and laid Justin down on it. Lucas helped Fiona down beside him. She watched in a haze of exhaustion and relief as Shane pulled up a flat rock and used it to elevate Justin's feet, took a blanket and medical kit out of the backpack, cut off Justin's shirt, examined but did not remove his bandages, checked his vital signs, and finally covered him with the blanket.

Laying a hand on Justin's shoulder, Shane said, "You're going to be fine, Red. You're hypothermic and a doctor needs to take a look at the gunshot wounds—"

Justin's eyes widened with reflexive alarm.

"A *shifter* doctor," Shane said. "The same one who took care of you last time. What did you think, I was going to drop you off at the nearest ER?"

Justin shook his head. He was starting to fade out, his eyes losing focus, his eyelids fluttering.

"Hey!" Shane snapped his fingers in front of Justin's face, jolting him awake. "Stay with me, Red. Just long enough to drink something hot. Then you can go to sleep. All right?"

Justin nodded. Staying awake, let alone speaking, was obviously a strain, but he managed to get out, "Take care of Fiona."

"Relax, Red. I'm on top of it." Shane dug into his backpack, removing a bundle of clothes and a thermos. "Lucas, I'm drafting you as a medic. Get Red into some warm clothes—*gently*—then help him drink this. Don't let him pass out till he's finished it."

Lucas looked slightly alarmed, but got to work.

"Here, drink this while I check you." Shane handed Fiona another thermos.

Cupping her hands around that warmth was one of the best sensations she'd felt in her entire life. Then she took her first sip of the hot, sweet, milky tea it contained, and thought, *No, that's the best.*

As Shane began examining her, she said, "How did you find us so fast?"

"I was hoping you could explain that, actually. We tracked you and Red to an airstrip, but then we lost you. We were still trying to figure out where you'd been flown to when some guy called the office. He said, 'A man named Justin who works at your company and a blonde woman who's apparently calling herself Fiona now are wandering around somewhere northeast of Fairbanks, Alaska. You better pick them up before they get frostbite.' Then he hung up before we could ask any questions. Any idea who that was? It sounded like he had some history with you."

Carter, she thought. *It has to be.*

"Yes," she said. "We have history."

In the brief silence before Shane replied, she could hear Lucas coaxing, "Come on, Justin. One more sip. Very good. One more now…"

"Whoever he was, he probably saved your lives," Shane said quietly. "Red's, anyway. He's a tough guy and you took good care of him, but you're still fifty miles from Fairbanks."

She shivered involuntarily. Shane offered her an armful of clothing. "Need some help, or should I turn my back?"

"Turn your back."

As she changed into the warm, dry clothes, she realized that the only reason Carter had been able to get them help was that Justin had told him where he worked. His compassion for a man he had every reason to hate had ended up saving his life.

"Last one," Lucas said, holding the thermos to Justin's lips.

Justin swallowed, his eyes closed, then mumbled, "Fi…?"

She lifted him into her arms and bent to kiss his cheek. It was still cold, but a little color had returned to his skin. "I'm here. Rest now. I'll be there when you wake up."

"'Kay," he whispered, and relaxed into sleep.

Shane took out a cell phone and sent a text, then packed up his backpack. "How are you doing, Fiona? Can you stay awake for a dragon ride?"

"I'm tired, but I'm not *that* tired," she replied.

Lucas stepped back, giving himself room to shift. A swirl of golden sparks whirled around him, then blinked out to reveal the dragon that he had become. Shane picked up Justin and settled him on Lucas's back and leaning against Shane's chest, then gave Fiona a hand up to sit in front.

Shane wrapped his arms around Justin's chest, then called out, "I've got him!"

Lucas spread his translucent wings and sprang into the air. Fiona had never flown on dragonback before, as dragons normally only let their mates ride them. Under other circumstances she would have enjoyed it, but now she just wanted to see Justin safely to a doctor and herself to bed.

She only realized that she had dozed off when she was startled awake by the thump of the landing. They were in front of Dr. Bedford's office, which she had last visited when they'd rescued Shane from Apex, and her teammates were running to meet them. Shane had his arms around her as well as Justin.

"You awake?" Shane asked.

"Yes. How's Justin?"

He let her go. "He's all right. Still out. Just as well. He reacted pretty badly the last time he woke up here."

"He had a flashback?"

Catalina, who had just run up, said, "He turned into a snow leopard and clawed the hell out of Shane. But don't worry, Dr. Bedford and I tried to make the place look less… medical."

The whole team had crowded around them now. Ellie was there too, having apparently come with Hal, and so was Raluca, with her hair disheveled and in what Fiona would swear was a nightie. A very beautiful and expensive nightie, but a nightie nonetheless.

"What are you doing here?" Fiona asked her.

"Searching for you and Justin," Raluca said. "The rest came by helicopter, but Lucas and I could fly faster than that. We can only carry three people each, and two of you were lost. I let Catalina ride on me, since she's a paramedic."

"And I really appreciate it," Catalina said enthusiastically. "It was awesome!"

Nick helped Fiona down, and Hal gave Shane a hand. Shane carried Justin inside.

They were greeted by Dr. Bedford, a serious-looking woman with cornrows and wire-rimmed glasses. She was swallowed up in a black coat so long that she tripped over the hem as she came forward. "Drat this thing."

It was only then that Fiona recognized Hal's coat. When Dr. Bedford indicated a bed to lay Justin on, she saw that the white hospital sheets had been covered over with a patchwork quilt.

"My grandma just gave it to me, so it was still in the trunk of my car," Destiny explained when she saw Fiona staring at it. "When I heard you two were lost in Alaska, I grabbed it and brought it with me in the helo. Lucky, huh?"

Since there was no way of disguising the IV stand and the medical monitoring equipment, Fiona didn't know how much the effort would help. But it touched her. Even people like Hal and Destiny, who barely knew Justin, had offered their own prized possessions to try to make him feel safe and comfortable.

She sat on the edge of the bed, holding his hand, as Dr. Bedford approached, a little nervously and holding up the edges of Hal's coat so she could walk. Shane stood on the other side and kept his hand on Justin's shoulder.

He woke up with a gasp when Dr. Bedford touched the stethoscope to his chest. Then he took in the room and relaxed. "Oh. Here again."

"Not for as long as last time, I think," Dr. Bedford reassured him. "Now take a deep breath."

Fiona sat stroking his hair as he obeyed the doctor's commands. But whether it was Hal's coat and Destiny's patchwork quilt or the presence of her and Shane or something that had changed in Justin himself, he didn't seem bothered by being in the hospital, and only tightened his grip on Fiona's hand a little when Dr. Bedford put an oxygen mask over his face.

He soon drifted off again, and stayed asleep for the CT scan. Afterward, Dr. Bedford reported, "There's no internal bleeding or organ damage—nothing his shifter healing can't take care of. He just needs to rest. And so do you, Fiona. You can share the bed if you like."

Fiona gratefully crawled into bed beside him, draping her arm over his chest so she could feel him breathing. The last thing she remembered was Hal pulling the patchwork quilt over them both.

She woke to the sound of voices. For a moment she had no idea where she was. Then she opened her eyes. Justin was sitting up in bed beside her, leaning against a pile of pillows and talking to Shane and Hal. She couldn't believe how much better he was—still tired and pale, but his eyes were bright and his voice was strong.

"Hey," he said, glancing down. "Did we wake you up? I can kick them out."

"No, it's fine." She sat up, rubbing her eyes. "How long did I sleep?"

"Almost 24 hours. You were exhausted. I hadn't realized how long you carried Red." Shane patted her shoulder. "Thanks for taking such good care of him."

"You're welcome." Fiona rubbed her eyes again. "Is there coffee?"

"I'll go hunt some down." Shane went out.

"Hal was just catching me up," Justin said. "We can't bust anyone for crimes they committed as part of Apex, since that doesn't officially exist. But Hal spoke with the FBI and MI6, and they're going to arrest Bianchi for arms dealing, Attanasio for making drugs, and Elson for attempted murder and a whole laundry list of other crimes."

"But what about Apex? Is it gone for good?" Fiona asked.

"I hope so," Justin said.

"Whether they are or not, I don't think either of you has to worry about them," said Hal. "Fiona's blown up two of their bases now. If they ever try to start up again, I bet they leave the US just to get away from her."

Shane returned with a cup of coffee, and a whole lot of people at his back. Fiona hurriedly tried to smooth out her hair as she realized that her entire team had apparently been lurking outside, just waiting for her to wake up.

"Hi," she said. "I'm fine. You don't have to worry about me."

That clearly didn't satisfy them, as they all crowded in anyway. And not just her team, but their mates as well. Grace and Journey, who'd had time to prepare rather than having to rush off to the rescue on a moment's notice, were loaded down with flower arrangements, a suitcase, and a familiar toolkit.

"Is that…?" Fiona began.

Grace nodded. "Journey and I dropped by the office to bring you some things we thought you'd like. Your toolkit…"

"Spare clothes..." Journey opened the suitcase, displaying the clothes Fiona kept at the office in case of emergency.

"And something to tinker with!" Grace pulled out a tiny robot dog.

Justin leaned over. "Oh, I've been wanting to see one of those. Does it fetch?"

"No, but it goes around obstacles. Watch." Fiona started up the dog and set it on the floor. It trotted across the room, avoiding everyone's feet, until it arrived at the door. There it sat on its haunches, pointed its nose in the air, and emitted an electronic bark.

"Good dog!" said Justin.

Now that Fiona had everyone gathered together, she decided not to put off telling them her secret. They all had to be wondering about the anonymous tip that had led them to Alaska, and Justin certainly wouldn't have said anything about that without checking with her first. Besides, they were her teammates and friends. Shane and Lucas had just saved her life. Raluca had jumped out of bed to go on a mission even though she wasn't on the team. Grace had brought her a robot dog.

"Everyone..." Fiona said. "There's something about me I'd like you all to know."

Justin put his arm around her waist and held her close as she began to talk. When she'd told him that story, it had been incredibly difficult, terrifying, and painful. But the second time was much easier.

When she finished, Nick shook his head in amazement. "And all this time I thought you used to be down on me because you were such a straight arrow."

"I apologize—" she began.

He cut her off. "Don't worry about it. It's cool, actually. You were a better fucking criminal than I was!"

That opened the floodgates. Everyone started assuring her that it didn't matter and they didn't care. But she'd already known that. The sheet of ice she'd kept between her and others had melted away for good, and her fear of their judgment had gone with it.

She leaned her head on Justin's shoulder. It would be a while before they made it back to Santa Martina, but as far as she was concerned, she was already home.

EPILOGUE
Fiona

Fiona's braids had come loose. They flew out, then whipped across her face as she ducked down to mold a snowball. "Fetch!"

She threw it in a high arc. All six of their dogs raced across their backyard for it, even Laila, the little white chihuahua, who had to wear a sweater to protect her from the cold. Foxy, the three-legged husky mix, leaped and caught it, then snorted indignantly when it broke apart in her mouth. Midge barked, then pounced on Foxy, bowling her over. The entire pack began to tussle with each other, leaping and rolling in the snow.

"I have to say, snow is a lot more fun when you have dogs," Fiona remarked. "I'd still never want to live in Alaska, though. Two inches is plenty."

Justin packed two snowballs tight and tossed them at the same time. Biscata, the Jack Russell terrier, and Lucy, the beagle and blue tick mix, went for the same one and collided. Biscata shrugged off the blow and bit down on the snowball, while Lucy yelped, then ran back to Fiona to be comforted. Angel, the Dalmation, caught the other neatly and intact, then trotted up to Justin and dropped it at his feet.

"Good girl." He fondled her ears, then glanced up at Fiona. "You know, I had a nightmare the other night, when you were off guarding that woman from the stalker."

"Oh, no. I was worried about that." They'd both had jobs with Protection, Inc. since they'd returned to Santa Martina, but only during the day. That had been the first night they'd spent apart.

But Justin didn't seem upset. "Angel woke me up. She was on the bed, nuzzling my neck and patting my arm with her paw. Lucy was on the bed too, licking my hand, and the rest of them were piled up alongside of me and at my feet. They knew. They'd all been in their doggy beds in the other room when I fell asleep. So you don't have to worry about leaving me alone anymore. I've got the pack. I'll be all right."

The rest of the dogs wandered back to sit, panting happily, at their feet. Fiona gave them each an ear-rub. "Just as well we couldn't agree on the same three, huh?"

"Actually, I did that on purpose. I always wanted six."

"You did not!"

He shrugged, grinning, until she dumped a handful of snow down the back of his shirt. "Okay! No, I didn't really." After a moment, he added, "But I would've if I'd thought of it."

Fiona lunged for him with another handful, but he ducked away and bolted across the yard. She chased him, accompanied by the delightedly barking pack, all around their big backyard. Justin ran easily, dodging around trees, kicking dog toys out of the way, and finally taking a flying leap across the swimming pool.

"Show off!" she yelled from the other side.

He laughed, not even out of breath, and teasingly beckoned to her. "Here, kitty, kitty!"

Instead of following him immediately, she took a moment to look at him from across the pool. His T-shirt was riding up, giving her a glimpse of one of the scars on his side. He'd put on a few more pounds of solid muscle, thanks to his own home-cooked meals and the Protection, Inc. gym, and was strong and lithe rather than thin. With his brilliant copper hair, black eyes, and sharp features, he looked like he should shift into a fox rather than a snow leopard. As he'd predicted, people did turn to look at him when he walked by. But it didn't seem to bother him now that he was no longer hiding in the shadows.

Fiona jumped across the pool and cornered Justin against the fence.

He threw up his hands. "I surrender!"

"You better," she said, and kissed him.

He caught her up in his arms and held her tight. Fiona relaxed into his embrace, enjoying the strength of his grip and the heat of his mouth.

She stroked his soft hair and broad shoulders, and he slipped his hands beneath her blouse to caress every inch of her that he could reach.

For a long time they stood and kissed as if they'd been parted for months instead of a single night. Then snow started falling again, melting on their faces and sprinkling their hair like confetti.

"Let's go in. I'll start a fire." Justin put his arm around her shoulders. And together they came in from the cold.

A NOTE FROM ZOE CHANT

Thank you for reading *Soldier Snow Leopard!* I hope you enjoyed it. The final book in the series, *Top Gun Tiger,* is coming soon.

If you enjoy *Protection, Inc,* I also write the *Werewolf Marines* series under the pen name of Lia Silver. Both series have hot romances, exciting action, emotional healing, brave heroines who stand up for their men, and strong heroes who protect their mates with their lives.

Please consider reviewing *Soldier Snow Leopard,* even if you only write a line or two. I appreciate all reviews, whether positive or negative.

Page down to read a special sneak preview of *Protector Panther,* the book which introduced Justin.

The cover of *Soldier Snow Leopard* was designed by Augusta Scarlett.

ZOE CHANT WRITING AS LIA SILVER

The *Werewolf Marines* series
Laura's Wolf
Prisoner
Partner

Standalone
Mated to the Meerkat

ZOE CHANT WRITING AS LAUREN ESKER

The *Shifter Agents* series
Handcuffed to the Bear
Guard Wolf
Dragon's Luck
Tiger in the Hot Zone

The *Ladies of the Pack* series
Keeping Her Pride

The *Warriors of Galatea* series
Metal Wolf

Standalone
Wolf in Sheep's Clothing

ZOE CHANT WRITING AS HELEN KEEBLE

Standalones
Fang Girl
No Angel

ZOE CHANT COMPLETE BOOK LIST

All books are available through Amazon.com.
Check my website, zoechant.com, for my latest releases.

While series should ideally be read in order, all of my books are stand-alones with happily ever afters and no cliffhangers. This includes books within series.

BOOKS IN SERIES

Protection, Inc.
Book 1: *Bodyguard Bear*
Book 2: *Defender Dragon*
Book 3: *Protector Panther*
Book 4: *Warrior Wolf*
Book 5: *Leader Lion*
Book 6: *Soldier Snow Leopard*

Bears of Pinerock County
Book 1: *Sheriff Bear*
Book 2: *Bad Boy Bear*
Book 3: *Alpha Rancher Bear*
Book 4: *Mountain Guardian Bear*
Book 5: *Hired Bear*
Book 6: *A Pinerock Bear Christmas*

Bodyguard Shifters
Book 1: *Bearista*
Book 2: *Pet Rescue Panther*
Book 3: *Bear in a Book Shop*

Cedar Hill Lions
Book 1: *Lawman Lion*
Book 2: *Guardian Lion*
Book 3: *Rancher Lion*
Book 4: *Second Chance Lion*
Book 5: *Protector Lion*

Christmas Valley Shifters
Book 1: *The Christmas Dragon's Mate*
Book 2: *The Christmas Dragon's Heart*

Enforcer Bears
Book 1: *Bear Cop*
Book 2: *Hunter Bear*
Book 3: *Wedding Bear*
Book 4: *Fighter Bear*
Book 5: *Bear Guard*

Fire & Rescue Shifters
Book 1: *Firefighter Dragon*
Book 2: *Firefighter Pegasus*
Book 3: *Firefighter Griffin*
Book 4: *Firefighter Sea Dragon*
Book 5: *The Master Shark's Mate*
Book 6: *Firefighter Unicorn*
Book 7: *Firefighter Pegasus*

Glacier Leopards
Book 1: *The Snow Leopard's Mate*
Book 2: *The Snow Leopard's Baby*
Book 3: *The Snow Leopard's Home*
Book 4: *The Snow Leopard's Heart*

Gray's Hollow Dragon Shifters
Book 1: *The Billionaire Dragon Shifter's Mate*
Book 2: *Beauty and the Billionaire Dragon Shifter*
Book 3: *The Billionaire Dragon Shifter's Christmas*
Book 4: *Choosing the Billionaire Dragon Shifters*
Book 5: *The Billionaire Dragon Shifter's Baby*
Book 6: *The Billionaire Dragon Shifter Meets His Match*

Hollywood Shifters
Book 1: *Hollywood Bear*
Book 2: *Hollywood Dragon*
Book 3: *Hollywood Tiger*
Book 4: *A Hollywood Shifters' Christmas*

Honey for the Billionbear
Book 1: *Honey for the Billionbear*
Book 2: *Guarding His Honey*
Book 3: *The Bear and His Honey*

Ranch Romeos
Book 1: *Bear West*
Book 2: *The Billionaire Wolf Needs a Wife*

Rowland Lions
Book 1: *Lion's Hunt*
Book 2: *Lion's Mate*

Shifter Kingdom
Book 1: *Royal Guard Lion*
Book 2: *Royal Guard Tiger*

Shifter Suspense
Book 1: *Panther's Promise*
Book 2: *Saved by the Billionaire Lion Shifter*
Book 3: *Stealing the Snow Leopard's Heart*

Shifting Sands Resort
Book 1: *Tropical Tiger Spy*
Book 2: *Tropical Wounded Wolf*

Upson Downs
Book 1: *Target: Billionbear*
Book 2: *A Werewolf's Valentine*

NON-SERIES BOOKS

Bears

A Pair of Bears
Alpha Bear Detective
Bear Down
Bear Mechanic
Bear Watching
Bear With Me
Bearing Your Soul
Bearly There
Bought by the Billionbear
Country Star Bear
Dancing Bearfoot
Hero Bear
In the Billionbear's Den
Kodiak Moment
Private Eye Bear's Mate
The Bear Comes Home For Christmas
The Bear With No Name
The Bear's Christmas Bride
The Billionbear's Bride
The Easter Bunny's Bear
The Hawk and Her LumBEARjack

Big Cats

Alpha Lion
Joining the Jaguar
Loved by the Lion
Pursued by the Puma
Rescued by the Jaguar
Royal Guard Lion
The Billionaire Jaguar's Curvy Journalist
The Jaguar's Beach Bride
The Saber Tooth Tiger's Mate
Trusting the Tiger

Dragons

The Christmas Dragon's Mate
The Dragon Billionaire's Secret Mate
The Mountain Dragon's Curvy Mate
A Mate for the Christmas Dragon

Eagles

Wild Flight

Griffins

The Griffin's Mate
Ranger Griffin

Wolves

Alpha on the Run
Healing Her Wolf
Undercover Alpha
Wolf Home

AND NOW FOR A SPECIAL SNEAK PREVIEW OF THE BOOK WHICH INTRODUCED JUSTIN!

PROTECTOR PANTHER

PROTECTION, INC. # 3

ZOE CHANT

Catalina Mendez strolled down the empty street at 3:00 AM, humming to herself.

It was her favorite time of day— night— well, technically day. Statistically speaking, a high percentage of bad things happened at 3:00 AM. It was a peak time for vehicle crashes, industrial accidents, medical crises, and violent crimes. For an adrenaline junkie paramedic on the late shift, it was the best and most exciting time to work, when she might actually get to save a life. It didn't hurt that Catalina was a night owl, working at peak efficiency by night and a little sleepy and slow by day.

But right now, she wasn't just at peak efficiency. She was *wired*. She'd just flown back from the small European country of Loredana, where she'd been working with Paramedics Without Borders to help restore emergency services after a catastrophic earthquake.

Her return trip had been a catastrophe all by itself. Her best friend and fellow paramedic Ellie McNeil had been supposed to pick her up at the airport, but her flight had been delayed, then canceled, then restored so many times that Catalina had finally texted Ellie to forget about it. Catalina was perfectly capable of taking a taxi whenever the hell her flight got in. Which had been originally scheduled for 6:00 PM on Wednesday, but turned out to be 2:00 AM on Friday.

By the time the plane took off, she'd drunk several gallons of coffee to make sure she didn't doze off in the airport and miss her flight. Then she figured she might as well drink some more, since she was already wide awake. By the time the plane touched down in Santa Martina, she'd worked up a pretty good caffeine rush. Her nerves tingled with excited anticipation that something exciting and important might happen at any second.

That was when she discovered that her luggage had been routed to Singapore. Which was certainly exciting and important, but not in a good way. She picked up her purse, which was all she'd taken on the plane, and made her way to the taxi stand.

As the taxi headed toward her home, she realized how little she wanted to go there. It would be boring. And lonely. She couldn't even reunite with her cats— Ellie had taken them while Catalina was away. Her bed would be cold and empty without any kitties to cuddle.

Thoughts of Ellie and bed led to thoughts of the man who now shared Ellie's bed, hot bodyguard Hal Brennan. And the other hot bodyguards at Hal's private security company, Protection, Inc. Ellie had promised to introduce Catalina to them when she got back from Loredana. She'd even offered to send photos, but though Catalina had been impressed with the pics of Hal, she'd declined to look at the ones of the single guys. She'd meet them in person eventually, and she liked being surprised.

The taxi stopped at a red light. Catalina recognized the silhouette of a towering office building a couple blocks ahead. It had been in one of the photos Ellie had emailed her, of her and Hal standing in front of Protection, Inc.

"Let me off here," Catalina said impulsively. "It's walking distance from my home."

The taxi driver craned his head at her. "Are you sure? It's a pretty long walk. And it's the middle of the night."

"I'm sure," she said.

Catalina paid him and stepped out on to the empty street. Sure, no one would be at Protection, Inc. But she'd at least get to take a closer look at the place she'd heard so much about. And she needed to burn off some energy before she went home, or she'd never get to sleep. Besides, night was the best time to walk around the city. The air was cool, the sky was a pretty purple-orange with light spill, and you never knew what might happen.

A vision of her mother popped into her mind as she walked down the street.

Walking alone at night in the city! Mom's remembered voice was loud in her ears. *You could be robbed! You could be murdered! You could witness a murder, like your poor friend Ellie! Why are you always so reckless?*

It's a good neighborhood, mom, Catalina replied to the voice in her head, echoing real conversations they'd had a thousand times over. *I'm not reckless. I'm just not afraid.*

You should be, Mom scolded. *Ever since you were a little girl, you haven't known the meaning of fear. I pray every night that when you do find out, it won't be too late.*

The street was empty and silent. As Catalina came closer to the towering office building that housed Protection, Inc., she saw that she was approaching a dark alley.

Normally she would have walked right past it. What were the odds that a mugger was lurking at a deserted street on the unlikely chance that someone would walk straight past his lurking area— especially when every woman Catalina had ever met, even her brave friend Ellie, would cross the street to avoid that alley?

But tonight Catalina hesitated. An odd feeling made her stomach clench and her palms tingle.

Oh, no, she thought, dismayed. *I spent months living in a tent in a disaster zone, and* now *I get sick?*

Then she recognized the feeling. It wasn't one she felt often, but she knew what it was. It was fear.

She stopped to take stock, wondering what had made her feel afraid. Some little thing in the environment, too subtle for her register consciously, must have signaled that something was wrong. Something was dangerous.

Catalina took a step to the side, meaning to cross the street. She wasn't *completely* reckless. If an action seemed both dangerous and pointless, she wouldn't take it.

A man staggered out of the alley, fetched up hard against the wall of the nearest building, and slid down to the ground.

Catalina ran to him. On her way, she took a quick peek into the alley to make sure the scene was safe before she entered it. That was the part of the paramedic test she'd almost flunked, but it was second nature now. She couldn't see all the way into the alley, but what she did see was empty and still, with nothing stirring but a few discarded candy wrappers in the light breeze. There was no obvious danger, no pursuing muggers or smoke or sparking electrical wires, so she was free to tend to her patient.

See? She told the mom-in-her-head. *Not reckless!*

Catalina knelt by the man's side, giving his body a quick visual scan before she did a more detailed examination. His eyes were closed. He was tall and muscular, but lean rather than bulky. His short black hair looked soft as a cat's fur. He wore dark jeans and a white T-shirt spotted with fresh blood. More blood ran down his handsome face from a cut at his temple. His chest was moving evenly, and when she bent over him, she couldn't hear any sounds that indicated breathing difficulties. His skin seemed pale, but it was difficult to tell in the hard white glare of the street lights.

Airway: good. Breathing: good. Visible bleeding: not severe. He wasn't likely to drop dead in the next few seconds, so she'd call 911 to get the ambulance on its way before she resumed her assessment.

She opened her purse and pulled out her cell phone, then stared at it in dismay. It was her phone from Loredana, which wouldn't work in the US. She must have accidentally packed her regular phone in her suitcase. Which was in Singapore.

"Dammit!"

Her patient woke as if she'd fired a gun in the air. His body jerked, he sucked in a sudden breath, and his eyes flew open. They were blue as ice, and they fixed on her with an unsettling intensity.

"Who are you?" he demanded.

Level of consciousness: alert and responsive, Catalina thought.

She spoke in the soothing tones she always used on trauma victims. "I'm a paramedic. Is it all right if I help you?"

Legally, she had to ask permission before she did anything to anyone. Almost all of her patients automatically said yes.

The man patted his hip, then his shoulder. His eyes narrowed in a quick flicker of dismay. "I've lost my weapons. And I can't—" He broke off, looking frustrated. "I can't protect you. So no. I don't give you permission to treat me. Get out of here."

He struggled to get up, but only managed to get as far as propping himself on his elbows. More blood ran down his face. He clearly wasn't going anywhere.

"Why don't you lie back down?" Catalina suggested, turning up the soothing. "Just let me take a look at you."

"No." Most men raised their voices when they were angry or upset, but this man lowered his. It was more forceful than if he'd yelled.

"I'm a paramedic," Catalina repeated. Sometimes trauma victims were too shocked or disoriented to take in what she said the first time. "I can help you. Can you tell me what happened?"

He might be a trauma victim, but he wasn't disoriented. Those ice-blue eyes of his seemed to look right through her, as if he knew things about her that even she didn't. "If you're a paramedic, then you need my consent before you treat me. I'm not giving it. Take your phone and go. Once you're in a safe place, call—"

"That phone doesn't work in America," she interrupted him.

The man let out an exasperated breath. He again tried to get up, and again failed.

"Why can't you stand up?" Catalina asked. "Are you dizzy? Or is something wrong with your legs?"

"Both," he muttered, sounding reluctant to admit it. "I've been drugged. They ambushed me with a tranquilizer rifle."

"With a *tranquilizer rifle?*"

She'd once treated a woman who'd been the victim of friendly fire from zookeepers trying to take down an escaped capybara. Catalina had never heard of a capybara before, but it turned out to be a guinea pig the size of a sheep. It had been one of her all-time favorite calls. But that tranquilizer dart hadn't caused dizziness and paralysis, it had immediately knocked the woman unconscious. And who would use one for an ambush? Criminal... veterinarians?

Then Catalina realized the important part of what he'd let slip. "If you've been drugged, it's the same as if you were unconscious. I can assume that you *would* consent to treatment if you were in your right mind. So settle down. I just want to check you for life-threatening injuries."

His eyebrows rose in disbelief, as if it was the first time in his life that anyone had the nerve to stand up to him. Then he took a deep breath, seeming to concentrate.

Her stomach clenched. Her palms tingled. Her heart began to pound. Nothing about the man had changed, but she suddenly knew he was dangerous. Very dangerous. Lethal. She had to run— she had to save herself—

The phone fell from her hand, the screen shattering. She scrambled to her feet, stumbling backward, desperate to get away.

But he hasn't threatened me, she thought. *He hasn't attacked me.*

He was still sprawled on the ground, bleeding, his gaze locked on hers. Deadly. Terrifying.

He's injured. He can't walk. He needs help.

All her instincts screamed at her to run. She was gasping, her pulse thundering in her ears, sweat pouring down her face and back. She'd never been so scared in her entire life.

Never abandon a patient.

It was the hardest thing she'd ever done, but Catalina took a step forward. Then another step. Then she dropped back down on her knees beside him.

Her terror vanished as if it had been switched off. The man rested his head on his arms, exhaustion etching lines around his strong features.

"I don't believe this," he muttered. "I hit you with both barrels. I laid it on so hard, I wore myself out! How are you still here?"

She stared at him. "You did that on purpose? How?"

"Practice." He raised his head. His intense gaze again fixed on her, but now she felt no fear. He had beautiful eyes. They were an astonishingly clear blue, like an early morning sky, fringed with thick black lashes.

"I've got some very bad people after me. You could get caught in the crossfire if you stay with me. But since you were playing hooky when God gave out fear…" As if against his will, he gave her an ironic smile. It transformed the hard angles of his face, making her notice again how good-looking he was. "If you can help me get up and walk a block, I can get us both into a building. Once we're inside, we'll be safe. I have friends I can call."

As an afterthought, he added, "I'll give you permission to examine me then. I know you're dying to check me out."

She couldn't tell if he was making a double entendre or a statement of fact. Strange guy. Strange hot guy who'd been ambushed with a tranquilizer rifle and could terrify you just by looking you in the eyes. Strange brave guy who preferred sacrificing himself to putting a stranger at risk.

Catalina crouched low. "Put your arm around my shoulders."

"I know the drill." He propped himself up on his left arm and put his right arm around her shoulders. It was warm, not cold with shock. Having his arm around her made her feel oddly safe and secure. As if he was protecting her, though he couldn't even walk.

She gripped his right wrist, unable to help noticing that he had amazing biceps. Amazing arms in general. Even his wrist was thick with muscle. Strange, totally ripped guy.

Strange sexy guy who knew unusual things. He knew how to do an assisted walk, and he knew the laws of consent for treatment.

"Are you a paramedic?" she asked, wrapping her left arm around his waist. He was warm all over.

He shook his head, struggling to get his legs under him. "I mean, yes, I am. But that's just a qualification, not my job. I'm— I *was*— a PJ. That's—"

"Air Force pararescue. Special Ops combat search and rescue," Catalina filled in. Quoting a poster she'd seen, she added, "Because sometimes even Navy SEALs have to call 911."

"That's right." His breath came harsh in her ear. He couldn't seem to move his legs at all, though she could feel his attempts through the tensing and flexing of his other muscles against her body. But though he thought bad guys could descend on them at any second, his voice and expression remained calm. "Did you ever want to be one?"

"Yeah, but they don't take women." Then she stared at him. "How'd you know?"

"You've got the right stuff. Mentally, I mean." Then he let out a frustrated breath and stopped struggling to move. "I hope you've got the right stuff physically, too, because we can't do an assisted walk. My legs are completely paralyzed. You'll have to drag me. Or I could give you the code to the building. It's only a block away. You could go in and call for help—"

"Forget it," she replied. "I'm not leaving you."

He smiled, but not the same amused, catlike smile she'd seen before. This one held infinite depths of sadness and regret over its pleasant surface. "Never leave a fallen comrade, huh? Are you an airman? A Marine?"

"No, I've never served," Catalina replied. "And I'd rather not drag you. I don't know what kind of injuries you have. Do you know?"

"I'm not sure," he admitted. "The tranquilizer knocked me for a loop. I don't remember the fight too well. I'm not even sure exactly how I got here."

She glanced at the blood on his shirt. If he had internal injuries, she definitely shouldn't drag him. "I'll do a fireman's carry."

He gave her a doubtful glance, which didn't surprise her. He had to be over a foot taller and fifty pounds heavier than her. Then he shrugged. "Okay. Let's give it a try."

Catalina wrestled him over her shoulders, thanking her lucky stars that she'd just spent months in a disaster zone without any high-tech amenities. If it hadn't built up her strength moving heavy equipment and patients, she probably couldn't even have gotten him into position.

She stood up, careful to lift from her legs, not her back. He weighed even more than she'd imagined. Her knees cracked audibly, and she staggered.

"Easy." He laid a steadying hand on her forearm. "Find your center of gravity and settle into it."

"Thanks," she gasped, regaining her balance. "Which way?"

"Forward. I'll tell you when we get there."

She took a step forward, trying not to pitch forward under his weight. Her breath burned in her lungs, and her back and legs and neck ached. She didn't feel like she could make it five more steps, let alone an entire city block. But her other choice was dragging him over the sidewalk and maybe making his injuries worse. She took another step, and then another one.

Another step. Another.

A quarter of a block.

Her face felt hot and swollen with blood. Her back was on fire.

Another step. Another.

Half a block. Catalina felt like she was about to pass out. She could see nothing but a red haze.

"You're strong," he said quietly.

Hearing that from a PJ— hearing it from this man, in particular— gave her strength.

Another step.

He suddenly whipped his arm out like he was slapping something out of the air. The shift in weight nearly knocked her off her feet. As she staggered, trying to regain her balance, she saw some tiny object rolling across the sidewalk.

"Put me down and run!" he said sharply.

"No!" A pain like a needle jab pricked her arm. "Ow!"

Everything spun around her, and she hit the ground hard. Catalina couldn't so much as twitch. When she tried to speak, she found that not even her lips would move. But now she was close enough to the ground to see the tiny object on the sidewalk: a tranquilizer dart. Another one was still embedded in her arm.

The PJ dragged himself on top of her and shielded her with his body.

"Last stand," he muttered. "Funny how by the time it comes to that, you're never actually standing."

Then he glanced down at her open eyes. "Oh. Didn't realize you were still conscious. Last stand for me, I mean. I'll make sure it isn't yours."

He laid his palm down on her back. It was warm. Comforting.

Catalina's vision kept blurring and the PJ was blocking her line of sight, but she could see some figures approaching them.

"The woman's a civilian," the PJ said. His voice carried on the still air, but his tone was calm as if he was having a perfectly normal conversation. "Just an ordinary good Samaritan. Leave her here. She doesn't know anything. I didn't even tell her my name."

Another man's voice spoke. If the PJ was cool, this man was ice cold. "We know. We've been observing from a distance. And we've seen some *fascinating* things. Her resistance to your power— her general lack of fear— even her physical strength. We're certainly not leaving her. She's the perfect subject for 2.0."

There was a brief silence. Then all of the hazy figures flinched back. One let out a hoarse scream of sheer terror, then spun around and ran away. A moment later, two more followed him, stumbling and arms flailing, apparently caught in the grip of total panic.

The man with the cold voice spoke again. "I'm impressed. My operatives all underwent intensive fear-resistance training. However, I anticipated that you might get to some of them anyway. That's why I brought as many men as I did. The three I have left should be more than enough to deal with one partially paralyzed, unarmed renegade."

The PJ replied coolly, "Send them over, and we'll see about that."

"It would be interesting to see what you can manage in that state. However, in the interest of expediting this, I think I'll just give you another dose."

There was snap of fingers, then a faint *whump* of compressed air. Catalina felt the PJ whip around. His hand brushed against her shoulder as he yanked something from his side and threw it back. One of the figures yelped in pain. Then the PJ gave a long sigh and slumped down on top of her. His breathing was even and deep, his hair soft against her cheek.

The figures moved forward, coming closer and closer. Catalina blinked hard, trying to clear her vision. The name on the building in front of her swam into view. She'd collapsed right in front of Protection, Inc.

Too bad no one's home, she thought dizzily. *Right now, we could really use a bodyguard.*

Everything went black.

Printed in Great Britain
by Amazon